THE ARM OF COINCIDENCE

*With best wishes from
Bill James Richardson
01832 272586*

The Arm Of Coincidence

BILL JAMES

SERENDIPITY

Copyright © Bill James, 2004

First published in 2004 by
Serendipity
Suite 530
37 Store Street
Bloomsbury
London

All rights reserved
Unauthorised duplication
contravenes existing laws

British Library Cataloguing-in-Publication data
A catalogue record for this book is available from the British Library

ISBN 1-84394-105-8

Printed and bound by Antony Rowe Ltd, Eastbourne

To Maggie, 'The wind beneath my wings.'
Thanks to all the 'real' people who agreed to names, and/or companies being included in this book. Special thanks to Christopher Capron and David Powell for their support and advice.
Very special thanks to Brenda Tomkins and Lyn Dowsett for their typing skills on the manuscript.

THE ARM OF COINCIDENCE

The whole of the village and parish of Halston and its inhabitants exist entirely in the writer's imagination. The characters from outside this area who appear in a bad light are also entirely fictitious and are not based on any individuals living or dead.

My grateful thanks to those individuals and companies who have allowed me to use their names in order to give the story an air of authenticity.

The ordnance survey map has been torn open to make room for this imaginary parish in North Northamptonshire!

The inspiration for this story springs from the extraordinary succession of coincidences that the writer has been involved with.

PROLOGUE

There had been quite sharp frost and Jamie was allowed out for the first time since his bout of chicken pox. He was well wrapped up and eagerly awaiting the arrival of the potato lorry.

'Just coming by the sound of it,' his father grunted. A shining green lorry trundled into the yard and stopped. Not the one that Jamie had expected, but he recognised the driver as he climbed down from the cab, after all he only lived at the Mill!

'Now then young Jamie, what do you reckon to this?' as he ruffled the lad's blond curls with a playful chuckle. Jamie walked to the front of the lorry and read 'Dodge' out loud. The previous lorry had Bedford on the front and hadn't been as noisy as this one. It had a peculiar motif on the radiator grill of four circles with a diamond shape running through them.

'That's because it's got a Perkins diesel engine in it,' explained the driver as Jamie traced his finger over it.

'First time out today,' the driver grinned at Jamie's dad, 'I hope no so and so runs into me otherwise I'll have to say can't you read!' as he pointed to the Dodge sign.

Jamie's uncle had gone to fetch the first trailer load of potatoes and he came round from the barn with a four wheeled trailer pulled by a shiny blue tractor. It had 'Fordson Major diesel' on the side and his uncle carefully drew alongside the lorry so that the hundredweight hessian bags could be transferred onto the lorry. The man that his father and uncle employed on the farm climbed up onto the lorry to help and soon all four men were busy heaving the bags from the trailer to the lorry.

'Best crop of King Edwards we've had for a long time,' Jamie heard his father remark to the driver. When they had almost unloaded the four tons onto the lorry. Jamie went with his father to fetch the other trailer which would make up the load to eight tons. This second tractor had to be started by hand on petrol. It was painted orange with the words 'Allis Chalmers' written on the side. Once started, Jamie was allowed to sit on the wide mudguard while his father drove out of the

THE ARM OF COINCIDENCE

shed round to the lorry. The four men worked hard and it wasn't long before the load was completed.

'Forgotten your sheets have you, Bailey?' said his uncle. Bailey pointed to a large box fitted to the chassis of the lorry.

'In there!' he grinned. 'Keeps 'em dry and no one can nick 'em, got all me ropes in there an all.'

He went to the passenger door and reached for a key under the seat, unlocked the box, and heaved out two sheets and some long ropes.

'Got to double sheet this weather,' he remarked, 'they won't have 'em if they think they've got frez in transit.'

'Gotter make an early start,' he grinned, 'got three drops and they all want me there at five o'clock! I do me first drop in Covent Garden about half three before the beggars get there, otherwise they'll keep me 'anging around whilst they put some on one van and some on another. I get to me last one at five, that'll be at Greenwich.'

Jamie saw his mum come out the house dressed ready to go to Oundle to do the weekly shopping. She asked if he would like to go but he preferred to stay and watch Mr Bailey with the intricate job of sheeting and roping, getting the ropes really tight with 'itch knots! His dad, uncle and the man had gone to feed the cattle and Jamie was eager to investigate his 'find' in the old Hall. It was his secret, he hadn't even mentioned it to his cousins. Of course, they weren't supposed to play in there, it wasn't safe, the parents insisted. It had been requisitioned by the military during the war and had housed some of the unfortunate Poles who had been killed at Arnhem.

Jamie was a big lad for his age, he had learnt quite a lot of reading before he had even started school. He was way ahead of the other children in his class. He crept into the workshop when he was sure no one was looking and took two large screwdrivers and a curved bar which a burglar would have called a 'jemmy'. He nipped into the house up to his room and collected his torch, he already had his prize possession, a Swiss army knife, in his pocket. He nipped over the road and made his way to the semi-derelict Hall. He knew that his uncle would like to have it renovated and live in it, but his father reckoned it would be too expensive. Jamie got in through a broken window and made his way down into the cellar. Before getting the chicken pox he had located a slab which wasn't as firm as the rest, where he had felt a draught which he quickly found again.

After a lot of prising and heaving with the screwdriver and bar he managed to get the slab up enough to get his hands under one end. He braced himself for a mighty effort and heaved the slab up till it leant against the wall. With mounting excitement he shone his torch into the hole and saw a rusty iron ladder going down into a tunnel. This was really exciting, what a surprise he would have for his cousins! He climbed down the ladder into the hole and saw steps going back up almost straight away into a tunnel, which was about three feet wide and nearly six foot high. Light filtered through from cracks near the roof of the tunnel. Everything was stone and the roof was arched like a bridge. Without even stopping to think, he was off up the tunnel, the cobwebs he encountered were no deterrent! The tunnel took a sudden sharp left turn and almost immediately there was more light from a larger hole so that he was able to see out by standing on the large stone which had fallen in.

He could see a large fallen elder tree whose roots had caused the stone to fall in. A patch of brambles made it difficult to see out but Jamie quickly realised that the tunnel was under the wall, which went from the Hall round the old orchard and on to the dovecote.

'Wow, a secret passage from the Hall to the dovecote!'

He reckoned it had been built when there was a priory on the site of the Hall. He had heard it said that the dovecote was a lot older than the Hall. They used it at the moment to store hay for the sheep as winter feed. It was, Jamie knew, nearly empty now as spring was on the way. He continued along the passage and soon came to a few steps leading up.

He was suddenly aware of sounds from the top of the steps. He crept to the top of the stairs and peeped through a square hole. He almost made a sound as he recognised his dad on top of his mum in the hay, his trousers down, his bottom heaving up and down, whilst both were grunting and groaning.

Suddenly the door opened, his uncle stepped in and Jamie realised he had a gun in his hand. There were two pops, one after the other in quick succession and his mum and dad went still, then the bodies started to jerk about and he saw blood pouring from the back of his dad's head.

Jamie screamed, his uncle swore and the gun swung in his direction. As Jamie ducked a bullet ricocheted into the tunnel. Jamie fled down the steps into the tunnel as another bullet screamed from side to side of the tunnel wall. Blinded by tears, terrified out of his wits, Jamie reached the hole in the wall and peered out. He could hear cursing behind him and knew that his uncle was trying to get into the tunnel. The noise stopped and Jamie saw his uncle running towards the Hall. He stayed still for a few seconds, then got out his army knife and started working at the mortar to loosen another stone.

He heard a dull thud behind him from the tunnel, then nothing. As he saw his uncle running towards the farm he realised that the slab had been dropped into place and most likely weighted down. Keeping an eye for what might happen next Jamie somehow got himself together. His parents were dead. WHY? He guessed that his uncle would eventually return and kill him. He had to get out. He had to escape.

He had almost freed the stone when he saw his uncle going to the dovecote with a wheelbarrow and some tools. He thought he saw a shovel handle and a pickaxe and guessed that the bodies were to be buried in the dovecote. He pushed as hard as he could against the stone, it moved a little, he scraped some more, he pushed some more. Eventually the stone went out. The roof stayed up. There was just enough room for him to squeeze through into the brambles. He used his knife to hack some of the brambles but got quite badly scratched as he crawled out. He ran to the Hall as fast as he could, down the old driveway to the chicane bridge, over the road into the wood.

He felt a little safer when he got to his 'secret' hollow tree and climbed inside. He tried to close his mind to the scene in the dovecote, but he couldn't. He knew that his situation was desperate, people would be looking for him and if his uncle found him first he didn't give much for his chances. He remembered the big box on the side of Mr Bailey's new lorry. It was virtually empty. If he could get to the mill end of the village without being detected he may be able to hide in the box. He knew that the lorry was going to Covent Garden which was in London. He would have to wait till dark and creep along the back of the houses and hope that no dogs barked. Fortunately he was wearing a dark coat and hat, and after what seemed an eternity it was dark but moonlit. He wouldn't need to use his torch.

He made it to the mill yard and breathed a sigh of relief as he saw the lorry, paintwork gleaming in the moonlight. His heart sank as he found the box locked. He managed to scramble onto the step by the passenger door and was amazed to find it unlocked. He found the key under the seat, and used it to undo the padlock and return it to its place. He very carefully pushed the door closed. The click seemed deafening. Nothing stirred, he removed the lock then checked whether the blade of his knife would go under the lid.

He got into the box with the lock and carefully made himself as comfortable as possible. He lowered the lid and heard the hasp drop into place. It was cold in the box and he thanked the lord that his mother had insisted that he wrapped up well. He had a job to stop himself from crying, he knew that if anyone heard him he wouldn't get away.

He awoke to the sound of the engine rumbling into life and they were on their way. It was very bumpy for the first few miles, then came the sounds of other vehicles and the road was less bumpy. In spite of the cold and the constant rumbling he must have slept, because he woke to a door slamming then almost silence. He lay listening hardly daring to breathe, Mr Bailey was undoing the ropes. He heard him working on his side of the lorry, then his hobnailed boots went back to the other side. Jamie poked his knife through the gap and released the hasp, got out as quickly and quietly as possible, lowered the lid and clicked the lock shut on the hasp.

He was sure Mr Bailey would have heard. He scrambled under the lorry and watched as the lorry man moved from side to side undoing ropes and lifting the sheets at the back of the lorry. He saw him take a bag onto his shoulder and deposit it in a doorway. As he started off with the second bag Jamie darted out from the other side of the lorry and dodged under the nearest stall. Every time Mr Bailey took another bag Jamie moved to another position until he felt confident enough to get up and run off into the night.

'HALSTON' 1981

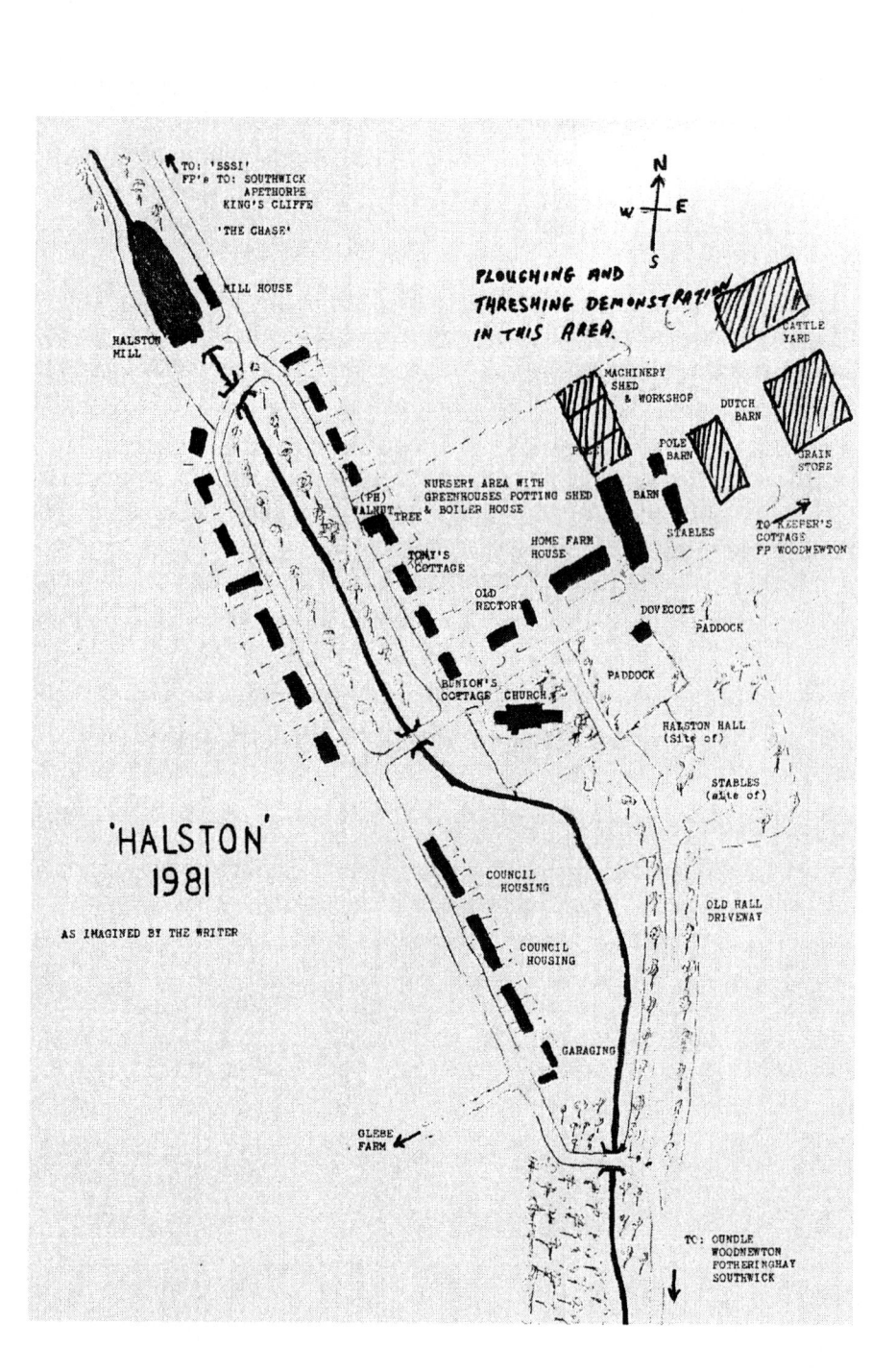

AS IMAGINED BY THE WRITER

CHAPTER I

It's Monday 6th April 1981, not the most brilliant of days, but visibility is good enough for me to look out of my windscreen at the panoramic view over the Nene Valley. My name is Jim Evans. I've been staying with my cousin on his farm in Hertfordshire, gradually getting myself fit after the accident. I've got my ordnance survey maps and typically the area I'm looking at is bisected onto sheets 141 and 142. Just as well I've got an old map as well, sheet 134, cost someone 44p in 1971. I got it from Oxfam. From my vantage point on Tansor Wold I can pick out Oundle, a water tower between Glapthorne and Southwick (although I can't see Southwick which is in a dip), Fotheringhay Church is clearly visible with its Lantern Tower. I've had plenty of time to pore over the maps and I feel that I know the area quite well already.

The village I'm heading for is called Halston. It has no through roads so you only go there if you want to. Only one way in and out, about three quarters of a mile from the through road with a sharp chicane bridge about half way along. I'm looking for Brynda Loring, my best mate's widow, killed in the accident which nearly killed me as well. I only actually met her the once, but I had heard plenty about her from Pete. I've got some of Pete's photos of her, some of them quite saucy. I didn't think he'd want anyone else to see them. His guitar had somehow survived the accident and as no one knew whether it was his or mine it had been left with me. The photos were tucked into a flap in the case. As I said, I only met her the once, but I understood why Pete had raved about her so much. In fact I had the most erotic dream featuring her during the night I stayed with them. It's just as well it was only the once or I'd have made a pass at her.

I doubt if she'd have been very thrilled, I was as bald as a badger then. I'd had no hair on my body for as long as I could remember. When I'd returned to the land of the living after the accident I was amazed to find that I was growing hair. There was no medical explanation for this, and although it's not as thick as one would like, it's changed my appearance beyond recognition. It was lucky that Brynda had kept in touch with our Sergeant Major's wife otherwise I'd have had no clue as to her whereabouts. She moved out of her married quarters as soon as possible, because she couldn't stand the sympathy and had got a job in a plant nursery in Halston. If you wanted to bury yourself in the countryside of Northamptonshire no doubt you could not find a better place.

I ate my sandwiches and headed off down the hill, across the A605 into Tansor, then to Fotheringhay. Less than 15 minutes after leaving the viewpoint I was through the chicane heading into Halston. On the right I saw two blocks of six garages, one block slightly newer than the other. A track led off to the left with a board announcing Glebe Farm, then three blocks of four council houses. I turned right at the T-junction, over the stream again then left past three rows of cottages, two rows thatched and one stone slated, then the pub which I was relieved to see, looked well maintained, and more importantly, did B & B.

It was called the Walnut Tree, obviously after the enormous tree between the pub and the stream. I got out of the car and walked down to the stream, picking my way through a host of golden daffodils. It looked absolutely fantastic, the daffs and assorted small trees all the way along the stream, on both sides until the roads merged again via yet another bridge. The two bridges had stone built arches with parapets, no doubt built many years before mechanical transport was invented, when the longest vehicle would have had four wooden wheels, possibly pulled by six horses.

On the other side of the stream another row of assorted houses, some relatively new, bordered the roadway. Beyond the bottom bridge I could see the watermill I had noted on my map. Turning back to the pub I could see that it was a substantial building, L-shaped with a stone slated roof, built of the local limestone, with attractive stone mullioned windows, parapets up the gable ends and three beautiful stone chimneys, each I guessed to be about five feet tall. I went back to the car and parked it up with several others in the large car park and went into the pub via the back door. I found myself in the bar.

Through the lounge/dining room several people were eating. Although it wasn't long since I'd eaten my few sandwiches I quickly decided that I would try their steak and kidney pie. I ordered from the fairly buxom lady at the bar and bought a pint of shandy (I'm no big drinker these days, although I'd had my stupid period in my youth). I enquired about B & B and found that they had no visitors and the terms were very reasonable.

THE ARM OF COINCIDENCE

'I'll show you to your room when you've had your lunch,' smiled the good lady who I quickly worked out from the conversation round me to be the landlady. Her name was Rose and her husband, who was both landlord and chef, was Jeff Walker. The dining room was very comfortable with old oak beams, nearly a foot square and all the oak floor joints were exposed as well. I couldn't fault the steak and kidney and declined a sweet although the list was very tempting. The last thing I wanted was to start piling on the weight, after all, it had taken two years to get fit after my long spell in hospital.

When there was a brief lull at the bar, Rose showed me to my room which was up a solid oak staircase to a room at the back. The room was furnished attractively and more comfortable than I had expected for the price. Rose left me to return to her duties and I went to the window to see the view. Amazingly I looked straight out over the pub car park, into a plant nursery with large greenhouses. Over to the right was another large old stone building with another building partly visible to the side, which looked like former stables converted to garages. To the left the view was over arable land to woods. Beyond the nursery was a cluster of large, mostly modern, farm buildings.

As I gazed out at what had to be Brynda's workplace I saw a boy of about three years old who had to be Jamie Loring, heading through the nursery towards a door in the high hedge, at the back of the pub car park. It took him a while to undo the door and I guessed it was bolted on his side to keep out unwanted visitors. He came to the back door of the pub and I soon saw him going back clutching a bag of crisps. It was a while before he appeared from behind the door and skipped down a path towards the house. The door either had a very stiff bolt or he had to have a box to stand on to reach it.

If his mum was as lovely inside as she was outside from what I had seen on our one encounter, Pete was always extolling her points, I was half in love with her already. But would she like me? Enough to let me take care of her and Jamie as I knew Pete would have wanted me to.

I went down to the car and started moving my gear upstairs to my room. I had several trips and the springs had noticeably risen when I had finished. My portable Yamaha keyboard, camera gear, clothes, a few books, mostly about birds and flowers etc, and Pete's guitar which I could now play reasonably well. Not up to Pete's standard, but nothing to be ashamed of. The keyboard I could play from music or memory. If I was singing I didn't play the melody except during a rest period.

THE ARM OF COINCIDENCE

At this point in time I had no idea how long I would be staying. It rather depended on how I got on with Brynda. When I'd got things stowed away to my satisfaction I got my camera bag and binoculars and went to explore. I took both the old and new maps with me. As I walked back past the cottages the way I'd driven in, I knew I'd have to get larger scale maps to pinpoint every building. I presumed that Oundle would have a bookshop where I could buy an up to date one and hopefully a library where I might be able to look at an even older one. I knew that the first really accurate maps had been drawn towards the end of the last century.

I turned left at the T-junction so the church was on my right. Stone built, with stone slate roof, a squat tower with no spire. The porch was open, but the door into the church was locked. The noticeboard informed me that the church of St Wilfred's and All Saints was a redundant church and was maintained by the redundant churches fund. The key holder was a Cyril Williams who lived in number 1 Thatched Cottage. I had just passed it and had noticed an old boy working in his garden. I went round the church studying gravestones. The most recent was nearly a hundred years old, then I noticed an extension at the back which still had lots of space left. The most recent stone, with a beautifully kept garden was to an Elizabeth Williams who had died in 1979. I suspected this was Mrs Cyril Williams.

On the opposite side of the road was the large house I had seen from the window in my room. The name Old Rectory was on a metal cast plaque on one gate. Imposing stone gateposts. No doubt sold off when the church had been declared redundant. Redundant or not, the churchyard was well cared for compared with many I'd seen. Next on the left was a big farmhouse which had been made into two. The farm entrance declared it to be Home Farm, D. Woodward Esq. Perhaps he fancied himself as the village squire. The last building on the left was a modern grain store.

After that the roadway deteriorated somewhat and an arrow pointed to Keepers Cottage and another with a large footprint engraved said Public Footpath to Woodnewton. By the looks of the track there was possibly a keeper in residence so I turned around and headed back.

Having been concentrating on the farm I had failed to notice a square building opposite the farmhouse. Four equal sides with a stone roof coming to a point and open jutting dormers on the three sides of the roof I could see without a closer look. A look at the map confirmed my thoughts that it may have been a dovecote. It was set in what appeared to be a small paddock. There was an imposing looking gateway between this and the churchyard with crests in the stonework of both pillars. The effect was rather spoilt by a rusty iron gate tied to the pillars with what in Hertfordshire was known as 'farmers' friend' (polypropylene baler twine).

I wondered briefly if it had the same title here. I looked at my map again and recalled seeing Halston Hall (site of) when I was preparing for this visit. I thought I'd walk along the other side of the stream and I stood on the hump backed bridge trying to see if there were any fish in the crystal clear water. Eventually I was rewarded by the flash of hundreds of very small fish as they sped under the bridge. I nearly missed them, hardly believing the speed at which they moved. Fishing plays no part in my life, so I had no idea what they were. Almost all of the trees on both sides of the stream were decked out with a mass of pink flowers, some with dark leaves, which I identified as purple plum or pissard. Not a very nice name for a beautiful tree. I think I'll stick with purple plum. There were also a few almost crimson hawthorns and in a sense that enormous walnut from which the pub derived its name, seemed out of place. Oh well, nothing is perfect.

Some of the houses on this side of the stream were relatively new so there had either been replacements, or infill. Some were old cottages with extensions and some hadn't seen much change since they were built possibly two or three hundred years ago.

I crossed the stream yet again, to where the road formed almost a triangle, almost, because the roads curved. The mill had quite a big yard. The mill house was at right angles to the mill and I could see the lake which formed the millpond extending further up the valley. The road quickly degenerated into a track, and I continued, as it was a public right of way leading to Southwick, Apethorpe and Kingscliffe. After about three-quarters of a mile I came to a parting of the ways, a different track to each village. Directly ahead the valley deepened and the entrance gate had a notice which said S. S. S. I. No public right of way, access only to Trust members or by permission from Dan Woodward, owner. Oh well, I'd have to ask Dan Woodward if I wanted to go in there. I knew that S. S. S. I. stood for Site of Special Scientific Interest, which meant that the farmer had agreed a management policy to protect a natural habitat for rare plants, and/or wild creatures.

I was wandering slowly back to the village, drinking in the peace and quiet, when a couple of Harriers roared over at low level. If I'd been wearing a hat I bet it would have jumped up a foot. So much for the peace and tranquillity. I sat on the bridge parapet watching the water come through the sluice under the derelict waterwheel. Considering how little distance it was from the source of the river the steam had a remarkable flow to it. I could only suppose that the spring which fed it came from underground reservoirs and could only escape at a limited rate. Northamptonshire, according to legend, is the county of spires, squires, springs and stately homes. Well this village had no spire, no longer a squire or stately home, but definitely a good spring.

I had been given a back door key along with my room key so I could get into the pub at any time. As the pub hadn't yet reopened I used my key and went into the Public Bar. Very similar to the lounge in size, with a dartboard, a skittle board of a type I'd never seen before (almost exclusive to Northants I found out later) and a piano. Rose heard the back door and came in to see if I needed anything.

'A glass of orange squash or something similar would be nice.' She nodded and reached under the bar for a squash bottle, put a generous amount in a pint glass and filled it with water. I held out some money but she waved it aside.

'No, as you're staying it's on the house. Cheap enough anyway, and we aren't that greedy.'

I thanked her and asked if the piano was playable.

'Oh, it's a bit honky tonk, but I play it good enough for Christmas carols.'

'May I?' I asked and when she nodded I lifted the lid and played a few chords. Surprisingly it was in tune so I sat down and played Twelfth Street Rag Russ Conway style. There was a double clap from the bar and I turned to see that Jeff had joined Rose. He grinned at me.

'We'll have to see how it goes down with the regulars. That's if you'd like to give it a whirl. We sometimes have a bloke in from Southwick who can make it talk, and the customers seem to enjoy it.'

He paused, then asked, 'Any idea how long you'll stay?'

'Not really, I have no definite plans, not less than two or three weeks, though. I've had a walk around the village and it looks like good walking country. I'm overdue for some holiday and having stuck a pin in the map, reckon I've struck lucky.' There was no way I was going to mention my real reason for being there. I looked at my watch, still only four o'clock, and decided to explore a little further.

THE ARM OF COINCIDENCE

'Any chance of a glass of water?' I asked. 'I'm still a bit thirsty.'

'You can have a pint if you like,' laughed Jeff, 'and by the way you'd better sign in. We don't even know your name yet.' He passed the visitor's book over to me and I signed in as James Evans, giving my cousin's farm address. I passed the book back.

'James eh, bit posh that.'

I grinned at him, 'That's just for the record, everyone calls me Jim.'

'Not from the valleys then?' with a passable Welsh accent.

'Nah, Sarth London,' I replied in like manner.

'Well you certainly don't sound like a Londoner, I'd never have guessed.'

'No, well my mum was a school teacher and believed in teaching us all half decent English. No thanks to the pint, it's kind of you, but I've learnt that I should have only a very small intake of alcohol.'

After I had drunk the water I went out again and this time headed past the council houses. Some of them had very well maintained gardens, others were badly neglected where it was obvious that the tenants were only looking for a roof over their heads. All were occupied. Some cars were parked near the garages which meant that either some people had more than one car, or some were off the road.

It didn't take long to get to the chicane. You wouldn't want to hit ice here, or thick fog. I suppose I was going quite slowly when I came in and hadn't realised how sharp the bends were. There was a wood on the right hand side, rising relatively steeply up away from the stream, no doubt the reason for the chicane in the first place. The wood had many different species of tree. I saw oaks, ash, sycamore, scots pine, larch, the odd beech, and even on closer inspection, a wild service tree. They were the Druids' fertility trees and not easy to propagate, they usually grow suckers around them, but I saw none. It was the most upright one I'd ever seen.

I heard a movement and looked round to see a guy striding towards me with a black retriever at his heels, looking none too pleased.

'What y'up to then?' was his hostile greeting.

'I was just admiring this fine service tree,' I replied mildly.

'Yer wat? That's a maple.'

'No my friend, it's a wild service tree, I know that the leaves look rather like maple, but the two points near the stem are completely different. It's in the same family as mountain ash or rowan, and the

THE ARM OF COINCIDENCE

whitebeam, in other woods it's sorbus, it'll have white flowers and reddish brown berries.'

He looked me up and down, 'Well so long as you're not after me birds. I s'pose you're not doing any harm. Where you from anyway? Aven't see you afore I don't think.'

'I'm on holiday staying at the pub, got any more interesting trees around here have you?'

'Some in the old hall gardens, you can come with me if you like, I'm on me way home an' we can cut through back up the track to my 'ouse.'

I fell into step with him and we crossed the bridge to a gateway which had once been grand, that I hadn't even noticed on my way in. We climbed over the gate through to an avenue of lime trees with overgrown privet hedges; the track was still sound under the grass. I looked up into the sixty-foot high trees at what looked like mistletoe. I got my binoculars out and said, 'Just as I thought, mistletoe.'

'Mistletoe grows on apple trees you daft 'apeth,' he snorted. I handed him the binoculars.

'Well damn my rage, I can see some berries on it still. I thought it only grew on apple trees.'

He passed the glasses back to me, shaking his head. 'O, well I s'pose you learn summat new every day.'

We reached the end of the avenue, the retriever trotting quietly at heel. 'The old house stood over there, so I've bin told, 'ad to be knocked down in the mid 50's, 'cos it weren't safe.'

'Some fine specimen trees still here though,' I remarked looking round. A fine cedar of Lebanon stood in the centre of what had once been a lawn with a driveway round it. There was a fine old Judas tree, a couple of wellingtonias, renamed sequoia gigantum after the Red Indian chief who invented a written language for his people.

'Bet you can't put a name to this un.' He pointed to a large shrub like tree with a pinkish glow to it.

'I don't suppose you'd care to put money on that would you? No I thought not. The flowers are just getting over, I bet it had a reddish glow to it a couple of weeks ago.'

I went over for a closer look. 'See how the branches grow back together wherever they touch. I wouldn't like to try to climb it, you'd probably get stuck.'

'So, OK smarty pants wot is it?'

'Persian Ironwood, Latin, Parrotia Persica named after the guy who first recorded it.'

'How d'you know?'

I shrugged, 'I just love trees, it's one of my hobbies, the more bizarre the better. I've got a book in my room at the pub which has almost every tree which grows in Britain. I'll show you if you like sometime.'

'Nah, s'far as I'm concerned you can go where you like, so long as you don't disturb me birds.'

I shook my head as he walked off up the lane towards the keepers cottage. Another country character, what would we do without them!

It was almost six o'clock by the time I'd wandered back to the Walnut Tree and I had a good look at the tree. Somewhere between a hundred and fifty and two hundred years old if sheer size had anything to do with it. Very rare for a walnut to go over two hundred years as they were quite fast growing. I went in the back door and eased off my walking boots, carried them upstairs, got washed, shaved, and changed and went down to the bar. The pub was open and already there were a few people in the bar. I asked Rose for a shandy.

'If I give you fifty quid now you can keep chalking things up till it runs out, then ask for more, is that OK?'

'That's very much OK! We know you won't do a runner just yet.' She leant towards me sotto voice, 'Join the old boy with the pipe, what he don't know about this village, isn't worth knowing.' I nodded my thanks, took my shandy and headed over to the fireplace where the old boy sat. Late seventies, I thought but still with a twinkle in his eye.

'We don't see too many strangers round here,' he said as he removed his pipe, which didn't appear to be alight. His eyes followed mine and he leant forward confidentially. 'It's almost part of me, I only takes it out of my mouth, to speak, eat, spit and sleep.' He made quite a performance of restoking it and getting it going.

'So what brings you to this neck o' the woods young fella? I see you're staying at the pub here, I expect that's your Cortina in the car park?' Back went the pipe for a few more puffs.

'I sort of closed my eyes, and jabbed in a needle into the map and here I am. I'm pleased to be here as it is a really attractive village,' I leant forward, 'once you get past the first dozen houses.'

He nodded, 'Nobody here had much say in it, the land was compulsory purchased, the only concession they gave us was the Warboys bricks which blend in half reasonable.'

THE ARM OF COINCIDENCE

I held out my hand, 'Jim's the name.' He shook my hand with a firm grip 'I'm Cyril but everybody calls me Bunion, don't care what I'm called as long as it's not late for meals.'

'Why Bunion?' I asked.

''Cos I had a good bunion for years. I have to wear really wide fitting boots otherwise it still plays up.'

'Did I see your name in the church porch as being a key holder? Is it you keeping the churchyard tidy?'

'Yeah, well, not many people are daft enough to work for nothing nowadays, I'd hate to see it covered in nettles. I've got a nice display of primroses in there at the moment and I reckon there are more wild flowers in there throughout the year than you get in a churchyard that's hardly touched.'

He had a few more puffs on the old pipe. I've never smoked myself, reckon it's a mug's game. But whatever he was smoking didn't smell as bad as cigarette smoke. 'That's God's Acre, you know, the churchyard, although the church was made redundant because hardly anyone supported it. I see no reason why it should become an eyesore not while I can manage it anyhow.'

Changing the subject slightly, I said, 'I had a walk this afternoon as far as the S. S. S. I. and it says people without trust membership should get permission from Dan Woodward.'

He gave his funny old grin. 'That might be a bit difficult, he's in Canada, been gone about three weeks and not expected back till early October. Still you can ask Tony, his son, he'll be in a bit later for his dinner.' He leant forward confidentially, 'His missis left him a couple of weeks ago, took the two boys with her. Apparently she tried to get him to pay himself more money whilst the old man's away and he refused. Mind you the old man treats him like dirt, can't think why, 'cos he treats Caroline OK. He only pays Tony basic wages which is totally unfair 'cos the lad went to agricultural college and is a damn good worker. He could leave I suppose, but his dad'll cut him off completely if he does.'

'Doesn't sound a very nice man, this Dan Woodward.'

'Very complex character, charming when he wants to be, especially to his peers. Likes to be the gentleman, rides round in a British Racing green Jaguar. Guess I know him too well, no son of mine would be treated like he treats Tony.'

'Got family have you, Bunion?'

'Yep, two sons and one daughter, nothing to keep them here of course. All married with two apiece, so I got six grandchildren. Lost me wife two years ago so I come in here every night for a good meal.'

His pipe had gone out but he stuffed it between his teeth and he didn't appear to notice. Rose called across, 'What's it to be tonight Bunion, before we get busy?'

'I'll have gammon steak please.'

'And the same for me please.'

'Right, be about fifteen minutes I should think.'

Bunion grinned at me and checked his watch, 'Make that fourteen minutes, it'll be here.' He looked around 'You're the only stranger in tonight. Three quarters of them at least are from outside the village. It's a very popular pub, real ale and jolly good food at the right price. They take the view that it's better to be busy and certain of their customers than drive them somewhere else by being greedy.'

'There's Tony just come in.' He put his hand up, and I turned to see a big blond guy of about my own age, looked almost Scandinavian, couldn't be though, unless that's why his dad didn't like him much. Still, plenty of fathers and sons didn't get on that well. He turned to Rose and asked what Bunion was having tonight, he opted for the same. Got himself a pint of Adnams (had I mentioned that this was a free house so they could sell what they liked?).

'Mind if I join you chaps?'

I pulled out a chair as invitation and introduced myself with the usual holiday bit. 'Bunion here says that your dad's taken himself off to Canada so I guess I need to ask you for permission to have a look in the S. S. S. I.?'

'No problem mate, I hear you met our 'ornery keeper this afternoon. With your knowledge of trees I could hardly refuse. It's not very often anyone makes an impression on him.'

Bunion snorted with a grin, 'Keepers, I've shit em, cocky young beggar, but he'll never make a first class keeper as long as he's got a hole –'

Tony interrupted, 'Yes, Bunion, we all know your opinion and you're probably right, I know he's not in Harry Churchill's class, but he's not a bad shot and he's got rid of a lot of vermin since he's been here.'

Bunion leant towards me, 'Tell you what, young fella, I'll take you up the hollow tomorrow if you like. Know a bit about the countryside flora and fauna you know.'

THE ARM OF COINCIDENCE

'Alright Bunion, we all know you're no muggins but there is no need to show off.'

It was pretty obvious that these two chaps were on the same wavelength and knew each other inside out. Rose came across with the cutlery and condiments then went back for our food. Bunion tapped his watch and winked at me. Exactly fourteen minutes. 'Yours will be here in a couple of minutes, Tony.'

'Great, don't wait for me, chaps.'

'We weren't going to, mate, think we're stupid.' Bunion grinned at him 'Here, have a chip while you're waiting.'

The evening passed quickly. Everyone seemed to know everyone else and I found myself drawn into conversation with so many people that I couldn't remember all their names. There was quite a lot of farming talk and I met a slim dark haired young man with a ruddy complexion called Robert. He had a milking herd at Glebe Farm. I'd passed the entrance on my way in although you couldn't see the house or buildings from the road because it was in a dip. I was invited to call by anytime. 'There aren't many footpaths across my land so I don't get problems with ramblers leaving gates open (unlike Tony here). I'll trust you not to let my cows out.'

At some stage during the evening Rose looked rather meaningfully at the Joanna but I shook my head and mouthed, 'Not tonight.' She nodded. Suddenly it was eleven o'clock and most people had gone home. Bedtime. I went to my room and crashed out. I hadn't seen Brynda, in fact she hadn't been mentioned all evening, but there was plenty of time. Softly. Softly.

CHAPTER II

I woke at 7 o'clock to a lovely morning so I had a quick wash and shave, grabbed my camera, crept downstairs and out of the back door. I didn't think I'd disturbed Jeff and Rose who no doubt had had a late night. The first people I saw were Bunion and Tony by Bunion's cottage. Tony looked a bit harassed, but waited for me to join them.

'I don't suppose you can drive a tractor can you?' asked Tony.

'Might depend on what tractor and what is behind it. I've done some work on my cousin's place in Hertfordshire, I'll have a look.'

'We've got mostly Massey-Ferguson, we use a 590 for drilling and I need to be in two places at once because my man's off sick. Bunion is going on a 595 for me with a big spring tine to level out the ploughing. My sugar beet land is ready for drilling at the same time and it's high time it was all in.'

I fell into step with them and we walked briskly round to the farm to the machinery shed. Bunion started the 595 which already had a wide springtime cultivator attached, drove it up to the fuel tank and started to fill up. I looked at the seed drill behind the 590, it too was a Massey, the same model as my cousin's which I had been trusted with once or twice.

'OK, Tony, I can help you out, I expect it's set up to do tramlines?' (Tramlines are when two rows of seed are cut off to leave a track for the sprayer to follow.)

'Sure is,' his face clouded over a bit, 'trouble is I've only got a limited budget while the old man's away, so don't know if I can afford you.'

I put my hand on his shoulder, 'I'm not in the habit of seeing people stuck.' I told him. 'I shall enjoy it, so you needn't pay me, I might need a bit of help myself one day.' His face lit up. 'Good man! I'll take the seed and fertiliser on the trailer up to the field, you follow me in the Land Rover to fetch me back. Bunion will need a good hours start on you so there's no rush.'

It was of course one of the more distant fields from the farmstead, up the chase past the mill and Tony parked the tractor, a 135, and trailer on the track just beyond the gateway. Bunion was already at work on the beautiful reddish brown soil, and the scent of newly moved earth was in the air.

'One of our best fields,' remarked Tony as he got behind the wheel of the Land Rover and I got into the passenger side. 'All of these fields have names, you know, and this one partly takes its name from the ironstone base which gives it the reddish colour. 'Far Bloom Furlong, the bloom meaning iron.' He turned the Land Rover and we started back down the chase.

'I don't know if they'll be up at the pub yet, and I didn't make any arrangements about breakfast,' I told him.

'No problem mate, if you can settle for cereals we can stop by my cottage, haven't eaten myself yet. I usually nip in at about nine o'clock for mine. It's a bit early, but circumstances alter from day to day.'

He pulled up at the second cottage from the pub, one of the stone slated roofed ones. He saw me looking at the roof.

'Collyweston slates, mined from the village of the same name near Stamford. Damned expensive now if your roof needs attention, because you have to use secondhand. If your house isn't listed you can sell the slates and put an artificial Colly roof on.'

'Is this one listed? I asked curiously.

''Fraid so, fortunately it's in good nick, that's one thing about the old man, he looks after his buildings.'

I followed him into the cottage which was reasonably clean considering his wife had been gone awhile. He had cornflakes and I opted for shredded wheat from his selection. Then we went back to the farm.

'We shall have to put the drill onto its transporter 'cos it won't go through the bridge,' explained Tony. 'And if there's any cars parked in the road we can't get past those either.'

Once again Tony took the tractor and I followed in the Land Rover. We unloaded the drill and filled up from the trailer ready to start. Barley in the front box, fertiliser in the rear. 'I expect I can bring the trailer into the field once the headlands are done?' I asked. 'Yep, you know how to set up the tramline system?' I nodded. Bunion had already covered a fair bit of ground and his headland was wider than mine needed to be, so he wouldn't wipe out my mark when he turned. The 'Mark' is made by a disc on the side of the drill to show where to drive. There is also the change in soil appearance which indicates what has been done.

Tony watched me start off and waited until I'd done the first round of the headland without getting hooked up in the hedge. He came to the tractor door. 'I'll see if my sister can bring you some sandwiches and a drink about one o'clock,' he told me. I gave him a thumbs up and away he went. It's amazing how much ground you can cover with these huge machines. When I first went to what was then my uncle's farm, the latest thing was the Fordson Super Major. Six forward, two reverse gears with a two stage clutch so that you could change gear without stopping, whatever you were powering behind you.

I suppose I was over about half the field and Bunion was nearly finished when I saw an old wartime jeep coming up the chase. Five to one, and I'd hardly noticed the passage of time. I drove along to the trailer as I was due for a refill on the drill anyway. A pretty dark haired girl slid off the seat of the jeep, she didn't look anything like Tony, but I supposed it must be his sister.

'Hi, I'm Caroline,' she held out her hand. 'You must be Jim, Tony's been telling me how you're helping him out.' I shook her hand and then she waved to Bunion. He raised his hand in acknowledgement and turned towards us when he got to his headland. Caroline reached for some folding chairs from the back of the jeep and I noticed a carrycot tied to a seat. I had a peep but the only clue I had as to the sex of the baby was the pink clothing. Taking a chance I asked what her name was. 'Fiona, her dad's got Scottish blood as well as a Scottish name.'

Bunion stopped a little way away and cut out his engine. I watched as he climbed carefully down from his high perch, then carefully straightened his limbs. He grinned, 'Not so young as wot I was before I got so old as wot I am now.' I knew from the twinkle in his eye that it was a phrase he regularly used. Caroline had set up a card table and placed a huge flask, plastic mugs and sandwiches on it. She gestured towards the food, 'Take a seat and help yourselves.' Bunion stuffed his old pipe into his top pocket and I waited for him to pick up his choice. Caroline had brought some for herself and there was more than enough to go around with hot strong tea.

We had been companionably munching away when the baby started to cry. 'O dear. Feeding time, I hoped she would sleep 'til we got home. I'll have to feed her or she'll get really upset.' She unstrapped the baby and lifted her out, settled herself in the chair and found a nipple for the baby. She didn't seem the slightest bit embarrassed. I was fascinated, I had never seen a baby suckling before.

THE ARM OF COINCIDENCE

'Oh blast!' Caroline had a wet patch by her other boob, spreading fast. Without even thinking I pulled her dress open and caught the stream of milk squirting out into my mouth, then closing the distance took the nipple gently into my mouth. I was suddenly hit by the enormity of what I'd just done and made to move away. 'No, please carry on. I make far too much milk and that's better than expressing it myself.' She sighed. 'I'll tell you when it's all under control.' So I kept gently going although I think my ears had gone pink. Caroline might not be embarrassed, but I was.

'OK, all under control.' I withdrew and she murmured, 'Thank you, Malcolm and I hadn't thought of that solution.'

'I didn't think of it either. I just did it,' I said.

'I'm glad you're pleased rather than cross.' She moved the baby over to the nipple I'd just abandoned. 'Still plenty for you, darling.' I took a further look at old Bunion and was surprised to see him rubbing his eyes. 'I'd better get me job finished,' he said gruffly. 'Thanks for the food, Caroline.' He climbed laboriously back into the cab, restarted the tractor, lifted the cultivator and went off to the other end of the field to his mark. Caroline burped Fiona, changed her nappy, and popped a contented baby back into the carrycot. We collected up the things and I stowed them in the back again. As I turned around I got a swift peck on the cheek, a cheeky smile and Caroline slid back onto the old lefthand drive and drove away.

I rubbed my cheek, then refilled the drill. I took the machine back to my mark checked the tramline device and was away again.

I saw Bunion drive over to the gate and watched as he folded up the sides of the cultivator from the tractor seat so that he could get out of the gate. He might be in his seventies but he certainly had all his marbles.

It wasn't long before I'd finished, or rather it didn't seem long. I had managed to almost run the drill out, so I loaded it back onto its transporter and set off back to the farm. The Land Rover was outside Bunion's cottage when I went by. He must have been watching out for me, because as I walked out of the big shed, he was waiting.

The pipe was well alight, and he gestured to the passenger seat. 'I'll run you back for the trailer in case it rains again,' he said. 'I doubt if Tony'll get finished before dark and he won't want to stop until he's finished. It's a bit slower paced job than ours.'

THE ARM OF COINCIDENCE

We were soon back to the field and I got out. 'Do you want me to take the trailer?'

'If you don't mind, I've had enough bouncing for one day.' He beckoned me a bit closer. 'I wouldn't tell you this myself you know, but I reckon you're the most alright fella I've met in a long while.' He let in the clutch with a grin and drove away. I watched him go. And so are you old boy, I thought, so are you. I started the Fergie and set off back to the farm with the remains of my load. Glancing at the mill house as I went by I was rewarded by Caroline assisting a small hand to wave from the window. I wondered briefly whether she would tell hubbie about the little episode and what his reaction might be. I shrugged, so what, what was done was done, and apparently for the best.

I found an industrial vacuum in the shed and sucked out the remains of the fertiliser. I emptied it into a plastic bag and tied it up tightly to keep it from going slimy. The seed could stop for another day, I decided. It was nearly six o'clock by the time I got back to the Walnut Tree.

I checked out with Rose if it was OK to have a bath and explained what I'd been doing. When I'd cleaned up and had a shave (after two years, the novelty had worn off. Now it was just a chore), I went down to the bar, got a glass of water, and asked for gammon steak, pineapple, and a couple of eggs. I grinned at Rose, 'It's hard work lugging those bags off the trailer into the drill, got to keep me strength up, no telling what I shall be doing next.'

Bunion was already in his favourite chair near the fire, so I took my glass of water and joined him. I put my hand up to my mouth and spoke into it, 'I wouldn't tell you this myself mind, but not many guys of your age would have done what you did today.' He nearly choked on his pipe, spluttering and laughing so much that he had to get his spotted hankie out to wipe his eyes. It was nearly seven before a dusty Tony came in, ordered a meal, and came over to our table with his pint. He said nothing but picked up Bunion's empty glass and had it refilled. 'Cheers,' as he and the old man clicked glasses.

'I've told Rose that all the meals are on me tonight.' He held up his hand as I would have declined. 'It's the least I can do in the circumstances. I'm very grateful. If the forecast is right, and we get some rain, it'll be just right for germination.'

Rose brought Tony's meal over and he tucked in. Bunion restoked his pipe and I watched a couple of lads playing skittles. The table had a net round the sides and back leaving only the front open for attack. There were three missiles called cheeses and Bunion took it upon himself to explain the intricacies of the game. If you were fortunate enough to floor all nine skittles with the first or second throw, you had a stack up, your score being the total number of skittles knocked down with three cheeses. Very good players could sometimes score the maximum of twenty-seven by getting a stack with each throw. The two lads playing weren't particularly expert as they rarely scored nine with all three cheeses.

'I used to be pretty good, even if I say it myself, but my throwing arm isn't what it was now.' Tony nodded agreement. 'He used to be the pub's star player and won many a pig at local garden fetes in the days when loads of people kept a pig and some chickens at the bottom of their gardens'. He continued, 'I can remember when the mill was still working and the miller used to mix up pig and chicken meal, even sheep grub. He used to take a load of spuds to London and bring back stuff like fish meal and soya from Silvertown docks to mix with his wheat and barley. All that stopped in the late sixties because the price of feed went up and made it totally uneconomic for people to keep pigs and chickens.' He grinned, 'Imagine the uproar now if anyone had a pig at the bottom of their garden. Our commuters would have the environmental health people out the first day.'

Bunion chimed in, 'The mill closed down in sixty nine and the miller took himself off to somewhere near Peterborough and just did general haulage. Dan kept the mill for grinding our own barley, and rolling a few oats. When the water wheel started falling to bits the mill was left abandoned.'

Tony began to speak again, 'When Caroline wanted to get married, she wanted to stay here, so dad gave them the mill house provided they paid for restoration themselves. Malcolm rolled his sleeves up and did all the labouring jobs himself, and even some of the so called skilled jobs like plumbing. He's not a bad old shit for a barrister.'

Bunion grinned, 'Don't give us that. I know the pair of you get on like a house on fire, and speak of the devil, here he comes.'

I turned to see a guy of around forty in an old sweater and jeans getting a pint of Adnams at the bar, then turn towards us. His face split into a huge grin and he held his hand out as I stood up. 'You must be Jim? I've heard all about you from Caroline. Quick thinking eh?'

'Not really. Just instinct I guess. Thought I might get my ears boxed. Boy, was I embarrassed afterwards.'

'Don't be. I tried it myself a little while ago. Damn sight better than messing around with that gadget she's got. Can't say I care a lot for the taste though, nothing like cows' milk.' This last remark in an undertone so that no one else could hear.

'So Jim,' Rose spoke behind me, 'you going to give us a tune tonight?'

'Would you be offended if I fetched my own keyboard down? It's a bit more versatile than the Joanna.'

'No of course not, just so long as we get a few tunes.' I turned to Tony. 'Want to come up with me and bring the legs down, save a journey?'

'OK.' He got to his feet and we went up to my room. I showed him my keyboard. 'Top of the range Yamaha,' I told him with a touch of pride. His eye was caught by Pete's guitar case in the corner. 'Play that as well do you?' I made a self-deprecatory movement with my hand. 'Not so well as the keyboard, but I'm improving.'

'Can I have look?'

'Sure help yourself.' He opened the case and stared reverently. 'Wow. A genuine Gibson. I've got a pretty bog standard guitar which the old man deplores, but I dug my heels in on that one. May I?'

'Be my guest.' He carefully removed it from the case and expertly began to tune it. Then he strummed a few chords, picked up the tuning fork and fine tuned it.

'Reckon you can play it as well or better than me,' I told him. 'Bring it down with the keyboard legs and we'll see what sort of a mess we can make together.' We started off down the stairs and I had a sudden thought. 'Do you sing along with it?' I asked.

'I try,' he rejoined.

We moved the table to one side in Bunion's corner and he moved a bit closer to the fire to give us room. I plugged into the nearest socket and we were as ready as we were ever going to be. 'Better get started before we lose our nerve. Do you know the Everley's All I Do is Dream?' He grinned, 'Let's go.' I played an intro and we began. I couldn't believe the way we harmonised naturally, almost as if we'd being doing it all our lives. If anything his voice was better than Pete's and that's saying something for an amateur.

THE ARM OF COINCIDENCE

I was struck by the fact that apart from us the pub had gone silent and when the last strains died away, and the applause sounded I realised that people had crowded in from the lounge and Rose and Jeff were beaming from ear to hear.

'Guys Mitchell's one of my favourites,' Tony whispered. 'How about And there's a pawnshop?' He nodded and away we went. Of course Guy Mitchell was a soloist so it didn't sound like him, but no one seemed bothered about that.

Tony and I were enjoying our evening when Brynda came in and came over to Tony. 'I went out to check the greenhouses and I could hear you singing, it sounded great out there and I couldn't resist coming in to see what was going on.'

I stood up and Tony introduced us. Brynda shook hands and I was certain that she hadn't recognised me; after all, the last and only time we met I hadn't any hair and Pete always used my nickname Lucky, the name my mum had originally called me. I knew from Pete that one of her favourite numbers was 'When you walk in the Room' by the Searchers, so I suggested it to Tony. He nodded and away we went with Brynda almost immediately joining in. Pete had always said she had a terrific voice and if it hadn't been for the danger she could have joined us in Northern Ireland. Thank God she hadn't. After that number I thought 'Stop while you're ahead' and Tony and I took our stuff back upstairs. When we came down Brynda was chatting to Bunion. Tony spoke to her, 'Auntie keeping an ear out for Jamie?' She nodded, 'He rarely wakes up when once he's asleep but so long as one of us is there he's OK. He's adopted her as his granny you know.' She smiled at Tony and nodded to me, 'See you around I expect. Next time you two decide on a jam session give me a shout.'

I stood up, shook hands with her and grinned 'Sure thing. Can't think of anything I'd like better.' I watched her walk towards the door and thought of our first number. Maybe I wouldn't have to dream for the rest of my life.

'Lovely girl that,' remarked Bunion, 'had the most rotten luck, her husband got blown up in Northern Ireland by a load of crooks, because he was driving an almost identical car to the intended victim. Wrong car, in the wrong place, at the wrong time. The killers weren't connected with the IRA or the Loyalists, just a load of gangsters trying to eliminate the opposition.'

'Did they get caught?' I asked, playing dumb. Bunion shook his head,

'Don't think so, mind, she doesn't say much about it, she showed me a picture of him once with a bald headed bloke. Both in army uniform. Apparently he nearly got killed at the same time and she hasn't heard from him since. They were on some sort of undercover work so it never came out that they were in the army. Didn't want to blow the cover of their mates, she said.'

Bunion resumed sucking on his dead pipe. I said nothing except, 'What rotten luck for her.' Tony spoke again, 'Anyway it's an ill wind etc., she's given my aunt a new lease of life, thinks the world of young Jamie and she's dead chuffed that he calls her granny. She's recovered quite well from her stroke, her speech has come back, but she's lost the use of her left hand. The doctors say that it may come back with therapy. She only goes out when Brynda takes her in the car to Oundle for her treatment.'

'Brynda's got green fingers you know,' remarked Bunion. 'She's kept the old lady's nursery going this last two years, and I believe things will get a bit easier when Jamie starts Tansor play group after Easter.'

Tony got up to leave. 'Turning the cattle out to grass tomorrow, it's been too wet up to now.'

'Want a hand?' I asked. He shook his head. 'I would like a shot, if I dare pay you, but I'm not going to take advantage of your generosity this time. Anyway, with a bit of luck Steve will be back tomorrow. He's no layabout so I know he'll turn up if he possibly can.' I watched him go, then turned to Bunion, 'What's with Dan Woodward anyway, how can he appear to be so generous on the one hand and so mean on the other?'

Bunion sighed, 'I dunno, it's only Tony he don't treat right, almost as if he's trying to get him to go. Tony loves this place though, and he'll see it through. Pity about his wife and kids though. She hasn't been in touch since she left and although Tony went to Peterborough to her mum's house he drew a blank 'cos she'd moved and left no forwarding address. He hasn't had time to go looking as yet and he won't have time for a few weeks. Not 'till the silage and hay is made. Then only a short time before harvest starts.'

He refilled his pipe, 'Don't suppose you fancy a game of five and threes do you?'

'Never heard of it.'

'OK. I'll show you, it's done with dominoes, usually with four players but it's alright with two.'

THE ARM OF COINCIDENCE

I'm a fairly quick learner and soon got the hang of it. If both ends added up to fifteen you scored eight. Three fives and five threes. You had to be careful not to make it easy for your opponent to score a maximum. The score was kept on a special peg board by moving the pegs along.

After an hour I was almost holding my own but the crafty old devil seemed to have a sixth sense about what dominoes I was holding. Eventually we packed up with Bunion saying, 'Don't know about you Jim, but I'm ready to hit the hay.' He stood up, 'Goodnight, see you around,' and off he went and I thought, as Pepys would say 'and so to bed.'

Wednesday wasn't so good so I contented myself with seeking out Oundle school bookshop and buying myself some next scale up maps of the whole parish. I spent most of the day studying them so I knew all the fields and footpaths. There were no bridleways, surprisingly, but Dan's land came close enough to one to be able to join it if you wanted to.

There was no jam session and we agreed with Jeff and Rose that perhaps one night a week was enough, so we planned to play again on Tuesday night, and Tony said he would tell Brynda to see if she could come.

The next day, Thursday, I accidentally met Jamie in the car park and he was initially very wary but when I told him that his mum had sung with Tony and me in the pub he lost some of his nervousness. 'Did you know that there are some tiny fish in the stream?' I asked him. He shook his head. 'If you'd like me to show you, you can ask your mum if it's OK, then she'll know where you are.' He scampered off and a moment later Brynda appeared in the doorway with him. Smiling she said, 'I think I'll trust you not to let him fall in.' So off we went with Jamie skipping along beside me, chattering all the time about the plants his mum was potting up and how she'd got to get the job done by tonight to catch the market. It seemed that a lorry came to collect the order in the evening to take it to an early morning wholesale market. We went to the bridge where I had first seen the tiny fish. I sat him on the parapet with my arms round him to make sure he couldn't fall and we quietly waited. He saw them before me, and pointed excitedly, but quietly. Then we had a bonus, a kingfisher flew under the bridge like a brilliant blue flash and settled to wait on a piece of driftwood ledged against a stone. It suddenly swooped and came up with a fish in its beak. Two swallows and it had gone. Then it moved further upstream to wait again.

'Wow, wait till I tell mum,' he crowed. 'I don't think she's ever seen a bird like that. What is it called?'

'A kingfisher,' I told him. 'It's actually quite surprising how large a fish such a small bird can swallow. Much larger than these I'm sure.' Jamie was anxious to get back to tell his mum all about the kingfisher and his catch, so off we went. I went with him into the nursery to make sure he'd got back safely. Brynda was potting up primulas, all beautifully in flower, making sure that the plants weren't damaged in any way and looked as though they'd been growing in the pots for some time. I stood watching in admiration as her tiny fingers fairly flew and the plants were transferred to pots as if by magic.

'I could give you a hand if you liked. I'll be very slow by comparison, but I'll be very careful and every little helps as the old woman said.' She looked a bit dubious but I started very slowly and carefully and after about five plants she said, 'OK thanks, carry on, as you said, every little helps.' I knew I'd never get to her speed but by lunchtime I'd doubled my output and was quite pleased with myself.

By the middle of the afternoon the order had been completed to her satisfaction and we loaded all the plants onto a specially built trolley where the trays of potted plants could be stacked in tiers. I asked Brynda if they'd been up to the SSSI and although she had been in the village for two years she hadn't been. I suggested a walk up the chase to see if there were any primroses.

'I'm not sure if Jamie could manage that distance,' she demurred.

'No problem,' I smiled, 'if he gets tired he can ride on my shoulders.'

'Alright, I'll just get us a drink and we'll be off. They're not coming for the plants till about six o'clock. I wasn't expecting to get any help.' She fetched out some orange squash, then we got off with Jamie chattering all the time. It was a full time job keeping up with his questions. 'Did we think there would still be fish in the stream? Would he see the kingfisher again? What animals lived in the reserve?' In between times he skipped along between us and I found myself hoping that we might one day become a real family. I pointed out the various trees along the stream. Pussy willows, hazel with its golden tassels, alders and their relatives the silver birch. One or two rowan (or mountain ash), and plenty of ash and oaks. Once we got into the reserve there were banks of primroses, cowslips and violets. Even a magnificent clump of oxlips or maybe false oxlips which were a cross between cowslips and primroses. There were some plants I couldn't name and I took photographs so that I could identify them later from my trusty Keble Martin Concise Flora. Jamie would have liked to pick some primroses but I explained that it wasn't allowed and he accepted it without a fuss.

There were loads of birds singing their hearts out. Blackbirds, a few song thrushes, jenny wrens (who make an amazing amount of noise for such a small bird). There were great tits which make a noise rather like a rusty hinge being opened and shut at high speed. We saw rabbits and squirrels and a couple of fallow deer who stood looking at us until a sudden movement by Jamie sent them bounding up the slope and over the perimeter fence. We didn't quite make it to the spring, it was obvious that Jamie was wilting. I promised that he could ride on my shoulders once we got out of the reserve and into the open and there was no danger of catching him on a thorn bush or briar.

Once over the gate I put my hands under his arms from behind, hoisted him over my head so that his feet dangled over my chest. I held his feet so that he couldn't fall off and away we went, somewhat faster than we'd come up. Caroline waved to us from the mill house as we went past. We were mostly talking about the nursery on the way back and Brynda was telling me how Mrs Spencer had started the nursery and made a success of it after her husband had defected with her sister. Apparently they had taken her son (another Jamie) with them and left Caroline and Tony behind. She had more or less brought Caroline and Tony up but had refused Dan's persistent advances much to his annoyance. Apparently the defection had become a taboo topic and she had only told Brynda because her little boy was called Jamie.

I left them at the gate into the nursery and went up to my room to develop my film. I hoped that some of the sneaky shots I had taken of Brynda and Jamie would be OK. As well as the shots, I was wanting to identify the plants I hadn't recognised. I was using a slide film and once developed, dried, and mounted into their frames I was able to look at them through my small portable viewer. Not bad, but I decided that a trip back down to Hertfordshire was imminent to fetch up my projector and screen.

I had dinner with Bunion and played a few hands of dominoes. All very relaxing. I told him how we had spent our day and showed him some of my slides. He identified one of my plants as deadly nightshade.

'Nothing like woody nightshade or black nightshade, the flowers are single, more bell shaped than the others with big black berries when they are ripe. The more common nightshades have flowers just like spuds and tomatoes,' he told me.

Well I knew the more common nightshades but had never seen deadly nightshade before. 'There's another nightshade in there as well,' he went on with a twinkle in his eye. 'It's called enchanters nightshade, no relation to the others at all, and its seeds stick to you like goosegrass when they are ripe.'

I showed him another slide which he identified as henbane, another poisonous plant, but not as dangerous as deadly nightshade. I didn't mention anything that Brynda had said about her employer. If this subject was taboo, I didn't want to rock the boat. Ah well, and so to bed, again.

CHAPTER III

I woke to a beautiful morning so I whizzed out of bed, quickly went through the necessary ablutions, grabbed my camera and quietly let myself out. I decided to explore the rest of the S. S. S. I. and set off at a brisk pace through the village. Other people were beginning to stir, getting ready to set off for Oundle, Peterborough, Stamford or wherever they earned their crust. I'd heard that some hardy souls drove to Peterborough, took the train to London, then a tube or bus to their place of work! Good luck to them. It wouldn't be for me.

There was the sound of Fiona letting rip as I went past the mill. Once into the reserve I pressed on through to the spring, which came out of the limestone rock at quite a considerable pressure. There was a slightly unnatural look to the way the sides sloped up. I reckoned it must be at least forty feet to the top of the bank. Perhaps this had been formed when they had quarried stone to build the older houses in the village. I must remember to ask Bunion sometime. I grinned to myself, the fount of knowledge of Halston, he was really the most amazing old man. Next time I go to Oundle I'll get a geological map from the bookshop if they've got one, I thought. There were quite a few rabbit holes in the banks, one under a hawthorn which looked larger than the rest with what looked like dusty hay scattered around the entrance. Of course, a badger sett. Why hadn't I thought of that before? I had noticed several holes scratched into the ground, some had been used as a latrine, a sure sign of badgers.

I looked at my watch, I'd been out for an hour and a half, guess I'd soon be able to get some breakfast. I wondered if Jeff would allow me to invade his kitchen for a cereal breakfast while they were still in bed. I very rarely eat a traditional English breakfast, very fattening, all that fried stuff.

Caroline spotted me on the way back and held up a tea cup in silent invitation. By the time I'd got to the door she had it open. A really solid oak door with studs and real long iron hinges. I ran my hand over the woodwork, obviously treated with oil quite recently.

'Malcolm treats all the woodwork with teak oil twice a year, it doesn't take long and it doesn't go black like linseed oil,' she explained. 'Anyway come on in, I have just boiled the kettle. Tea or coffee?'

'Tea please, I was just on my way back to the pub to see if anyone was up to grab a few cereals. Got to stop the worms from biting, you know.'

'I think I can run to a bowl of cornflakes' she laughed.

'Oh heck, I wasn't thinking you know.'

She shook her head. 'I didn't think you were, you great lummox, sit down and help yourself.' She put a bowl and spoon, a packet of Kellogg's and a bottle of milk in front of me. 'We don't stand on ceremony here' she grinned. 'No more washing up than is necessary.'

I put what I thought was a reasonable helping into the bowl and as soon as I put the packet down, she picked it up and heaped up the bowl. 'That should last you till lunchtime, pity you weren't here half an hour ago when I was feeding her ladyship.'

'Oh no, that was a one off. Could become addictive you know, then where would we be?'

She smirked archly 'I doubt whether anything that I, or Malcolm did would make any difference to our relationship. We would never do anything that we don't tell each other about. A good marriage is built on honesty and trust. If that isn't there, you're doomed to the divorce courts.'

'That sounds like a very good philosophy, but I doubt if many couples adopt it. Not many people go through life without fancying some people other than their spouses. If they're honest that is.'

'Yes of course, and we are the same as everyone else in that respect. There's only one thing that would damage our marriage, and that's if I were stupid enough to get pregnant by someone else, or he fathered a child with someone else.' She spoke so matter of factly, without a shred of embarrassment, that I realised that what she was saying in a roundabout way, you can take my knickers off if you like. I didn't think it would do my chances with Brynda much good if I took her up so played dumb and changed the subject to the mill.

'Has the mill still got its machinery?'

'Oh yes. Malcolm would like to restore the wheel and get it working again, just for a hobby of course, but the estimates he's had so far are too expensive.'

I looked around me. 'Really nice country kitchen you have here.' I remarked taking in for the first time the scrubbed pine table and chairs, the flagstone floor, the cream Aga and all the pine units with their barley twist pillars and carved acorns and wheat heads. The tiled area around the cooker and Belfast sink areas had country scenes. I made a vow that Brynda could have a kitchen similar if it was what she wanted, and more importantly, I acknowledged to myself, if she wanted me.

'Tony was telling me about your session in the pub on Tuesday night. I understand that you're having another session next Tuesday?'

I nodded. 'That's the plan at the moment.'

'If Malcolm is home and can baby-sit, I'll come down after I've fed her ladyship. I like singing, Tony and I sang together in church before it was closed and no one complained.'

'Quite a musical family' I remarked. 'What does Dan play?'

'Absolutely nothing. He's tone deaf and thinks that anything to do with music is a waste of time. It comes from my mother's side of the family.' Her face clouded over when she mentioned her mother, I noticed.

'I've got my aunt's piano in the sitting room. After her stroke it upset her to see it and not be able to play it. It's a lovely Broadwood and we'll take it back if she gets so that she can play again. You can have a look at it if you like. Oh, and play it of course and give me the benefit of your opinion.' This said with a cheeky grin.

She took me through to a spacious room, which looked out over the mill pool. 'Nice view,' I remarked, then turned to the piano, which she'd neglected to say was in fact a well preserved baby grand. On top of the piano was a pile of sheet music and the top sheet was Grainger's Country Gardens, a piece that I could usually play from memory. I played safe (and modestly) as I put the sheet on the music holder, sat down, and played. The piano had a lovely tone and was perfectly in tune. When I had finished the piece, I had a quick look through the stack and selected a piece by Mozart, Rondo Alla Turca in A Major. This was a somewhat longer piece about three and a half minutes. I returned the sheet and shut down the lid. I turned to Caroline and was surprised to see her with a dream like expression on her face and her eyes closed.

'I wish I could play it as well as that, why ever aren't you a professional musician?'

'Because, my dear, there are more good pianists than there are jobs for. A lot of musicians struggle for years hoping to be discovered. Like all artistes you need that bit of luck to be noticed by the right people. I did get on New Faces years ago but I didn't get anywhere. I had a steady job so I didn't bother any more and just played for pleasure.'

'You play classical like a dream, you play and sing pop with keyboard or guitar. You know how to help out a farmer when he needs a hand. What else can you do?'

I laughed. 'I can see you want my CV. Let's see, I've done a bit of stunt riding as part of a motor cycle team; I've got an HGV licence Class II for all rigid vehicles. I play a bit of jazz on a Tenor Sax that I left back at the farm and I manage to get a few decent photographs.'

She was laughing so much that tears were running down her face. 'Enough, enough. I don't know whether it's the truth or porkies. But don't tell me any more or I'll have a heart attack.'

'OK, so we change tack again. Tell me about the jeep. Have you had it long? I noticed it had a temporary registration number but forgot to ask about it.'

'Actually we've only had it about a year. Malcolm had to go to a farm down in Warwickshire that hadn't seen much change in the last twenty-five years. I don't ask much about his work, what I don't know I can't talk about. Anyway he noticed the old jeep in the back of a barn, covered up under a pile of old sacks and was struck by the registration plate MAC 2. He thought if he made an offer on the jeep of more than it was worth the old boy might snatch his hand off, and he did. Malcolm reckons the plate is worth over two grand and he's had it transferred to his new Audi Quatro. We bought a battery for the jeep and cleaned it up and it started, so Malcolm had a new set of tyres put on it and got it tested and now it's our fun vehicle.'

'I didn't notice it this morning. Where do you keep it?'

'In the mill at the moment, with my Fiesta. The doorway is just wide enough, even if it doesn't look it. If Malcolm ever gets the mill wheel turning again we'll build a garage on the end of the house. It might get a bit dusty in the mill.'

'I'd like to look in the mill sometime when it's convenient.'

'You can look now if you don't mind going on your own, at your own risk of course. If you haven't brought the key back in an hour, I'll send a rescue party.'

I took the key from her and thanked her for the breakfast. I decided to look at the wheel first. I knew there were three basic types of wheel, the most popular being the overshot which required the greatest head of water; the undershot which required the least, but wasn't as efficient as the first; and the breast which was cross between the two, the least common, and that was the one fitted here. It was in a sorry state, the main axle and hub seemed OK as did the spokes, but the paddles/buckets were almost non existent. I took a few pictures then unlocked the door and went in. There were three floors. The top floor was the grain store, which had a hoist which would have been driven by the wheel. The first floor had two sets of milling stones and the ground floor was where the flour was bagged up or mixed with other things. I noticed a rolling mill on the first floor behind the stones for rolling oats or barley. I had to use the flashgun to get a few pictures of the various components, which were covered in dust and cobwebs. I had to be careful on the stair/ladders, taking a firm grip on the handrails in case a step gave way. Amazingly it seemed remarkably sound. I heard Caroline getting her car out, so went down and gave her the key and promised a set of photos when I had them developed. I had a print film in this time, a departure from my normal slides.

When I got back to the pub I looked over the hedge into the nursery and called over to Brynda, who was working on the cold frames, to see if she needed any assistance. She shook her head, 'No thanks, all under control, but it was much appreciated yesterday.'

'Right, I'll just check a few things out with Rose and Jeff, then I'm off to Hertfordshire to my cousin's place for the weekend. I'll look in on Monday when I get back.' Half an hour later I was on my way, travelling light. I planned on bringing back my tenor sax, slide projector and screen, some sheet music and a few more clothes. I had high hopes of being allowed to get to know Brynda and Jamie a lot better, no matter how long it took. Money wouldn't be a problem, I'd got my army pension when I got my honourable discharge and the sale of mum's house had brought in a considerable sum, which was invested as safely as possible. I'm definitely no gambler. I expect Brynda got quite a good widow's pension from the army, as Pete had been killed whilst working in the line of duty, even if he wasn't the intended victim.

Rose had insisted on packing me up a few sandwiches and a flask of tea, so I pulled the Cortina into a lay-by at about twelve o'clock, went in front of a tree for a pee (well how do you know whether you're in front or behind), ate my sandwiches and had my tea.

I arrived at my cousins' just after they'd had their lunch and received

THE ARM OF COINCIDENCE

the usual warm welcome. One thing for sure, on this farm there was always someone around, cows have to be milked. We went about the early afternoon chores together and I told him all about the village, and old Bunion in particular. I left him to the milking, I only went in there to do relief milking for him. Cows don't like a change of personnel. I'd taken over so that they could have some holiday when I had leave, and they usually went for a couple of weeks because the milk yield invariably went down a little till the cows got used to me again.

I spent an enjoyable weekend with Roger and Sue, and their two boys and one girl, setting off for Halston after breakfast. The day was fine but with a cold wind, what's known as a lazy wind, blows straight through you instead of going round. I got to Halston in time for lunch. After lunch I unloaded the car and set up the projector in my room to view my slides. Good thing it was a decent sized room. Nothing bad, but nothing to shout about either, one or two half decent shots of Brynda. I didn't think any were good enough to show her. I went off to find Bunion, he was busy in his garden in spite of the cold wind.

'I like to grow a few vegetables,' he said. 'I take 'em round to the pub in due season and they knock a bit off me bill. Nice to know that the stuff you're eating is off your own garden.'

I left him to it and went off to find Brynda. She was in the potting shed, at least in the warm. Jamie was building with his Lego but complained of being bored so I asked if he wanted to see the slides I had taken when we went up to the chase. 'Good idea,' exclaimed Brynda. 'Get him out from under my feet for a bit. I don't like to leave him with his Gran too long at a time. I know how wearing he is with his continuous questions.' I gave him a shoulder ride the long way round by the road. Bunion was still at it and Jamie gave him a wave as we went past. Jamie liked the shots of himself the best. Surprise! It didn't take long to get through the film so I showed him some slides of my cousin's family and farm. As with most small boys his chief interest was in the tractors. Being reluctant to return him to his mum so soon, I told him a story about one of Roger's old farm tractors, making it up as I went along. After that I had to take him back as I'd run out of ideas to amuse him. I made a mental note to buy him a few toys when I went to Peterborough.

Tuesday dawned fine and cold, so I decided to explore the footpaths. After my cereals Rose packed me sandwiches for lunch and I put all my gear into my rucksack and set off up the chase. First I walked through the forest to Southwick. The Hall was just visible through the trees as I went down the valley into the village. Someone was cleaning the church so I took the opportunity to have a look. The first thing I saw was a Holdich organ dating from about 1840 and the cleaner, noticing my interest, opened it up for me and plugged in the electric blower. It was a strange instrument, the footnotes started in a different place from every other organ I'd every played. I soon closed the lid and put the key back where it had come from. The only other thing of note was a fine marble monument off the chancel to a George Lynne who had died in 1758.

The pub was much smaller than Halston, thatched, with a name I'd never heard of before, The Shuckborough Arms. I made a mental note to ask Bunion about it. It didn't take long to walk the length of the village to a bridge. There were three blocks of what looked like council houses beyond the bridge but I didn't investigate. I went back up to the forest and this time followed a footpath to Kingscliffe. It was quite pleasant in the forest, protected from the worst of the wind. I crossed a stream and eventually reached a hard track. Left to Morehay Lawn, I looked through the binoculars but although I could see a farm which I worked out to be Boars Head, all I could see where, according to my old map, Morehay Lawn should be, were a few trees. Right went to Apethorpe via Cheeseman's Lodge. I went straight on, crossing another lane, which led to Spa farm from Apethorpe and eventually came to a rough lane, which I found to be called Morehay Lane. I walked round the village, which was much bigger than either Southwick or Halston. All the old houses appeared to be built of local stone, and roofed mostly with the local Collyweston slates. I ate my sandwiches in the churchyard then made my way back to Halston via the shortest route.

Rose said she'd got a copy of Arthur Mee's Northamptonshire, which she found for me, so I took it up to my room and read up about the villages around.

At six o'clock I went down for a meal and Rose suggested that we set the organ up in the lounge where there was more room and we wouldn't get in the way of people who wanted to use the dartboard. Bunion reckoned he could hear well enough from his usual perch by the bar room fire. When Tony had finished his meal we went through to the lounge and set up the organ. Tony opted to use the Gibson again, as it was so much better than his guitar. I'd brought more sheet music back with me from Hertfordshire and we were sorting through when Brynda arrived with Caroline who was carrying yet more sheet music. I bought the three of them drinks and after a bit more discussing we decided to try a few Abba numbers. Even though I say it myself it was incredible how the four of us blended in together. Obviously not in Abba's league, but good enough for us to acquire an appreciative audience. There were more people in the pub than the previous Tuesday so perhaps word had got round.

Apparently Malcolm was working relatively close to home and had got home in good time to take charge of a well fed baby. Mrs S was listening out for Jamie, so time was forgotten and we had a really good time. Inevitably we got our wires crossed a few times but the audience didn't seem to mind. Brynda said she had a big order to pot up and if I wasn't doing anything special could I give her a hand in the morning? I was only too pleased to get more time with her, so I was up bright and early Wednesday morning and on parade by eight o'clock. We took trays of plants out of the cold frames and got potting in the relatively warm shed. I hadn't really thought how the heat was derived till Brynda suggested I could throw a couple of bales of straw into the straw burner, in the barn adjoining the potting shed. She said it was very efficient, providing heat for the greenhouses as required. Tony kept her supplied with bales of unwanted straw, Mrs S only had to pay expenses. We were finished by lunch time leaving Brynda time to spend with Jamie before the lorry came.

Whilst I was eating my lunch a motor cyclist came in and ordered a pint of Adnams. When he took his helmet off I thought he looked vaguely familiar. Every time I glanced in his direction he seemed to be glowering at me. He was on his third pint when I went upstairs to fetch my wallet and anorak. I was going to Peterborough to get Jamie a pedal tractor. As I entered the bar I found myself face to face with the motor cyclist.

'I got a bone to pick with you, mate,' he growled. 'Stop giving my girl the eye on Tuesday nights or I'll smash your face in,'

'Sorry mate, I don't know who you are, you look vaguely familiar, but I don't know your girl friend and I most certainly haven't been making eyes at any girls in the pub.'

I made to go past him but he grabbed my arm. 'Well she reckons you fancy her an' I'm likely to get the elbow 'cos of you,' he snarled.

THE ARM OF COINCIDENCE

'Look mate, if she's here next Tuesday point her out and I'll gladly be brutally frank with her. I expect I've inadvertently looked in her direction whilst I'm singing.' I shook off his hand. 'Now if you don't mind I'm off to Peterborough.' I went out to my motor and drove out of the car park. He was walking towards his bike, which I recognised as a Yamaha RD35OB. Two stroke twin, M reg. I was nearly to the chicane when I saw him coming like the clappers behind me. I couldn't believe my eyes when he kept coming and cut me up as we entered the chicane. His back tyre just caught my front bumper as I got as close to the verge as possible. He lost control, his bike hit a tree stump and tossed him up into a Scots pine.

I blew an SOS on the car horn then managed to back my car alongside the tree on the nearside. He showed no signs of falling down and I could see his head and right arm were over a branch. He was either dead or unconscious. I scrambled onto the roof rack and realised that a small broken branch had penetrated his leathers at the waistband. I felt for a pulse and found one so he wasn't dead. I leapt down and got my towrope from the boot, back onto the roof rack and was tying him to the tree when Caroline pulled up in her Fiesta, on the way back from somewhere. I asked her to get Tony to bring the forklift, a door, rope and a hacksaw, 'And phone for an ambulance,' I yelled as she started off.

It seemed like an eternity before the cavalry arrived but it could only have been a few minutes. I jumped down when I heard them coming hoping that he wouldn't come round and start struggling. I moved the car out of the way. The grain bucket was on the Sanderson fork lift truck. Steve, Tony's man, was standing in it with a six foot garden gate and some rope. Tony lowered the bucket for me to get in and I guided Tony into position so that the bucket was just under his feet. Steve held the gate whilst I tied him to it. I gently sawed through the small branch about one and a quarter inches through, untied him from the tree and Steve guided Tony away from the tree as I eased his head and arm from the branch. I could hear the siren of the ambulance and within minutes he was loaded into the back on the gate. Tony told the driver that someone would come after them with the Land Rover to recover the gate. They sped off to Peterborough just as the police arrived. I took a couple of photos then. We recovered the bike. There were now two pieces, the front wheel and forks, which were completely smashed off. We loaded it into the bucket and Tony and Steve took it back to the farm. The police wanted a statement so I suggested we went back to the pub so that Rose could verify what had been said between us, and she would probably know his name.

I had to draw a diagram of the scene and Jeff was able to name the chap who came from Oundle. The police called back to the station for someone to go round to his home to see if his parents were in. Tony came round to the pub and suggested that I take the Land Rover to Peterborough so I could bring Bunion's gate back, which he and Steve had appropriated. Apparently they had heard my SOS and were on their way in the Land Rover when they met Caroline by the bridge. 'We nearly forgot the hacksaw, couldn't think what you wanted it for.'

Fortunately with Rose's statement, and the fact that he'd had three pints of Adnams in quick succession the police said I'd have nothing to worry about. My car wasn't damaged, it had only taken a touch to put him out of control. I handed the keys to my car to Tony so he could use it whilst I was gone, if need be, and set off to Peterborough in the Land Rover. First stop Peterborough District Hospital. I pulled up outside the A and E entrance, I could see Bunion's gate just inside. No information was available on the lad's condition, so I put the gate into the back of the Land Rover and followed signs to a car park. After asking a few people about a toyshop (you can't believe how many you have to ask before anyone knows) I got the information I wanted and set off back to the park so that I could drive round and pick it up. Bloody one-way streets. I eventually got to the shop, put my purchase on the front seats and went back towards the hospital. I thought I'd go back the way I'd come on the A47 to Wansford then cross-country.

Someone was trying to get out of the lay-by in front of the hospital so I flashed them, put my indicator on, then parked in the vacant space. I locked the car and went to reception. All I could discover was that he was still in theatre, but his injuries weren't thought to be life threatening. I had to be content with that and made my way back to Halston. I stopped outside Bunion's and put his gate back on, then went round to the farm. My car was outside the big shed where most of the machinery was kept. I parked alongside and Tony came out to see if there was any news on the lad. I told him what little I knew, took my keys, got the toy tractor out of the Land Rover and set off to find Brynda, just in time to help load the plants into the lorry.

'If I'd known I'd have kept away for another half hour,' I joked.

Brynda wrinkled her nose at me 'No you wouldn't, you'd have been

THE ARM OF COINCIDENCE

here at the same time as the lorry if you'd known.' We'd finished loading and the lorry had gone before she noticed the big box.

'Wow. Is that for Jamie?' I nodded. 'He'll be thrilled to bits. I'll fetch him and we can get it out of the box together.' Jamie's eyes boggled when he saw the size of the box. I broke into it and Brynda helped get the tractor out. It was bright red, like the Massey Fergusons favoured around here. It took him all of thirty seconds to master it. Brynda's eyes were suspiciously bright when she turned to me.

'Thank you very much, it's just what he wanted. He's had his birthday so this is a bonus. You shouldn't have spent so much money though, but I'm not going to ask how much it cost.' She reached up to kiss my cheek but I turned it into a real kiss, just gentle, with no demands, just enough to let her know she'd been kissed.

I went back to my car and drove it back to the pub park where I was immediately surrounded by people wanting to know what had happened. I noticed a couple of middle aged people waiting diffidently on one side and guessed they were the lad's parents. I went over to them and the man immediately took my hand and gave it a hearty shake. 'We've just come from the hospital and they tell me that you saved his life by leaving that piece of wood in his tummy. He's a hot headed young fool. Rose was telling me about how he reared up on you in the pub, no doubt bolstered up by dutch courage.'

I grinned at him. 'When you see him to talk to, tell him it's lucky he didn't try to smash my face in. He may have finished up worse off than he is now.'

'I can well believe it,' his dad said. 'Anyway we just wanted you to know that we don't hold you responsible in anyway, and hope that he manages to learn something out of it.' We shook hands again and I went into the pub with several curious people following me in. It has always amazed me how people seem drawn to any sort of incident. I bet that if a plane crashed here the place would be swarming with souvenir hunters in a very short space of time. I was quite pleased to get my meal over with and I persuaded Bunion to join me upstairs with a box of dominoes. Seems he had been swearing about his missing gate until Tony enlightened him.

CHAPTER IV

Thursday morning dawned bright and cold, and I decided to walk to Fotheringhay to get the feel of the village that might have become another university town or city, if the college hadn't been destroyed all those years ago. Quite a large part of the church had been destroyed at the same time but it still had the lantern tower and magnificent flying buttresses that I'd noticed on my way into Halston on my first day.

Incredible when I thought about how much had been packed into the last ten days. As the book had said, there was very little to show of the birthplace of one monarch and the death place of another. Richard the III was born here and there is a society who studied his life as much as possible. Mary Queen of Scots was executed here. Her claim to the English throne, if she personally made one, must have been more valid than Elizabeth acknowledged, after all, her son James the Sixth of Scotland, succeeded Elizabeth to the throne as James I of England. I took a few photographs of the mound and the one block of masonry preserved within some iron railings. I went over the narrow humped back bridge and along the river to get a shot of the bridge with the church behind it. Old stone bridges make wonderful subjects for photographers.

I timed it right to get back to Halston for lunch, so Rose made me a few sandwiches. I'd nearly eaten them when Caroline rushed in. 'Have you seen anything of Tony? I can't find him.'

'What's the problem?' I asked.

'I've just had a call from Jill Mason, Robert's had an accident and is unconscious in Peterborough Hospital with head injuries and the cows will need milking at about half past three. The boys had gone to play with school friends in Woodnewton. They can stay the night if necessary, no problem there, but the cows. I doubt if Tony's done any milking since college.'

I slid off my stool. 'We better have a look then, hadn't we? See if I can work out his system.'

'You saying that milking cows goes on your CV as well?'

THE ARM OF COINCIDENCE

I grinned. 'I've done a bit. Tell you what, I'll follow you down to the farm and give you a verdict when I've seen his system, OK?'

'Right, let's go then.'

I followed her down to the farm and could see Robert's herd of Friesians eating their way towards the corner of the field nearest the farm. No doubt their body clocks would be telling them that it would soon be milking time. Caroline led the way to the milking parlour and it was with great relief that I saw almost a replica of Roger's layout. Alfa-Laval equipment, each standing had a list of ear numbers and amounts of supplementary feed they were to be given. Very organised.

I turned to Caroline. 'We're in luck, I've used a system exactly the same as this one, and Robert's milking cap, overalls and wellies are all here. If I put them on they might not notice too much difference. They don't like change from their routine you know. I see there's a radio, I expect he has it on when he's milking so I'll have it on as well.'

'You'd better check the food pellets, but you'd better be careful. That's what Robert was doing when he had his accident.' There was a relatively small food hopper nearby which was nearly empty. It was fed by an augur from a larger bin in the next shed. I switched on the motor but no pellets came through so I went round to the other shed. A wooden ladder lay on the ground with a patch of blood near it. One rung of the ladder near the top was broken. I tested the other rungs then put it upside down against the bin so that the broken rung was near the bottom. I carefully climbed until I could see inside the bin. There were still pellets in there but they weren't reaching the augur. An aluminium shovel lay in the bottom, obviously dropped as Robert was trying to transfer himself to the inner ladder. I carefully hoisted myself over, down into the bin and heaped the pellets up over the augur. I climbed back out and down to where Caroline stood anxiously waiting.

'Do you think we can get into the house? I need to find out who his supplier is and order some more. You'd better ring the hospital to tell his wife that she needn't worry about this end.'

Caroline found the key under a stone and let us in. Their address book was open on the kitchen table at the page with the merchants phone number. I rang through and found that Robert had already placed an order which would be delivered tomorrow I was told. I stood and waited as Caroline phoned the hospital and asked for the intensive care unit. When she got through she asked for Jill Mason. She explained what the arrangements were, then passed the phone over to me.

'I'm Jim Evans and I've met your husband briefly. Don't worry about this end, I've used exactly this type of equipment before and I've been into the bin and heaped up enough pellets to augur through for today and tomorrow morning. I'll empty the bin before the new load goes in.'

'Thank you very much. I'll be back later, the doctors are confident that Robert isn't going to die, but he's still unconscious. He has a fractured skull, they said that only the thickness of it saved him from being killed outright.' This last with a catch in her voice. I tried to reassure her again then passed the phone back to Caroline and went out to start up the augur. The bin was half full by the time the augur started clattering empty. Caroline came back in.

'I shall have to go, Fiona is getting restless, it's nearly food time'. She climbed into the Fiesta and wound down the window. 'The key is under the stone if you need to go in.' Then she drove off. I checked through all the equipment to make sure everything was in order. I was struck by a thought and went round to have a closer look at the ladder. The rungs were all sound and had an eighth of an inch wire under each rung (now on top as the ladder was upside down). The wire of the broken rung had pulled out when the rung broke. Then I noticed that where the wire had pulled through the washer, the riveted end had been cut away with something like a drill. I pulled the ladder down and there was a dent on both sides of the break. It had been cracked deliberately with a hammer. By whom? Why? I thought that Robert was well liked, I hadn't heard anything said against him. I decided there and then to say nothing for the time being, but to be vigilant and see if any clues turned up. I was pretty certain it wasn't his wife. If she'd been trying to get rid of him she wouldn't have heard the clatter of the fall and would have left him lying there to die.

By this time the cows were queuing up to come in so I put Robert's kit on, switched the radio on, then opened the gates to let them through. Cows have their own pecking order, they go into their regular cubicles in the same order every day to be fed and milked. It was a simple matter for me to give each cow its allotted ration. The cow's yield was recorded and the food varied according to yield. I gave their udders a good wash before attaching the machines. These milking parlours are a far cry from the days when you sat on a three legged stool and each cow had to be milked by hand. Nowadays you worked from a pit so that the cows' udders were at a nice convenient height.

When the last cow had trundled through the gate back into the field,

THE ARM OF COINCIDENCE

I went through the routine of sterilising the equipment and washing all the muck from the concrete floors. I switched off the radio and hung up Robert's overalls and cap. I think some of the cows had been a bit suspicious. The morning milking yield would show whether they were unduly upset or not. I completed the records then decided that now was as good a time as any to empty the bin. I found a face mask in a cupboard in the dairy, set the augur going and climbed into the bin and started shovelling. I was pretty confident that the smaller hopper would hold what was left, besides, there was an automatic cut out on the augur when the hopper was nearly full.

I got back to the Walnut Tree just after six o'clock, had a bath, and went down for a meal.

'Jim Evans to the rescue yet again,' Rose teased. 'How long are you going to milk for? I expect there's an agency who supply relief cowmen.'

'Guess I'll carry on as long as I'm needed. No point in paying a lot of money out to an agency when I'm here, and available.'

'Well I expect they'll pay you. Jill won't expect you to do it for nothing. You'll need to be up at five tomorrow morning. Can you cope with that?'

'I can if you've got an alarm clock I can borrow. I'll try not to wake you up when I go out.'

'We've got one, but we only use it when we have to be up early for some reason, I'll get it now then I shan't forget.' She bustled off and returned with an old fashioned one with the bell on top. I looked at it and grinned at her. 'Good job you sleep at the front, and got no other visitors at the moment.'

I took it up to my room, wound it up and set it so that by the time I came to bed I could check it was going OK. When I went back down to the bar Caroline was there with a petite brunette who looked harassed to death and who would blow away with a good gust of wind. I shook her hand. 'Jim Evans, you must be Robert's wife, I met him in the pub here one evening last week, has he come round yet?'

She shook her head. 'They say it might take several days and it'll be a few days after that before he can start work again. It's very kind of you to help out like this, seems like a miracle you being here, but I'll phone the agency in the morning and see if they can get someone.'

I shook my head. 'No need, no point in rocking the boat any more than is strictly necessary.'

'But your holiday.'

'It's not important,' I interrupted her. 'I shall enjoy keeping my hand in. I've got nothing spoiling anywhere, and it gives me a great deal of satisfaction to think that I'm able to do someone a good turn.'

'Well, thank you indeed, but of course we'll pay you and you can move down to the farm tomorrow if you like. Relief milkers have stayed in the house on the rare occasions when we've had a holiday.'

'That sounds like a good idea, I shan't wake anybody up that way. I take it that Robert starts milking just after five?'

She nodded. 'He works long hours as do all cowmen who do the job properly. I'll get the spare room ready when I get home. See you tomorrow.' I followed them out and saw two very subdued boys in the Land Rover. Caroline got into her car and they went their separate ways. I told Rose that I would keep my room on and pay for it.

'Only if we have to turn anyone away,' she said. 'We've got another two rooms, a twin bed and a double. I told you before we're not that mercenary. Anyway it is as much as we can do seeing as how you're helping the Masons out.' I thanked her and got a glass of shandy and joined Bunion in his corner by the fire.

'Fancy making up a foursome of dominoes with these two other old codgers?' He gestured with his pipe towards another pair of OAPs.

'Sure, why not, I'll have to partner you though, it would be unfair to lumber either of them up with me.'

Bunion called over. 'Hey Frank and Les, fancy a game of dommies with me and my young friend here?' They picked up their beer and joined us. Introductions were made and I gathered that Frank and Les were from Oundle, but were regulars at the Walnut Tree. Bunion got the dominoes out, face down, and shuffled them round. We each took a domino in turn until we had six each and the remaining four were dead for the duration of the hand. After an hour's play I was amazed at how small a margin we had lost by.

'Well lad, I don't think you disgraced yourself. You'll soon be playing like a veteran.'

I found it quite stimulating trying to remember what the others hadn't got. It wasn't helped by not knowing what the four dead ones were. I had an early night. 'Got to get me beauty sleep you know,' I grinned at the others.

'Pah! When I was your age I often managed with four hours a night,' from Bunion, Who else? I thumped his shoulder and took myself off to bed. The alarm was still showing the right time so I thought I could trust it.

I was down at Glebe Farm at quarter past five and the cows mooed their greeting. I put all the lights on and opened the gates to let the cows through to the holding pen, switched on the machine and got busy. I was finished by half past seven and all cleaned up and sterilised by eight. Jill came out with a cup of tea, saying that breakfast was available as soon as I was ready. 'Thanks, I only have cereal for breakfast, so I'm not too difficult to please.'

'In that case I'll leave a selection on the kitchen table, I get some milk before the lorry arrives. It's usually here 'bout nine.' She fetched a jug and filled it. 'I'm just going to run the boys to Woodnewton to their friends again, then I'll ring the hospital to see what's happening.'

She took them off in the Land Rover and I let myself into the kitchen and got two Shredded Wheat and topped up with Kelloggs. The milk lorry arrived just as Jill came back with the Land Rover and I left her to talk to the driver whilst he pumped out the tank. He gave her a receipt for the amount taken.

'Hardly any change from yesterday,' she managed a smile at me.

I grinned back. 'I nicked Robert's gear so I suppose the smell was about the same so they hardly noticed.'

She invited me back into the kitchen and phoned the hospital. Little change but apparently he was doing a lot of muttering which required cotton wool in the ears. 'Strange really, because I rarely hear him swear unless something is seriously wrong.'

'Well you could say this was serious enough for a good curse,' I replied. 'Now, what's the routine? What would Robert have been doing if he had been here?'

'I think he'd said something about getting the silage pit cleaned out ready for this year's crop,' she said thoughtfully.

'OK, that's what I'll do, now you get off to Peterborough. I'll nip up to the pub for lunch.' Then I had a thought. 'Why don't you take my car, it's insured for any driver over 25 and I might be glad of the Land Rover here.'

She had a think. 'You've got a point. I'll put some petrol in.'

'I don't think it needs any at the moment,' I told her. 'I filled up on my way back from Hertfordshire on Monday.'

I showed her where all the switches were and waved her off then made a tour of the farm buildings to see what tackle was available.

There wasn't much left in the silage pit, just enough to warrant a muck loader. I found an old Ford Super Major with a loader and did the necessary checks. What the old army boys called WOFL TB – pronounced woffle TB: water, oil, fuel, lights, tyres and battery. Well the lights were knackered but the tractor started all right so I took it round to the pit. Next I found a 135 Fergie with a three ton trailer and I was in business. By lunch time, I had it all cleared out and tipped up on the muck heap. I'd hose it down after lunch. Then it would be time to milk again.

After lunch I loaded what I thought I would need at the farm into the Land Rover and went back. I found an outside tap not too far from the pit. There was a six hundred gallon tank nearby which I suppose was used for filling the sprayer. A short length of hose reached from the tap to the tank. When I found the long hose I also found a high-pressure washer, so I carted the lot round in a wheelbarrow and set to work. The cows started chelping at me and I realised it was half past three again. Their clocks kept good time, I thought. I was ready to start milking when Jill arrived back with her boys, Bill who was almost eight and John six. They shook hands gravely. Jill said she'd bring me a cup of tea and ushered them into the house. The milking was underway by the time she brought the tea. She stopped long enough to tell me that she'd spent the whole time talking to Robert but apart from an occasional flicker there had been no change. When I had finished I got my gear out of the Land Rover and took it in. She showed me to a room with a double bed, which she said was the guest room.

'I'll be able to sprawl out in there. I'm used to single beds,' I told her.

'The bathroom is at the end of the corridor. We always have our main meal in the evening and it will be ready when you are.' With that she left me and went back downstairs. I had a bath and change of clothes, good job I favoured jeans, T-shirts and sweaters.

We settled into a routine, every day she went off to Peterborough to be with Robert, talking at him, trying to bring him round. I hardly noticed that we'd gone right through the Easter weekend and it was Tuesday, music night again. Every day Jill had left the boys with various friends in Woodnewton, picking them up when she came back from the hospital.

When I arrived back at the pub Rose told me that they had a couple of guests in the double room. Bunion said he'd be down to the farm in the morning to see what sort of balls up I was making of the job. 'What do you do with yourself between milkings?' he asked.

'Oh, I find plenty to do, I've been working on the forage harvester, getting it serviced ready.'

'Quite right,' Tony chimed in. 'They only break down when you're using them, and you don't want it to happen as soon as you start.'

We had a really good session. Caroline had sorted through the music sheets and we set a tape recorder going so we could play it back later, the only danger with that being that we might not like what we sounded like! When we had finished Tony asked how long I was likely be down at Glebe Farm and how was I getting on with Goody Two Shoes. I must have looked puzzled because he laughed and said, 'That's what we call Jill Mason. Very prim and proper she is, I've never heard her swear or anything in the three years they've been here.'

'I hadn't realised that they were relative newcomers. I thought it had been Masons farm for years.'

'Well, so it has been, Robert's uncle and his father before him. Robert's mother blotted her copybook with the parents and they disowned her. She married the guy who'd made a mum of her and never came back, not even for the old folks' funerals. Can't say I blame her. Funnily enough she married a man named Mason, no relation, so she didn't even change her name. Anyway the first Robert knew of even having an uncle was when Fred Mason's agent got in touch with him and told him that his uncle had just died aged fifty two and had left him the farm.'

'What did he die of?' I asked, thinking about the broken ladder.

'Heart attack. He had a relatively mild one and was taken to hospital and his agent got a relief milker a bit sharpish. Two days later, just as they thought he was getting better, he had a massive heart attack and died. The relief cowman stayed until Robert and family got here and Robert was allowed to take over the running of the place. When everything was sorted out, the death duties nearly crippled the job, but he's stuck it out.' He continued, 'The old man tried to buy it off him, but he wouldn't entertain it, said he'd been to agricultural college and been working as a cowman in Worcestershire and it was what he had always dreamed of doing.'

Brynda went back to the farmhouse and Tony said he'd see her home, rather to my chagrin she accepted, so I had no chance to making the

THE ARM OF COINCIDENCE

offer myself. Caroline looked at me with a smile. 'You'll have to pull your finger out or you may lose her before you've even made it to first base.'

'Am I that transparent?'

'I've seen the way you look at her, mate. Seriously though, I'm hoping against hope that Donna will come back with the boys, but I don't suppose Tony will wait for ever, and if she doesn't want to be found it will be difficult for him.' I chewed that over for a few minutes and decided that as soon as Robert was home and back in harness, I'd go looking for her myself. Caroline laughed.

'I had to smile when Tony called Jill Goody-two-shoes. What he doesn't know, is that we went to the same school. We were quite good friends there and got into various scrapes together. In fact, she was no goody-two-shoes then. We lost our cherries lying side by side with a couple of lads from the local secondary school.'

'Where did you go to school then?' I was curious.

'We went to Roedean, nothing but the best for us. We lost touch when we left school, so it was a nice surprise when she turned up here with Robert and family. Robert's got her on a pedestal. If only he knew. He's the good-goody. Never seems to give the rest of us a second glance.' She looked at her watch. 'God is that the time. Malcolm will think I've run away with a black man.'

'Why a black man?'

''Cos they're supposed to have big whatsits of course.' She laughed and departed.

I went back to Glebe Farm and found Jill in the kitchen working on the paperwork which accompanies any business. 'If I don't keep everything up to date we'll get in a hell of a muddle. It's my job anyway, so Robert being in hospital makes no difference in that respect.' I was looking at her with new eyes, trying to imagine her as a naughty-naughty, and I couldn't. I said goodnight and left her to it. The rest of the week passed uneventfully, Robert still unconscious and the boys stayed with various friends each day. Then Monday morning it was back to school for them.

I had just finished all the routine chores, and the milk lorry had been and gone, when I saw Bunion coming down the drive with a beautiful Alsatian trotting alongside. I walked out to meet them, then stood and waited with my hand slightly extended towards the dog. He came up and had a few sniffs, then licked my hand. Bunion stood grinning, 'Didn't take long to make friends did he?'

'Didn't know you had a dog, Bunion, never seen you with one before.'

'Not mine mate, belongs to the people in the old rectory. I have him when they go away. He and I are old friends aren't we, Buster?' The dog put his head on one side looking for all the world as if he understood every word. Maybe he did.

We turned towards the farm. 'Heard some houses got flooded in Southwick yesterday; second time in eight months,' Bunion remarked. 'Thank God we don't get that problem here. Our watershed is much smaller, owing to the lie of the land, our water mostly finishes up in the Willow-Brook at Newton or the stream that runs along the forest perimeter.'

Bunion relit his pipe and had a few sucks. "Course Southwick has got a hell of a watershed. They get water from Benefield and Deenethorpe aerodrome,' he continued. 'Last August all the land was dry but hadn't cracked. There was heavy rain particularly at Benefield. I didn't see it but they reckoned that at half past seven to eight o'clock in the morning there was four feet of water up the street an' it had all gone by lunch time. People were driving through in bright sunshine wondering why carpets were hanging over the hedges. Most of the year their stream is bone dry as soon as you get out of the village, half a mile upstream, whereas ours is pretty constant all year round. I've never known it to run dry.'

I grinned at him. 'I expect after that long speech you could do with a cuppa couldn't you? I'm just going in for breakfast so Buster can have a warm by the Aga.' We went into the warm kitchen and I shifted the kettle onto the hob. Buster had a sniff round. 'No doggy smells here, mate.' I told him. Then to Bunion, 'I never gave it much thought till just now, but there are no farm dogs here at all. Not many dogs in the village come to that. Most of them in the council houses.'

'That's right, Woodward's haven't had a dog since they sold their sheep. Can't say I was sorry to see them go. Smelly things and you have to handle them so much, what with all the dipping, feet trimming and the shearing. To say nothing of being up half the night during lambing time.'

'I haven't done anything with sheep since I was a lad,' I told him. 'My uncle had a sheep farm in Wales but it was compulsorily purchased years ago because they needed more water. They flooded his valley to make a reservoir. He bought the first farm that he fancied when it came on the market, and moved to Hertfordshire.'

I made the tea and heaped my dish up with cornflakes. 'Crikey, you're not going to eat all that lot are you?'

'Sure am, but I don't have anything else. No toast and marmalade, no bacon and eggs, nothing.'

'Only teasing mate,' Bunion grinned. 'I'll inspect the premises, make sure you're doing the job right, then I'll give Buster a good run. Only got him till Saturday, they've gone to Nottinghamshire for a three day conference.'

'What do they do?' I asked curiously.

'Dunno mate. They tried to explain to me once or twice but it was all Greek an' Latin to me.'

Bunion had his inspection then went off. I went down to where the cows were grazing to move the electric fence over to give them fresh grass. We had our usual music session on Tuesday evening and even if I say it myself I think we were getting quite good.

The days passed quickly and on Saturday morning Jill took the boys to see if their chatter would jog Robert out of his long sleep. Just after lunch they were back and I knew as soon as I saw them getting of my car that the miracle had happened.

'Of course, his first questions were about his beloved cows,' Jill said with a rueful twinkle in her eyes. 'He did say one thing that jogged my memory though. We've got three followers due to calve any time, we'll get changed and fetch them to the yard where we can keep an eye on them.' I must admit I hadn't thought too much about the followers. I'd checked most days to see if they were all right, but hadn't thought to ask when they were due to calve. I knew that some of the current milkers were getting to the end of their lactations.

Jill had written the cow tag numbers on a piece of paper in case we forgot before we got to the field. I wondered if it was safe for a couple of children to be doing this but they seemed to be very confident, came with being brought up with the job I suppose. It was easier than I'd thought and we soon had the three back in the yard with nice clean straw to lie on and some hay to munch. Turned out we were only just in time because by Sunday evening we had three nice bull calves.

On Monday I went with Jill to see Robert to update him on what I'd been doing and to get instructions on what I should be doing to keep up to date. He asked me to check the fuel supply and if necessary to order a delivery from Rutland Oil. He also said would I get in a ten ton load of top dressing fertiliser from Bradshaws of Cotterstock. The hair had been shaved off the back of his head where he had been stitched and he was still showing his bruises from the fall. He was fortunate not to have broken any bones, he'd landed flat on his back judging by the bruises. We left him with the latest *Farmer and Stockbreeder* and, the *Farmer's Weekly*, and Jill said she would ring Keith Morris about the calves. We stopped off at the Wheatsheaf at Alwalton for a spot of lunch on the way back. I mentioned that Caroline had said they were at school together, but had lost touch until she and Robert took over Fred's farm.

'What else did she tell you?' asked Jill.

'Not a lot,' I replied. 'Just the basic facts like your school was Roedean, bit posh I understand.'

'Supposed to be one of the best girls' schools in the country, although some of us were more amenable than others. All I ever wanted to do was get married, have some children and live in the countryside. Very ambitious!'

I smiled and thought it was perhaps lucky that she managed to do it in the right order. 'Where did you meet Robert?' I asked.

'Agricultural College, never dated anyone else. He was ambitious and it never entered my head that he might not be successful. I hadn't realised just how difficult it is to climb the farming ladder. Then our dreams came true when Robert was left the farm.'

'I should imagine that it would be nigh on impossible unless you were born into it, made, or got a lot of money from some other source first,' I remarked.

'That's right, we nearly didn't make it. The death duties meant that we were almost hand to mouth for the first two years. Things were just improving when this happened.' Jill insisted on paying for the lunch and I got behind the wheel of the Cortina. I grinned at her, 'Back to the grindstone.'

'This car is a dream to drive after the Land Rover,' she sighed. 'Maybe if nothing else goes wrong, we may be able to afford to run a car as well as the Land Rover by the end of the year.'

'What about the boys' education? Wouldn't you like to send them to Laxton school in Oundle?'

'No chance. We couldn't afford it for one thing, and for another they've got a very good middle school and upper school in Oundle and I see no point in crippling ourselves unnecessarily. If they've got it in them and work hard, the schools will make sure they reach their potential.'

'You seem very confident,' I remarked.

She shrugged. 'I've seen their results, considering they have to take kids from all walks of life, quite a lot go on to higher education, even Oxford and Cambridge.'

When we got back I checked the diesel tank, no need to order yet. I ordered the fertiliser and was given Wednesday as delivery day.

CHAPTER V

Well it's Tuesday 5th May, I came to Halston on the 6th April. I find it hard to reconcile a month with what has been packed into it. The amount of rain we've had! If it doesn't rain in the day it rains at night. Good job Robert's land is free draining or it would be a hell of a mess with the cows outside.

When I'd completed the regular milking jobs I went in for a few cereals. Jill rang Keith Morris and it was agreed that I should deliver the calves to him on Thursday. Jill said she would draw me a map because it was out in the sticks near Kettering. I went out to get the fertiliser spreader ready so it could go as soon as it was dry enough but it looked as though Robert had already done it. The chain drive from one wheel was well oiled, all grease nipples had been serviced. The Fergie 165 it was attached to was full of fuel and water and the oil on the mark of the dipstick. Nothing to do then. I went back to the house just as Jill was getting ready to go to the hospital so I nipped up to my room, changed, and went with her. I updated Robert on the fuel and fertiliser situation.

'I see that the spreader is all ready to go when the weather is right; I take it that it's set up to deliver the correct amount?'

'Sure is, I don't go mad with what I put on, it's pretty expensive stuff, and the price of concentrates keeps going up. Do you know what the price of wheat and barley is nowadays?'

I shook my head. He continued, "Bout £120 a ton, the grain growers are sitting pretty at the moment! Trouble is, I'm stupid and stuck with the cows! Can't afford to change though, we have to go with what we're geared up for. It would cost a fortune in machinery to change. Dan Woodward bought a brand new caterpillar D6 with hydraulics last year, I dread to think what that cost.'

I rubbed my chin. 'I haven't seen anything of it.'

He thought for a minute. 'Have you seen the steam ploughing engines? No? I expect it's in the same shed as them, it's part of the machinery shed, but separate if you see what I mean. Wait till Bunion gets the steamers out. There's one of the first Fordson Major diesels

THE ARM OF COINCIDENCE

in there; 1952, I think Bunion said, and a pre-war Allis Chalmers all done up by Bunion, so it looks better than new.'

'I'm surprised that's allowed,' I remarked. 'Do they belong to Bunion or Dan?'

'Oh, everything is Dan's but it suits him to have Bunion keep everything shipshape. Bunion and Tony have been taking them to Peterborough Showground every August Bank Holiday for years demonstrating steam ploughing at 'Expo Steam'. I dunno if they'll go this year though because they've sold a lot of land and there's nowhere to plough now.'

'Perhaps they'll find somewhere else to go,' I said.

'Maybe, but it's only ten miles to the showground so they could drive them there. Still, now they've bought the 'Cat' they might get a low loader, then they could go further afield.'

I moved away to let Jill talk to him in private and found an old boy with no visitors who had had prostrate surgery. I noticed Jill looking in my direction. 'Time to go, by the looks of things.' I wished matey a speedy recovery and went back to Jill and Robert.

'They say I've got to stay in another week; still I daresay it's for the best, I don't suppose I'd be able to leave the job alone.'

We went straight back to Halston and had lunch in the farmhouse. I caught up with the news in the local paper, and then it was milking time again. I must admit that I wouldn't want the job for the rest of my life! I didn't see much of Jill's boys because they'd usually gone to school by the time I cleaned up in the mornings and when they came home they went into the sitting room and watched television, after they'd done their homework.

Tuesday evenings were of course the highlight of the week. Music night at the pub. Caroline and Brynda had put their heads together at some stage during the week and sorted out what they wanted to sing. Caroline had done some arrangements, she was more talented than she had admitted to. After we had finished we sat chatting and Tony remarked that he'd had a postcard from the Rockies. 'Reading between the lines, reckon the old man's found himself a bit of company.'

'I saw a grain lorry leave this morning,' said Caroline, 'not as loaded as usual judging by the way he accelerated away.'

'No, that was the last load. I can get the grain store cleaned and fumigated ready for this year's crop whenever I like now.'

'You know, I think we could do a gig in the grainstore,' said Caroline

THE ARM OF COINCIDENCE

thoughtfully. 'It's big enough to hold about 400 people and we could start a mill restoration fund. We could open the mill to the public on a limited basis, set up a charity or something. What do you say, Tony?'

'It's feasible I suppose, we could park cars in the field opposite, hire some portable loos for the ladies and make something for the chaps. Dare say Rose and Jeff could organise a bar, what do you reckon Jim?'

'Think we'd be good enough?'

'Well I should think we could learn enough numbers, and if Caroline does the musical arrangements as good as we've had tonight, I dare say we wouldn't make fools of ourselves. When would we be aiming at?'

'Between hay, silage time and harvest, say end of June or early July.' I got a pencil and paper off Rose. 'We'd better make a list of what we will need,' I said. 'Portable loos, sound amplification equipment, staging, card tables and chairs, cloakroom tickets, Performing Rights Licence, stewards, door keepers, car parkers.'

'Quite a formidable list,' remarked Brynda. 'Guess you can add publicity posters and advertising. No good without that, and direction signs to put out on the night.'

'OK so far, If anyone thinks of anything else to add to the list let me know. I'll see to the sound equipment. I'm sure someone will hire to us. As soon as Robert gets back in harness I'll have a bit of time.'

Bunion had been quietly puffing away at his old pipe. 'Staging is easy, all you got to do is put those two matching low four wheel trailers you use for bale carts side by side on one side of the shed and there's your stage.'

'Good thinking, Bunion,' grinned Tony. 'You can be head bouncer.'

'Daresay I could manage that job if you give me a pickaxe 'andle,' he quipped back. I remarked that I'd got a load of fertiliser coming in the morning and Tony said that if it was on pallets I should nip up to the farm, and he'd get Steve to unload it with the Sanderson. 'It'll probably be mostly one and half tons on a pallet and you can load whatever you can straight onto trailers to save handling too many times.'

'Ten tons altogether,' I told him.

'That'll most likely be four at one and a half and two at two tons then,' said Tony.

I thanked him and turned to Brynda. 'How's Jamie getting on with his tractor?'

'Fine, he's rigged up a little trailer with a box and his old pushchair wheels, so he can help move trays of plants. I think he's going to be a farmer or an engineer. If you come over with me I'll show you.'

I nodded. 'Great, ready when you are.' We said our goodnights to people and went through the door to the nursery. 'As long as it's shut most people assume that it's bolted, because most of the time it is.' I shot the bolt home then somehow or other found her hand in mine as we went towards the house. I was quite impressed with Jamie's trailer. Pretty good for a three year old, even if it was all tied together with 'farmer's friend'.

I pulled Brynda gently towards me giving her plenty of scope to pull away, but she didn't and I kissed her gently and she responded very satisfactorily. Then she pulled away. 'We hadn't better get carried away, 'cos it's the time of the month when we'll only get frustrated.'

'Well it's nice to know that we might get carried away,' I joked. 'I'd better say goodnight, it's up at five again in the morning.' I kissed her again and went back the long way to pick up my car, quite chuffed with the way things were going.

The fertiliser arrived just as the milk lorry was going and as Tony had predicted it was on pallets. While the driver was undoing his ropes and sheets I shot off up to Tony's and found Steve eating his sandwiches. He took them into the forklift with him and came after me still munching. I got two fourwheel trailers out into the yard with the Super Major and the other trailer on the 135. It didn't take Steve many minutes to transfer the pallets onto the trailers. The lorry driver grinned at me. 'That's a relief. We usually have to unload by hand here 'cos Robert says he can't afford a forklift at the moment.'

He folded his sheets and wrapped his ropes, climbed into the ERF lorry and departed with a wave. I got all the trailers under cover because even though all the pallets had a plastic seal over them I know that there's nothing worse than handling wet fertiliser bags.

Thursday morning after milking I took the three calves away from their mothers and loaded them into the back of the Land Rover. The cows didn't like it one little bit, but what has to be has to be. I'd put some straw in the Land Rover to make them as comfortable as possible and tied a wire mesh over the back so they couldn't get out. Armed with Jill's map I set off. Three quarters of an hour later I'd found the place and was greeted by an Amazon of a young woman who introduced herself as Gloria Morris, Keith's wife. Individual pens had been prepared for the calves and I carried one and Gloria another then I fetched the third one. I was quite impressed with the set up. Two rows of pens, one each side of a long shed. Each with its own feeding set up. The sound was something else, all those calves vying for attention in the most vocal manner! Gloria explained the set up, heifer calves from Robert were reared then he had them back, as did several other dairy farmers. The bull calves were sold on once weaned fully off milk substitutes, and old enough to fend for themselves. Dan Woodward apparently bought most of his beef cattle off them. It saved market fees.

This Gloria was something else, hell of a figure, long blonde hair and as strong as a horse. I wondered briefly what she'd be like to ride. She offered me a coffee, which I accepted while she wrote out a cheque for £270 for the three calves. I told her that Robert was recovering well and would be home next Tuesday all being well. Then we chatted for a few minutes about the state of the world in general before I went back to Halston.

First thing I noticed when I got back to the farm was that the swallows and martins had returned from their winter quarters. They were a welcome sight. Maybe things would improve now. I washed out the back of the Land Rover and chucked the straw on the muck heap. You wouldn't believe how much muck three small calves could make. The rest of the week and weekend passed off without incident. Sunday it even began to dry a bit so I thought with a bit of luck I might be top dressing on Monday. When Jill came back from hospital she had instructions from Robert as to what gear and engine speed to use. I think I'd have got it about right because I'd had a word with Roger over the phone on that very subject. Better to be safe than sorry, the number of times I hadn't gone into too much detail because I'd assumed that the delegated person would know, only to find out that they hadn't known.

Monday after milking I took a load of fertiliser down to the far meadows and Jill fetched me back with the Land Rover to save time. She said she'd bring me some lunch down about one o'clock to save time, and off I went with the 165 and spreader. The most difficult part was judging the distance to drive away from the last run so as to get even coverage. I'd done a couple of fields and was starting on the third when Jill arrived. My eyes must have been bulging out of my head when she got out. She had a pair of jeans cut high into shorts which were too big for her (most likely Robert's), a somewhat see through blouse with an almost non-existent bra which left the nipples proudly over the top. She appeared to be completely at ease with herself in spite of the out of character get up.

She took a couple of rugs and a large bag out of the passenger side. She handed me a rug and a Tupperware box of sandwiches, got out a large flask and poured two mugs of coffee. There were a couple of oak trees in the corner of the field where I threw the rug down and leant my back against a tree and started eating. Jill took the opposite tree and did the same. It was the first half decent warm day we'd had so I supposed this accounted for the outfit. We didn't talk, just sat eating our sandwiches and drinking coffee. I'd actually finished and was thinking of starting work again when I realised she had changed position and I could see *it*! She'd got no knickers on and the wide cut legs of the too big shorts were revealing everything. Not only that but everything was all puffed up and damp. JT went into automatic and sprang to attention in a most uncomfortable way. I tried to surreptitiously adjust the situation, lay back on the rug and tried to blot out the image. I heard a rustling sound and a shadow fell over me. My zip was snatched down, JT freed from the confinements and engulfed in a wet pussy. I felt her nipples brushing my nose as she swung her tits over my face. No point in keeping my eyes shut any more. She was completely naked with a half smile on her face. 'When rape is inevitable, relax and enjoy it.' She started rising and falling, her eyes closed, and her breath came in ragged gasps. 'Oh God! I can't make it last.' I felt her muscles contracting on JT as she went into orbit, great spasms racking her body. JT responded in seconds and I had to let the lot go. Her breathing returned to normal. 'God, I needed that! 'Fraid I've made mess of your underpants.' She rose to her feet and pulled a roll of kitchen towel from the bag, tore off some sheets and passed them to me, then cleaned herself up. Reaching into the bag again, out came a serviceable pair of knicks and bra, which she put on. Then out came her usual working jeans and check shirt. In the meantime I'd put my clothing in order.

'So what brought that on?' I wanted to know. She sat down on the rug and stacked everything back into the bag.

'Remember I said I was going to the accountants before I saw Robert?' I didn't remember her saying anything, but said nothing. 'Well, when I got there his secretary apologised saying that he had to rush home over some crisis with one of the children. So I left the stuff with her and went round to the hospital a good three quarters of an hour before

THE ARM OF COINCIDENCE

visiting time. I hoped they'd let me in. As I walked into the ward there were doctors and nurses around a bed with a panic on, no-one on the desk and when I got to Robert's bay, two of the beds were empty and the old boy in the corner was asleep. Robert's bed had the curtains drawn round, I thought, oh God, something's gone wrong. Then I heard a slurping noise and a muffled giggle so I peeped in a crack in the curtains and that pretty staff nurse who sports an engagement ring was doing what I've just done! I crept away down to the cafeteria and got a coffee, I was bloody furious. Then I thought, right mate, in this case what's sauce for the gander is going to be sauce for the goose! I had another coffee, then went back up to the ward. Everything was back to normal except that the bed where all the doctors and nurses were was now empty, so I assumed the patient had either died or gone back to intensive care. Robert was sitting up reading the *Stockbreeder* and if I hadn't seen what I'd seen, I'd never have known. The fact that he said nothing just hardened my resolve to have some of the same.' She turned towards me and gave a quick kiss. 'Anyway it was great, you really filled me up, best come I've had in years! I hope that if you and Brynda get together she appreciates what she's got.'

'If we get together, as you put it, I shall be a very happy man. You're a lovely lady Jill, but that was a one off. I have always made it a rule to steer clear of married women, but I doubt if many men would have been able to resist you just now. You took me unfairly by surprise.' I stood up and pulled her to her feet, gave her a quick kiss, climbed into the 165 and got going again. When I turned at the end of the lane the Land Rover had already gone. I used up what was on the trailer then it was time to milk again. I took the 165 back to the farm, the 135 and empty trailer wouldn't hurt till morning.

Jill went straight from the school run to Peterborough and was back with Robert by half past ten. I'd already taken the Fordson and a fourwheel trailer to where I'd left off the day before taking the 135 and trailer back for the spreader.

'Boy, it's good to be home and alive,' Robert stretched when he got out of my car. 'I'm raring to go. I'll have a walk round the farm and do the afternoon milking.'

I knew it was a waste of time arguing that he should take it easy for a few days so I said, 'Right, if you pack me a few sandwiches now I can take them with me and I can carry on with the top dressing till dark.' Jill went in to do the sandwiches and I topped the tractor up with fuel, greased and oiled the spreader so that I was ready to go when Robert came out with the sandwiches. He'd already changed and put on a pair of boots so I left him to his own devices. By night I'd fetched the other trailer and completely finished the job. I had a quick bath and changed and ate the meal with the family, then off to the pub. Reckoned that this would be my last night at Glebe Farm. Robert would want to be in full control again.

I was a bit later than usual getting to the pub so the others had the music sorted ready to begin. 'Reckon I'm redundant at Glebe Farm, Robert came home today, straight back into milking this afternoon. It'll be waste of breath trying to get him to take it easy. They were very wise keeping him in that bit longer.' I let them have all their own way with the music they had chosen. They, or rather Caroline, had dancing in mind with her arrangements this time. The Gig was on.

'What the old man doesn't know about he won't try to stop. It'll be too late by the time he gets back. Bunion reckons we should stage our own ploughing exhibition after harvest, as we're not going to Expo this year. Make a bit more money for the mill wheel.'

They'd obviously got the bit between their teeth, things were going to snowball pretty rapidly. Tony managed to walk Brynda home, I wondered if he was going to be kissing her. I'm not usually a jealous sort of person but I knew that I was certainly feeling that way at the moment. When I got back to Glebe Farm it was to find Jill ironing my clothes.

'I raided your room and got all your used clothes and put them into the washer, then the dryer.'

'I was going to take them to the launderette,' I protested.

'Well you'd have had quite a journey there isn't one in Oundle. Anyway it was the least I could do after all your kindness to us.'

'Think nothing of it, I've enjoyed myself.' I told her firmly.

'Especially yesterday?' she queried with a cheeky grin.

I was about to say something when Robert came through from the sitting room. 'You can have a lie-in in the morning. I'll be up to do the milking. Can't wait to get back into full going gear.'

'OK mate, have it your own way, but be careful.' I took myself off to bed and switched off the alarm clock, but I was wide awake at 5 o'clock. Automatic pilot as they say. I heard Robert moving about downstairs so I went down for a cup of tea and asked Robert if there were any books I could browse. 'In the front room there is a book case with quite an assortment to choose from.' I got a copy of *Cider with Rosie* and went back to bed. Typically after a few pages I went back to sleep and didn't wake again until Jill and the boys got up. I went through my ablutions, collected up all my gear and shoved it in my holdall and went down. I had breakfast with the boys then Jill brought my clean clothes through and I stowed everything in my car. Jill tried to give me some money but I refused point blank. 'And don't hide it anywhere in my stuff because I'll only bring it back. The only thing is, from now on I'll stick to doing a couple of weeks milking as holiday relief in future.'

I waited till Jill had gone off with the boys and Robert was turning out the cows, then I went to him. 'I've got something to show you mate, it's going to come as a bit of a shock, but I'd hate anything else to happen to you.'

'You going to give me a lecture on dodgy ladders? Don't worry I'll sling it and get an aluminium one.'

'This is where the shock comes, there wasn't anything wrong with it until someone sabotaged it. I didn't tell Jill because I didn't want to worry her.' I showed him how the wire had been weakened so that it would pull through and the rung had been cracked with a hammer or something. His face paled. 'I wonder why anyone would do that? I've never done anything to hurt anyone. I refused to sell the farm and Dan Woodward didn't like that much, but he'd been gone to Canada best part of a month before it happened. I doubt whether he'd get someone else to do it. I don't know why he's so desperate to get the farm anyway. I'd have thought he could manage with 650 acres.'

'Well you'll have to be on your guard because someone's got it in for you. I shan't mention it to anyone, but I'll keep listening, maybe whoever did it will try again. I'd get a good guard dog if I were you, I know it'll be another mouth to feed but it'll be a good deterrent. I'll be off now back to the pub, but if you need me for anything at all, just shout.'

We shook hands and Robert muttered something about paying me. 'Forget it mate, Jill's tried it already. Get it into your heads. If I want help some day you can return the compliment.' I jumped into the motor and left him looking after me. I drew into the pub yard and parked in my usual spot and let myself in.

Rose was busy cleaning. 'Back again then? Couldn't keep away from Jeff's cooking eh?'

I grinned. 'I'm not going to complain about Jill's talents, but it's good to be back and finished with cows for a bit. I was glad to help but I wouldn't do it day in day out like they do.'

I carted my stuff upstairs and found that the dirty washing I'd left behind had all been washed and stacked in the chest of drawers. I crept up behind Rose and gave her a hug. 'I hope you're going to put the washing on the bill, that was a nice surprise, on top of Jill doing my washing yesterday. I won't let it accumulate so much in future.'

She leant on her broom. 'No problem, boy, just let me have it once a week, the washing machine stands there, it may as well be in use. The nearest launderette must be Corby or Stamford.'

'Only if you let me pay you,' I said sternly.

'You can bugger off. If you can do good turns for people so can we.' That was the end of that conversation.

'I'll be in for lunch, Rose. I'm off to see what's happening on the other establishments.' No one around in the nursery, perhaps Brynda had taken the old lady for treatment or something. Everything was silent round at the farm so I took myself off down to Caroline's. Her Fiesta stood outside the mill so I reckoned she would be in. When she came to the door she invited me in for a coffee. I went round the kitchen as she was making it, looking at the assortment of snaps on show. I saw one of her and Malcolm's wedding taken outside the church. 'How long has the church been redundant?' I asked.

'Quite a while, but they let you use it for weddings and funerals at your own risk.'

'Did Tony and Donna get married here?' I wanted to know.

'No, it's usual to get married in the bride's local church if she wants a church wedding. I've got a picture of their wedding in the sitting room, I'll get it for you, their photographer was better than ours.' I had a really good look at Donna so that with a bit of luck I'd recognise her if I saw her. Shouldn't be too difficult as she had red hair, not the most prevalent colour.

'Who got married first then, you or Tony?'

'Oh, I did, but we've only just started a family. We'd nearly given up hope. I got pregnant when we'd stopped trying, if that makes sense.'

'There's loads of things that can't be accounted for,' I said, thinking of the mysterious regrowth of my hair.

I took myself off when Fiona started to yell for attention. I went up to the S. S. S. I. I hadn't had time to walk up there since taking over

Robert's milking. There is always something new in the country, some wild flowers had died and others had emerged to take their place. I saw several fledgling blackbirds. A cuckoo was calling in the forest and I heard the distinctive call of a woodpecker, rather like a cockatoo.

I got back to the pub at lunch time, had a plate of sandwiches, then decided to go the Peterborough. Instead of going to Wansford to the A47 I went round the back roads and got onto the A605 at Elton. I passed the sugar beet factory on the way in. All quiet there until September when the new season would get underway. I found a park just under the railway bridge and walked into the city over the river bridge. I bought a street map of Peterborough from a newsagent and discovered just how much it had grown since I'd visited the showground as part of the White Helmets motor cycle display team. It occurred to me that Donna's mum may well have moved out into one of the New Ortons. The old Longueville and Waterville were hemmed in by new parkways and townships. There was now Orton Malborne and Orton Goldhay and lots of building going on all around. Orton Malborne school was opened in 1977 so I decided to try there first. It was too early to go yet so I had a good look round the city centre shops to see what was on offer. I didn't buy anything and got back to the car park with time enough to drive round to Orton Malborne in time to catch the kids coming out of school. Following my map I went back up Oundle road, past the beet factory, over the Botolph Bridge and left into Shrewsbury Avenue, from there to Malborne where I soon found the school. Mums and sometimes grandparents arrived, then the children started to stream out. No sign of Donna although I did spot one or two redheads.

It was no use going to any other schools, I expected they all came out at the same time, so I made my way towards the Orton shopping centre. In Orton Goldhay I spotted the Winyates Primary School and thought it might be worthwhile enquiring if they had any children called Woodward. I found the head teacher but drew a blank and a suspicious look, so I said I was a private detective trying to trace a wife and family for a man who couldn't spare the time to look himself. The Orton Centre when I got there had a large car park, shops round a square, a Co-op supermarket and a DIY store. I had a nose round then went back to Halston. I decided not to enquire directly to schools again because they may alert other schools that someone was looking for the Woodward family. If Donna did not want to be found she could go into further hiding. I didn't want to go to Peterborough more than once a week without good excuse, Tony might tell me to mind my own business.

I went round to the nursery and found Brynda watering what looked like thousands of French marigolds all in individual segments of 10-hole containers. Jamie came out of the house, very importantly, to tell me about his playgroup. He was making lots of new friends and there were loads of toys to play with but gratifyingly he still liked his tractor best.

Brynda said she'd got a big load of plants going on Thursday and she'd appreciate a bit of help. Just what the doctor ordered. The more time we spent together the better we'd get to know one another. You have to either live or work with someone to really get to know them, so many couples can only meet socially when they're on their best behaviour, and only find the niggling habits after they are married. I heard of one case where the girl told her fellow that she wanted 'to wait till they were married' then he found out that she had been having an affair with her married boss for years. Fortunately for him he found out before the knot had been tied.

When Thursday arrived I presented myself in the nursery when Brynda came back from playgroup. 'Amazing how he's taken to it,' Brynda remarked. 'Some of the children cling to their mums and cry when they go. Not Jamie, as soon as he gets there he's off. I might as well be on another planet. He never wants to leave. Anyway we'd better get cracking while he's out of the way. It is a massive order this time, thousands of bedding plants going to various markets. Marigolds, tagetes, lobelia, alyssum, ageratum, antirrhinum, African marigolds, begonias, busy lizzies, stocks, petunias, nemesias, monkey flowers, pansies, Sweet Williams, in short most of the popular annuals.'

She had a list of what quantities of each variety and we went round the cold frames loading them into the special trolleys and lining them up at the back of the loading bay. We managed to get finished before it was time to fetch Jamie.

'Want to come with me to Tansor and have a look at the set up?' she asked.

'You bet!' We went round to the shed where the car was kept. First time I'd seen it, a bright yellow Renault, pretty utilitarian. The gear lever had to be pushed and pulled and twisted through the dashboard. 'Bit different from your Ford,' Brynda grinned. It started first time and she backed it out of the shed.

'They're economical to run, go nearly anywhere, and you can push a lot of stuff in the back, anyway I like it.' When we got to Tansor Jamie insisted on a guided tour. We were the last to leave. I think we were hindering the people who ran it from clearing up.

I went to the pub for lunch when we got back, saying that I'd give a hand with the loading when the lorry arrived. After I'd eaten I spread my Peterborough map on a table in the lounge and studied school locations. I had a sudden thought, I needed to know what Donna's folks looked like, maybe mum or dad met the kids from school. Be a good idea to see if I could invite myself into Tony's cottage again so that I could see if he had any pictures dotted around. I needed to see him anyway to get a date organised for our gig. We had a fair bit of hiring to organise.

CHAPTER VI

Brynda's lorry arrived at about 2 o'clock and I went round and helped load as promised. When we had finished Brynda said, 'You'd better come in for a coffee, Mrs Spencer is dying to see this mysterious man who seems to be the answer to everyone's prayers.'

Well, I thought that Caroline's kitchen was big, this one was huge. A double Aga no less. Everything in old pine. A Welsh dresser with traditional willow pattern china arranged on it. I don't usually take much notice of people's houses, only when something smacks me in the eye, either end of the extremes of good or bad. This was good. Brynda made three cups of coffee, put them on a tray with a glass of orange, sugar, milk and a biscuit tin. She led the way to the sitting room where Jamie was sitting at the feet of his gran playing with toy cars. Mrs Spencer wasn't as old as I'd been led to believe, late fifties maybe, but her illness had probably aged her. Brynda introduced us and I came under the scrutiny of a pair of searching grey eyes. I must have passed, because she smiled and held out her good hand, her right, for me to take.

'I understand that Brynda takes you for physio and your hand is gradually getting better?' She nodded and managed to open and close the fingers of her left hand, quite slowly, but surely. She asked me lots of questions about myself which I answered as truthfully as I dared while we drank our coffee. I caught Brynda watching with a little secret smile and wondered briefly what she knew that I didn't. I told Mrs Spencer to hurry and get back the full use of her left hand so that she could play again.

'I shan't take the piano away from Caroline now,' she said, then with a twinkle in her eye 'But I may buy myself an electric keyboard which will do some of the work for me. I hear that you're going to try to raise some money for Malcolm's water wheel?'

'Not just me. Tony, Caroline and Brynda have as well. I've got to see Tony to arrange a date so that I can get stuff ordered and booked. I've got more time than the others.'

Brynda looked at her watch. 'I'd better go and tidy up outside, if Jamie gets to be a nuisance, send him outside.'

Mrs Spencer ruffled his hair, 'He's a good boy, most of the time.'

I rose to my feet. 'Nice to have met you, Mrs Spencer, I'll call in and see you again another day.' I followed Brynda out. 'Got much to do now?' I asked.

'No, just clearing up, start to get busy again on Monday.'

'Does Jamie go to playschool tomorrow?'

She shook her head. 'Not Fridays, I was only going to take him two days a week, but he likes it so much that they agreed to take him four days. It's about as much as I can afford anyway.'

'How about a day out at Wicksteed Park then? Mrs Spencer might come too if she liked.'

Her face lit up. 'Jamie would love that, and Mrs S might come too now her face is more or less back to normal. She didn't like people to see her when it was all twisted from the stroke. Not from vanity, it just embarrassed her to feel people's pity.'

'OK, what time in the morning?'

'I think I'll have watered and done everything that has to be done by ten o'clock'

'Great, then I'll bring my car round to the house so that if Mrs S decides to come she won't have far to walk.'

I took myself off round to the farm where I could hear someone working in the machinery shed. Tony and Steve were working on the forage harvester, making sure that it would be ready for use when needed. 'We hedge our bets,' Tony explained 'We make some hay and some silage, how much of each depends on the weather. So long as we get some good meadow hay for the old man's hunters it doesn't matter much.'

'Where are his hunters? I haven't seen or heard any horses?'

'Oh, he doesn't trust us with them while he's away, they've gone to some hunting friends of his to get properly looked after.'

Steve grinned at me, 'Bloody good job too. I don't want to have to ride the brutes to keep 'em exercised.'

'Robert was telling me that Dan bought a new crawler last year, I haven't seen it yet, where do you keep it?'

'Oh, it's in with the vintage stuff at the moment. Steve's pride and joy,' grinned Tony. 'All sheeted over so the birds can't shit on it, everything in there is sheeted over at the moment so you can't see anything.'

'Changing the subject,' I said, 'when can we fix a date for the 'gig', we need to get booked for this amplifying stuff, loos and everything?'

'We could have a conference on Tuesday night. I don't know what commitments Caroline has, they usually go on holiday in June sometime.'

He looked at his watch. 'It's about knocking off time, fancy a coffee?'

'Sure thing,' I didn't tell him I'd just had one, saved me from inviting myself.

Steve went off and Tony locked up all the doors, then we walked round to his cottage. While he was making the coffee I looked round for photographs. I didn't think there were any, when I spotted one lying face down on the bookcase. I was looking at the photo of two little blond boys when Tony bought the coffee in. His face crumpled. 'I put it face down because I get upset every time I look at it,' I could see that he wasn't far off tears.

'I take it you haven't heard from Donna then?' I asked.

'Not a whisper, when I went round to her mum's house and found she'd moved I didn't know where to look. The new people said they didn't know where she'd moved to except it was a new house somewhere in Peterborough. I went round to the Council Offices but they either couldn't, or wouldn't help. I suppose they thought I might have been knocking her about or something.' He sat despairingly down in an old armchair gazing into his coffee.

'Look, mate, I know you haven't got much time but I've got plenty. I'm taking Brynda, Jamie and possibly your aunt to Wicksteed tomorrow but I could make a few discreet enquiries next week if you like. I saw your wedding picture at Caroline's so I know what Donna looks like. I've seen the boys now, but I don't know what your ma-in-law looks like.'

He brightened slightly. 'I had thought about asking you to stand in for me for a few days so I could look myself, but perhaps yours is the better idea. At least they won't recognise you if they spot you before your see them, if you see what I mean.'

I nodded. 'That way I can find our whether she has any intention of coming back or not, if I find them that is. Have you got a picture of herself I can look at?' He nodded and went off upstairs coming back with a group photograph. It was fairly easy to pick out ma-in-law, she

THE ARM OF COINCIDENCE

was still a relatively attractive woman, an older version of Donna gone grey.

'Her name is Norma Eastwood, and the boys are Brian and Ben, Brian is six and a half and Ben is five so they should both be at school. Ben started at Woodnewton last September.'

I nodded, 'Can I borrow the photos for the time being?' I asked, 'Just in case I need to check if I think I see them.'

He passed them over almost in tears again. 'She is pretty proud, is Donna, she most likely thinks I should have found her by now. Doesn't realise the reality. If I fall out completely with the old man any chance I have of inheriting his half of the farm will go out of the window.'

I finished my coffee and took myself off back to the pub. 'See you later for dinner then,' I said.

Friday was at least fine and I was pleased to see that Mrs Spencer had decided to come too. We arrived at Wicksteed Park, Kettering at about a quarter to eleven. Jamie was in seventh heaven with the swings, slides, see-saws, roundabouts and everything. He soon made friends with some other children and they vied with each other to see who could swing the highest and who could slide the fastest. Hardly any of them were much over four because the older children were all at school. Mrs S had her hand firmly through my arm. 'I shan't fall over if I've got a big strong man to hang on to,' she said with a grin.

We all went on the little train, all the way round the lake. Brynda took Jamie on the water chute. This was like a big boat, which was hauled up a steep slope by a strong cable. When it was released it went into the water with a great splash. Needless to say they both got a bit damp! And I got shots of it all. We went to a cafeteria for lunch then went to the swings and slides again which were all free. You had to pay to go on the train and water chute. Jamie was desperate for another ride on the train so I treated us all again then it was time to go home.

I made a slight detour in Geddington because I wanted to photograph the Eleanor Cross, one of only three surviving in the country. They had been erected to commemorate the resting places of the cortege taking Edward the First's wife's body back to London. One of the other two is at Hardingstone just outside Northampton, and the other at Waltham Cross, North London.

When I'd taken my pictures I thought we may as well go home the scenic way, i.e. the back roads. We went to Grafton Underwood, Brigstock, past Fermyn Woods house, to Lower Benefield, to Glapthorne via the gated road. At Southwick I stopped and took a few pictures of the Hall, the daffodils were dying, but buttercups were replacing them. The horse chestnuts were a magnificent sight with their upright pinkish white flowers. I took a few pictures of the house with branches of flowers on the left hand side. When I got back into the car Mrs S remarked that the place was open to the public on Bank Holidays. I made a mental note to bring Brynda and Jamie over at the end of the month when the next Bank Holiday came.

When we got home I was invited in for tea. I played with Jamie on the floor while Brynda got the tea. Mrs S had a doze in her chair. She woke when Brynda came in with tea and cakes and started talking about the current situation in Ireland.

'I haven't watched any television lately,' I confessed, 'so I've not got much idea of what's going on in the world.'

'What about papers?' she asked.

'Hardly every look at them; you don't know what to believe in them anyway. Most of them have different versions of the same story and no matter how dramatic the events are, they are usually exaggerated.'

'Well I tell you what I'd do if I were a Catholic out there. I'd try to persuade my neighbours to dress up, join the Orange parades, and generally make fun of them. Bet that would have a far better effect than trying to fight them.'

I grinned, 'Well, it's an interesting thought, I suppose, but I doubt whether they'd try it. Loads of people of both religions over there just want to live a peaceful and fair life. Trouble is, they've had hundreds of years of brainwashing and provocation.'

She nodded, 'It's very sad, so many lives lost. I once heard of a woman who lived in Rothley near Leicester. They moved a boundary so she was living in Mountsorrel and she played merry hell!'

She thought for a minute, 'I may have got that the wrong way round, but it doesn't matter, I mean what difference did it make, she was still in the same house in the same street. It doesn't make much difference how many times you change the names of countries or places they are still the same. It's the people who change, if you get the wrong people in power, like Hitler for instance, you're in big trouble. They make all sorts of promises but once in power they can do as they like.' It was a long speech and I daresay she had a point or two, but I didn't want to comment, so I said nothing. I took another slice of chocolate cake and carefully ate it, not wishing to get crumbs all over the carpet.

THE ARM OF COINCIDENCE

I took my leave and went back to my room at the pub to develop my films. I'm impatient and don't want to wait for them to come back from the professionals. Bunion, Tony and I had dinner together, we all had shepherd's pie. Tony spotted someone called Barry from the Council houses and suggested a game of dominoes. Barry worked for 'Squerkins Wheezles' which turned out to be Perkins Diesel. Bit unfair, I thought, they make pretty good engines, export them all over the world for different applications.

Barry grinned at me, 'Just my little joke, I'm what they call a 'sliphand', I can step into the breach anywhere on the line if someone doesn't turn up for their shift. Some guys who consider themselves skilled workers don't even know what engines they're building!'

Tony was busy shuffling the dominoes. I was to play with Bunion against them. Conversation ebbed somewhat as the serious business began. More by luck than judgement I'm sure, Bunion and I filled our side of the pegboard first. I looked up to see a determined looking chap heading towards us.

'You Jim Evans?' he addressed me. 'Don't know if you can help me out, I've just been talking to Malcolm in the lounge and he seems to think that you've got an HGV licence and may be free?'

I nodded, 'Yes, I've got a class II, what's your problem?'

'My chap was rushed into hospital with appendicitis this afternoon, I'm too busy to go on the truck myself, and the lorry's booked for Northampton Market in the morning. I could pay you £2.50 per hour if you're willing.'

'Early start?'

''Fraid so. Does that mean you'll do it?'

I grinned at him, 'I expect Malcolm told you I've done little else but step into breaches since I came here. I don't like to see people stuck when it's no fault of their own. You'd better wise me up about the lorry and what you want me to do.'

He thought for a moment. 'I'll give you directions of how to find my place and meet you at 6 o'clock. It's only a four-wheeler, not new I'm afraid. Ford D1000 Turbo charged. Quite easy to drive. Ever driven a cattle truck?'

'No, but I'm used to animals, so it shouldn't be a problem.'

'The difference between cattle trucks and almost everything else is that you have to read the road as far ahead as possible, so you don't have to brake too sharply. If you drive too fast and too close to the vehicle in front and have to brake suddenly you finish up with all your animals in a heap at the front. If you corner too fast they go to one side and tip you over. I've seen one tipped over and it's not a pretty sight! You still game?'

I nodded, 'I've got some maps in my room, I'll nip up and get them and you can pinpoint your place and the other places I have to go.' I nipped upstairs for 141, 142 and 152, which had Northampton on it.

We spread 141 out on the table and he pointed out his farm near Oundle, the farm near Sudborough where I had to pick up my load, and the location of the market in Northampton. 'When you've unloaded the lorry will need a wash out on the high pressure wash. Then if you park up and get yourself a cup of tea you'll probably be approached by someone who wants some animals brought back this way. 'Bout time I introduced myself, Terry Grant.'

I shook his hand and promised to be at his farm at six the next morning. Rose must have heard most of the conversation because she offered a packed breakfast and lunch. I grinned at her, 'Thanks very much, how about a packet of cornflakes, half a bottle of milk, a dish and spoon for breakfast. Anything you've got for lunch.'

'Right, I'll leave you some milk and sandwiches in the fridge and the flakes and other stuff on the kitchen table.'

I looked at the clock and was amazed to see it was already past ten o'clock, time for the roost.

I duly presented myself at Terry Grant's place at six o'clock and I quickly familiarised myself with the controls. Terry showed me how the inner partitions worked and how to put the decking in if anyone bought sheep. The motor was in good nick, well maintained, so I had no qualms about taking it out. By the time I got to Sudborough I had the feel of the motor, not so much different to a car but I had the feeling that all that was about to change. The animals were penned up ready for loading, ten fat cattle ready for slaughter. It didn't take many minutes to load them up. I gathered that he'd been warned that it wouldn't be the usual driver. The first few miles the motor rocked about something rotten, which made me concentrate totally on the steering! After that things settled down and I had an uneventful journey into Northampton. I found the market easily enough and someone guided me between two other trucks into a vacant bay. A market man came up to me for my notes, consulted his clipboard then asked me to unload. The cattle were herded into a pen and lot numbers pasted

THE ARM OF COINCIDENCE

on to them. I refastened the back and took the lorry over to the wash and parked alongside a four wheel Guy. The driver showed me how to operate the water jet. 'You need to chuck the straw out first. There should be a muck fork and some clean straw in the box at the front.'

It was as he said, and I chucked out the soiled straw. He inspected my truck. 'You're lucky today, there's no dead shit in there! Terry's driver doesn't clean out any more than he has to.'

My new friend was German judging by his accent but he seemed to be popular with everyone in the market. The lorry on my other side pulled out and another took its place. The driver came and let his ramp down. My new friend greeted him with, 'How's the old gatepost, mate?'

'Jealousy'll get you nowhere, Henry.' The bloke winked at me with a broad grin 'Private joke! He's referring to a certain part of my anatomy!' They both fell about laughing. I turned on the high-pressure jet so didn't hear any more of their conversation. By the time I'd finished they'd both parked up and disappeared. I parked alongside and found them in the café, got myself a coffee and joined them. These two guys were as crazy as coots! Obviously good mates but half the time I had no clue as to what they were talking about. However they said that if there was any spare work they'd see that I got it. It appeared they were pally with Terry's driver and were sorry to hear he'd got appendicitis.

I went back to my truck and ate my cornflakes, then had a wander round the market. The sale ring was quite an eye-opener. I had no idea how the auctioneer knew who was bidding. Sometimes the animals were brought in singly and sometimes in groups. Once sold they were put into different pens so there was little time lost between sales. The sheep and pigs were sold in separate rings and I didn't get to them until it was nearly lunch time. I ate my sandwiches whilst watching proceedings.

I finished up with a load of sheep for Cotterstock, which my new friends assured me didn't need the extra deck.

'If you take this on till Graham gets back I expect we'll see you around,' they said. We set off almost in convoy and didn't split up until we got to Oundle.

When I returned the lorry to Terry's place, I signed off the log book and as he wasn't around left my hours on the seat with a note that if he needed me, to call the pub and I'd do my best, provided I got sufficient notice. When I got back to the Walnut Tree, I had a bath and change of clothing. My clothes were a bit niffy to say the least so I handed them over to Rose to bung in the washing machine. She wrinkled her nose in mock displeasure. 'Good job we're used to country smells,' she joked. 'I'll put them in the tumble drier when they're washed, but if you want them ironed it'll be a DIY job!'

I grinned at her, 'Don't think I'll bother, it'll be good enough to get rid of the pong.'

I went round to find Brynda. She was in the house. I felt unusually nervous when I asked, 'Would you like to go to Bulwick for a meal this evening? I've heard that it's very good, do you think Mrs S would mind?'

She smiled, 'I'll go and ask her!' She went though to the sitting room. At least she wasn't going to turn me down out of hand. She was still smiling when she came back 'No problem, I should be ready with Jamie settled down about seven.'

'Great, see you at seven, then.' I went back to the Walnut Tree walking on air and hoped Rose wouldn't mind my eating elsewhere for a change.

When I told her, Rose looked almost as pleased as I felt. 'She's a lovely girl, you could do a lot worse than marry her, even if she has got a child.'

'Reckon Jamie would be a bonus if she's thinking along the same lines as me. I'm keeping everything crossed!'

'I hope you're serious, I wouldn't want to see her hurt again. You haven't known her five minutes as the saying goes, but I must admit, I've noticed that she gives you quite speculative looks when she thinks no-one's watching.'

I asked if I could use the phone and insisted on paying 10p for the call. I looked up the Queen's Head in Bulwick, rang through and booked in for 7.30. I got changed about quarter to seven and took extra care with deodorants. I found a white shirt and tie, blazer and grey flannels. When I went down it was to be greeted by Bunion grinning from ear to ear, 'My, my, Lord Muck of Turd Hall! Too good to eat with Tony and me, only joking boy, but you take good care of that girl!'

I wrinkled my nose at them and went out to my car. Brynda was ready, she looked absolutely smashing, her hair tied in a ponytail, wearing a green velvet dress. I opened the passenger door and settled her in. It didn't take long to get to Bulwick and we were soon in the warmth of the bar. Brynda had a white wine whilst I stuck to my usual orange juice. I explained to the landlord that alcohol and I weren't very good friends. We were studying the menu when in came the guy who had been in the market, not the German, the other one, it looked as though he had his wife with him. I heard him tell the landlord that his mum was sitting in for them. I was quite relieved when he simply acknowledged me with a wave and he and his wife joined another couple. I told Brynda that I'd met him in the market in the morning. She smiled at me, 'When did you meet his wife then?' I must have looked puzzled. 'At the playgroup you lummox! She runs it.'

I looked round and recognised her in retrospect.

We both chose gammon steak with pineapple, peas and boiled potatoes. Then we followed it with lemon pie and coffee. There didn't seem to be any point in staying longer so I paid the bill and we went out to the car. Brynda's hand found its way into mine, I turned her round and she came into my arms. I kissed her gently. 'Where now?' I asked her.

'Somewhere we can have a cuddle without being spied on of course!' She scrambled into the car and I went round to the driver's side.

'I think I saw some sort of turning off near that chicane bridge about halfway to Southwick.'

'Let's go see then.' She cuddled up as I started the motor. When I got to the bridge I saw a roadway going up to a farm on the left and over the bridge a track off to the right. I drove as far as I could until I came to a barrier. Then she was kissing me.

'I hope these seats fold down, I need a really good seeing to! It's been a long time, my panties are wet through, and if you don't give it to me good and proper I'll never forgive you!'

Her tongue darted into my mouth and her hand started to squeeze through my trousers. J. T. was already at full stretch and it didn't take her many seconds to free him from all restraints. 'This is what I want,' she whispered.

I pulled away slightly. 'There may be a problem, I can't protect you, I can't use those wretched things anyway.'

'No problem,' she sighed, 'Just what I like, Pete wasn't circumcised either, although his wasn't as big as this. Anyway, there's nothing to worry about, just wind this back down and let's get on with it.'

We finished up completely naked except for our shoes and made love until we were both exhausted. At one time she wanted the interior light

THE ARM OF COINCIDENCE

on so she could watch what we were doing. I looked at my watch, getting on for midnight. 'I hope Mrs S isn't waiting up for us!'

'No of course not, silly. If Jamie needs anything he'll go along to her room when he finds I'm not in mine.'

'You know I was worried a bit back when Tony seemed to be taking an interest in you, I know now that he desperately wants Donna and the boys back and I'm going to try and find them for him.'

'Mmm, I only let him walk me home to see how you'd react! He was only being friendly, I don't think he realised that I was interested in you.'

'I didn't either! But I'm very glad you are, I was so nervous of being rejected that I couldn't bring myself to make a pass.'

'I know, why do you think I was so blatant? Come on, we'd better get sorted out and get back to Halston. Think you can back out without getting us stuck?' she teased.

I put my hazard lights flashing to give better visibility, the track was well defined, so I had no trouble in spite of the long curve. By the time I'd managed to tear myself away from her and park up the car it was well past midnight. I was reminded of the song 'She had kisses sweeter than wine'. I practically skipped to the back door and let myself in.

We had some rain in the night, but by afternoon it had dried up and the sun was shining. It made you feel good to be alive. Brynda, Jamie and I took a picnic up the chase to the S. S. S. I. I spotted some young fox cubs at play, three of them. Fortunately they were upwind of us and they hadn't heard, smelt or seen us. We had a vantage point from where we could watch over a slight ridge. I eased the groundsheet out, put a travel rug over it and we all three lay on our tummies to watch. Brynda on my right and Jamie on my left. Jamie was entranced.

I felt Brynda's breath on my ear. 'Rub my bum,' she whispered. I reached over with my right hand and obliged, still watching the cubs and whispering to Jamie. Her bottom started to make circular up and down movement. She would suddenly speed up, then stop and lie perfectly still for a moment, then off again. Suddenly she went into overdrive, which culminated in her whole body quivering and shaking for several seconds. She turned her head and looked into my eyes with a sexy smile. 'See what you've made me do! That was lovely thank you, I'll return the compliment later when we haven't got company.'

Jamie was wrapped up with the foxes and they didn't notice us at all until Dad fox came home with a rabbit for them to share. He was more alert to danger than the cubs and spotted us, quickly ushering his brood into the hole. Considering that there was a badger sett not far away, I was surprised that the foxes were so close. A fox is no match for a badger in a fight.

We had our picnic with Jamie chattering all the time about the foxes. I warned him not to tell anyone else about them because if George found them he'd most likely shoot them.

We went home with Jamie on my shoulders and Brynda carrying the much lighter rucksack and holding my hand. It was brilliant, like a dream. I wondered how Jamie would react to having me for a substitute Dad. Don't cross bridges before you come to them, or count your chickens, Jim boy, I told myself. I stayed round at Mrs Spencer's house until long after Jamie had gone to bed and we spent a relaxing few hours talking about everything and nothing.

I found myself whistling as I made my way back to the pub. Rose and Jeff were busy washing up all the glasses and putting them back in their places.

'Terry rang,' said Rose. 'Are you available on Tuesday to pick up four lots of pigs and take them to Brierly Hill near Birmingham? He said you'd be back in time for the music session. He hasn't got much on tomorrow, so he can fit round it himself. Could you let him know by nine o'clock tomorrow otherwise he'll have to try and get another haulier.'

I looked at my watch and grinned, 'I doubt if he'd appreciate a call right now! I hope these messages aren't being a nuisance to you?'

'Not at all,' from Jeff, 'being helpful to our customers is all part of our philosophy.'

I said goodnight, went to bed and dreamed that Brynda was cuddled up with me, well sort of.

I rang Terry just before nine and assured him that I could do the job. 'I'll leave all the addresses on the seat.' He said. 'You can pen each lot up individually, you won't need any deck in, they'll have plenty of space without. I'll also leave an atlas and a street map in the lorry with the slaughterhouse marked. You need to be at the first pick up at seven so you should get here just before half six.' I said I'd be there and rang off. I had my cornflakes, then nipped round to the nursery to see if there was anything I could do. Brynda had just got back from taking Jamie to playschool.

'You can take Mrs S for her therapy if you like, it's only half an hour, so it's hardly worth coming back for. Leaves me free to work on the plants.'

'What time?' I wanted to know.

'She needs to be there by ten o'clock so if you fetch your car it'll be time to go, unless you want to take mine?' She grinned with raised eyebrows knowing perfectly well that I wouldn't. I fetched my car round to the front door and got Mrs S settled into the front seat. 'You'll need to tell me where to go in Oundle,' I said. She gave directions when we got to the Talbot Hotel and we were soon parked outside. I went in with her and found some magazines to look at while she had her treatment. When we got back in the car I asked if she fancied a visit to the coffee tavern. 'That would be nice, haven't been there since I had my stroke, might see a few acquaintances.' That proved to be an understatement. Practically everyone in there knew her and came over for a chat. We didn't manage to get away until we'd had two coffees and two slabs of cake each. I returned her to the front door and went off to find Brynda. The yellow peril was out, of course she had gone to fetch Jamie. It was gone twelve so she wouldn't be long.

I wandered round the nursery, poking my nose in everywhere until she got back. Jamie ran down the path to me and I swung him straight up on to my shoulders. Brynda looked up with a smile, 'You can take him off my hands after lunch if you like. We shan't get anything done if you stay here to help me!' She had a point!

'Tell you what, I'll take him to Sacrewell this afternoon, there's a mill and lots of different animals there.'

'Where's that?' she asked, 'Is it far?'

I shook my head. 'No, it's only at Wansford, I'm surprised you haven't noticed the sign.'

'I haven't been that way much, I don't like the junction with the A47. OK, I know you'll look after him.'

That's what we did and I think Jamie enjoyed it as much as Wicksteed Park. We had a look round at all the old machinery as well as the animals. David Powell, the manager, took us round the mill explaining how it worked. Jamie surprised me with the intelligent questions he asked for such a young child. He was fascinated by the big stone revolving above the stationary one, the grain feeding into the centre, and the flour coming out round the edges. It went down a chute to be bagged up on the ground floor. I took a happy, exhausted little boy back to his mum at about five o'clock.

CHAPTER VII

I got to Terry's place at twenty past six and found him waiting for me. He laughed his head off when he saw the packet of cornflakes, milk, dish and spoon, to say nothing of a large pack of sandwiches. 'Boy, do you get looked after at that pub! You'll never want to move.'

'You could be right. Now show me on the map where this slaughterhouse is at Brierley Hill and I'll be off.'

It only took half an hour to the first pick up. The pigs were penned up ready for loading, so all I had to do was back into position, let down the tail ramp, open the gates, and we were in business. The farmer had a couple of boards, which we held behind the pigs to encourage them forward. Once to the front of the lorry, I shut them in with an aluminium partition, closed up the back, and off again. I looked at my watch. Fifteen minutes. If none were harder than that, it wouldn't be too bad. In the event, none of the loading was difficult. The pick-up points were not too far apart, getting slightly nearer to Birmingham with each one. It was a well-organised set-up. The traffic round Birmingham was pretty horrendous and I found myself ground to a halt several times with no apparent reason for it.

I arrived at Brierley Hill just after ten and was guided into the unloading bay. This was when the fun started. The pigs sensed that this was the end of the road. The smell was nauseating, and they kept running back into the lorry. I was pretty well shattered by the time they were all shut into the holding bay. I left the smell behind as quickly as possible and found a place to eat my cornflakes, a bit later than usual.

Once back on the M6, the traffic had thinned out. The lorry could just about manage 60 mph empty. I went back to Oundle via Lutterworth, Market Harborough and Corby, getting back to Terry's about lunchtime. There was no-one around, so I ate my sandwiches before washing out the lorry. There was an obvious place for doing this job, with a high-pressure electric water pump. You had to use water from a two hundred gallon tank, which had its own ball valve to refill it. It had a very powerful jet which quickly blasted all the straw and muck out the back and down the ramp. I filled in all the necessary lorry documents, locked up the cab and put the keys and my time sheet through Terry's letterbox.

It was still only half past two when I got back to Halston. I parked up and took my sandwich box, dish and the rest of the cornflakes in to Rose, then wandered round to the nursery. The Yellow Peril was out, so I went back to the pub, collected my camera and went off for a walk. I went through the forest to Southwick and then on to Short Wood, a nature reserve belonging to The Northamptonshire Trust. The Trust is still raising money to pay for it, and there would be a Mediaeval Fair at Ashton in June as a fund-raising affair. There were acres of bluebells, an absolutely magnificent sight. I took several photos, especially where I found some 'white bells' or early purple orchids. I wondered if Brynda had a red dress she could wear in the bluebells. If not, I'd pay a visit to the Oxfam shop in Oundle and see what they'd got.

On the way back I passed an old railway wagon. I'd seen it before, but hadn't had a good look. There was an old stove in it, so I supposed it was a shelter for the forestry workers at one time. A bit further down the footpath I caught a flash of blue over to my right and found the most magnificent area of bluebells that I'd ever seen. It was different from the rest of the forest, mostly sycamores, and I made a mental note to ask Bunion about it. I made my way round to the nursery when I got back; still no yellow car. As I turned to leave, I saw Mrs S wave from the window. I waved back and she indicated that I should go in. I went in the back door and made my way through to the sitting room. She greeted me with, 'I don't expect Brynda will be long now, she's taken a load of small plants to an old customer of mine at Wellingborough. I told her not to rush back, so I expect she's having a look round the town with Jamie.'

I thanked her and turned to leave. 'If you're a scrabble player, you can keep an invalid company till they get back.' She pronounced it in valid, no doubt to indicate that she was no longer an invalid. She got the scrabble set out and we sat at the table. There was a pen and pad in the box ready for scoring and a bag to put the letters in. It was a while since I'd played and this board had double and triple letter scores as well as double and triple word scores. Mrs S was very good at finding high scoring words to go on these. Mind she was lucky enough to get the Q and U at the same time!

We were just chatting away when she got to what was on her mind. 'I hope you won't take Brynda and Jamie away. I doubt if I shall be able to take over the work of the nursery again. It was getting a bit much even before I had the stroke.'

I looked at her rather woebegone face. 'If I'm lucky enough to get accepted, do you think there'd be room for one more here? I know Brynda likes this work and I've got a pension and was lucky enough to inherit some property, which I have sold, and I've invested this money.'

The transformation of her face was like the sun coming from behind a cloud. 'When are you going to ask her then?'

'Do you think I stand a chance? I'd like perhaps to be a little more certain. I wouldn't like to be turned down.'

'Pah, faint heart never won fair lady! I'm sure she's only waiting to be asked.' I heard the unmistakable sound of the Renault returning and we were concentrating fully on the game when Brynda came in with Jamie. He was clutching a brightly coloured ball about the size of a regular football. I grinned at him, 'Reckon we shall have to take that over into the paddock to kick it around. Glass and footballs don't mix!'

'That's what I told him, but he loved it so much I let him buy it.' Brynda gave a little grimace and held up crossed fingers. She had a nose at the scores. Mrs S was about 100 in front. 'She keeps picking the high scoring letters out of the bag,' I said with mock complaint.

Brynda looked at her employer. 'If you want to carry on with your game I could get dinner for all of us?'

Mrs S looked up, 'Now there's a good idea.' She winked at me, 'Save you a few pennies at the pub as well. AND you can sample Brynda's cooking.'

Jamie took the ball to his room and came back with a great box of Lego, which he amused himself with while we got on with our game. We got finished just before Brynda announced that dinner was ready. Mrs S had a comfortable win.

We went into the kitchen. 'I've done spaghetti bolognaise, quick and easy. I hope that's all right?' She grinned at me. 'You can wash up while I get Jamie to bed before we go round to the pub.'

'Oh, lor! I'd forgotten it's music night. I wonder what Caroline's sorted out for this evening.'

It was after seven when we got to the pub. Tony and Caroline were already there. 'I took the liberty of fetching the keyboard down,' said Tony. By the time we got started on some Abba numbers, the room was about full. We called a halt about 9 o'clock. We needed to sort a date for the gig. In the end we settled on June 6th, a week before

Ashton Fair, which meant that I could get busy with Yellow Pages and try to find someone we could hire amplification stuff from and other people for toilets, etc.

Brynda and I walked back to the house hand in hand. It always seemed strange to see one half of the house lit up and the other, Dan's half, in darkness. We stood, kissing, in the kitchen. 'If we're quiet, we can go up to my room,' whispered Brynda. Needless to say, I didn't get back to the pub till the early hours.

I was late up the next morning!! I got the Yellow Pages out after I'd had a few cornflakes. It didn't take long to look for toilets for the ladies. Eventually I found a guy in Pytchley Road, Kettering, who could hire us the amplification gear: mikes, speakers, in fact everything we'd need. I could collect it all with the Land Rover on Friday 5th June to give us a chance to get set up and have a trial run. I got organised with the Prince William School cadet force to take care of car parking. We would contribute to their funds. Central Printers in Peterborough would do posters for us as soon as I got them our requirements. They could also supply cloakroom tickets. Jeff said he would organise a licensed bar and get people to man it.

I went down to Caroline's for her ideas on posters. She suggested that we call ourselves 'The Halston Swingers'. Sounded OK to me.

After about half an hour we had something that we thought would be eye-catching without too much detail. Admission would be £2 and we thought we ought to include 'Halston Water Wheel Appeal'. I took our ideas and showed Brynda. I found Tony once again in the workshop, and then I set off for Peterborough and Central Printers. I parked in the same car park as before, near the railway bridge.

Over the bridge into Bridge Street, I had a nose in Oxfam and bought myself a nearly new pair of jeans, then off down to Cowgate and the printers. Having got the posters organised, I decided to have a look at the market. There was a café near the market where I had a bit of lunch. As I wandered round the market I saw a material stall and some lime green nylon material that had an almost reflective sheen to it. Our uniforms for the gig. Surely Caroline would know someone who could make it up into 'boiler' suits! It wasn't silly expensive and the lady advised me to have it all to be certain of getting four suits out of it. On another stall I found 4 red elastic belts with 'peacock' interlocking buckles. As I was walking back up Bridge Street I remembered the bluebells and had another look in Oxfam, this time at the ladies section. I found the ideal dress: a red bridesmaid type with a lowish neckline, which would show a bit of cleavage! I couldn't resist it, and was pretty well laden as I made my way back to the car. It was surprising how long I'd taken mogging round the market, etc. It would soon be school out time.

I got the street map out and decided on the new area of Dogsthorpe near the Paston Parkway. I found the school, but no sign of the people I was looking for, so I headed for home. Amazing I already thought of Halston as home.

I went straight to Caroline's with my market purchases, hoping that she would be as enthusiastic about the idea as me. She was. 'I know someone at Glapthorne who'll do it for us. I'll get everyone measured up and see if she can start straight away.' I left the material with her, after we had measured each other up.

'I don't think the others will object, do you?' I asked.

She laughed. 'I'll get the thumbscrews out if they do!'

I went round to the nursery with the red dress in a bag, with a mixture of excitement and anticipation, hoping that I wasn't taking too much for granted. Fortunately she went in to try it on straight away. She looked absolutely smashing with her blonde hair streaming down her back. 'I've left my bra off, it showed over the neckline.' She did a twirl. 'Is this for the gig?'

'Actually, no. I want to take pictures of you in a sea of bluebells. I've got something else lined up for the gig and Caroline needs to measure you up to get it made. We're all going to have nylon lime green boiler suits with red belts and 'peacock' buckles.' I uncrossed my fingers from behind my back when she said: 'It sounds great! I could embroider 'Halston Swingers' on the front if they're done in time.'

I was giving her a sound kissing when Jamie burst in from the garden. He stood looking round eyed for a few seconds, then he smiled. 'I'm glad you like my mummy. Are you going to be my new daddy?' he asked hopefully.

I squatted down in front of him, 'I'd better ask her, hadn't I? Do you think she'd like that?' We both looked at Brynda hopefully.

'As a proposal, I don't rate it much,' she smiled. 'But if you're asking, the answer is yes!' I grabbed Jamie up and danced the pair of them round the kitchen. I was so happy I was almost crying, so much for macho man.

'Does that mean I can have a little brother or sister?' demanded Jamie.

'Well, with a bit of luck, sort of, but you'll have to settle for half brother or sister.'

'Actually he won't,' Brynda interposed.

That stopped me in my tracks and what passes for my brain went into overdrive, remembering my dream. Brynda went on, 'It was Pete's idea, I'll explain later.'

'How long have you known who I am?' I asked thoughtfully.

She laughed, 'Ever since you got here, of course! I knew from Katie that your hair had grown. I knew where you were, and hoped that one day you'd come. Sometimes, you great lummox, you're too slow to catch a cold.'

I smiled ruefully at her, 'And there I was thinking we could get to know one another before I revealed myself. I kept in touch with Sgt Major Graham and you kept in touch with Katie. I don't know what made me think you wouldn't know what was going on. I'll come back later for the rest of the answers.' A quick kiss and I bolted.

I hadn't been dreaming after all! And she'd said it was Pete's idea. They must have spiked my drink. I remembered having a hangover the next morning and couldn't work out why.

I had my evening meal with Tony and Bunion as usual and I was walking on air to such an extent that I had to tell them that Brynda had agreed to marry me.

'Does that mean you'll soon be leaving us?' asked Tony slowly.

'No, it means that I'm going to move over to your aunt's house.'

'Oh, good,' Tony's face cleared. 'I had visions of her having to get someone else and losing Jamie, too.'

I shook my head. 'I like it here. I like your aunt. Look, chaps, I'm afraid I've been holding out on you. I didn't think Brynda had recognised me. I'm the bald headed fellow in the picture she showed you of Pete. When I eventually recovered consciousness in hospital after the big bang, I found I was growing hair! I hadn't had any for as long as I can remember. Pete and I were best mates in the Army, in the Signals to be precise. We were going round pubs playing and singing and trying to pick up titbits of useful information. Pete picked up most because he had learned to lip read when his younger brother went deaf. He went to classes to keep him company, also just in case the same thing happened to him.'

Tony and Bunion both gave their seal of approval and I remembered to ask Tony if he'd have time to pop down to his sister's to get measured up. I said I'd bring Brynda down when she'd got Jamie to bed.

Rose came over to our table, 'Terry on the phone for you, Jim.'

'Oh, thanks.' I went to the phone and found that there was work for me for the rest of the week if I could do it. I accepted and agreed to meet him at six o'clock. I went back round to Brynda soon after seven and found her talking animatedly to Mrs S in the kitchen. Mrs S had obviously heard the news and seemed very pleased about it. 'Look, it seems a bit ridiculous for you to be calling me 'Mrs Spenser'. I've been trying to get Brynda to call me Mavis for nearly two years!'

I grinned at her, 'Tell you what, we'll call you Auntie, same as Tony and Caroline. Doesn't seem quite so disrespectful.'

'I suppose I'll have to settle for that. When is it all going to happen, then?'

I put my arm round Brynda. 'As soon as I can arrange a licence. Unless you want a church wedding?'

She shook her head. 'I don't think so. I had that with poor Pete. It would cost more than a registry office and take longer to arrange. Anyway, we can still dress up for it if you like?'

I agreed to that and said I'd arrange with Oundle Registry Office. Brynda and I set off for Caroline's hand in hand. 'You know I said it was Pete's idea? Well, we'd been trying for a baby for some time and I went to the doctor's to see if there was something wrong with me. There wasn't so Pete went and found out that he was infertile. We were devastated; we discussed adoption, but rejected it on the grounds that we wouldn't know anything about the genealogy of the children. We rejected AID because Pete wanted to be sure of the father. Then he came up with the idea of getting you tipsy, because he said that he couldn't think of anyone else whose child he would rather bring up.'

'I wasn't dreaming after all. It never entered my head that it had really happened. You didn't give any sign that you'd recognised me either.'

'Well, I was hoping that you wouldn't love me and leave me. I knew damn well that you knew who I was, you're the first person who hasn't asked where my name came from!'

I grinned at her ruefully, 'Not as clever as I thought I was. No, Pete told how your Welsh dad had really wanted a boy, and how both your parents died trying to rescue sheep in a blizzard, and how your gran brought you up.'

She squeezed my hand a bit harder. 'With a bit of luck I might be just a teeny weeny bit pregnant already.'

'Hey, I though you were protected.'

'Are you cross?'

'No, of course not. You're a minx and I'm absolutely crazy about you.' I dragged her into my arms and kissed her soundly.

'I'm glad of that. Most women would love the father of their child. If Peter hadn't been killed, I think he might have had to share. I'd have wanted another child, and we couldn't have tried the same stunt twice!'

We'd arrived at the mill house without really noticing. Tony opened the door to us and took us through to the sitting room. 'Your turn now, Brynda,' he grinned. 'Another size twelve, I bet.'

Caroline ran the tape round, arm lengths and leg lengths were the most important! 'I've had a word with my friend and I'm taking the material and measurements over tomorrow morning.'

Malcolm was away on a case and we stayed and worked out a programme which didn't require all of us singing all of the time. Most of our favourites were from the sixties. We reckoned on a two hour programme, with a half hour break for us in the middle, when we could play stuff we would record beforehand. That settled, we decided that we would need a few extra practice sessions at Caroline's before the gig so that we would be confident of not falling on our faces, or even getting egg on our faces.

The grain barn had two big sliding doors at the end facing the road. One of them had a smaller door set into it, which we could use for admittance. The big doors could be opened at the end of the gig, or in emergency.

Tony, Brynda and I walked back together. We parted from Tony by his cottage and I went back with Brynda. Unfortunately, with an early start in view I thought I hadn't better stay.

The next three days I had early starts and late finishes. The problem with market work was that you had a fair bit of time in the middle of the day, waiting until one of your clients had bought some animals. If they didn't, you went home.

One evening I remembered to ask Bunion about the bluebells in the forest. Apparently, the main forest was leased to the Forestry Commission on a very long lease from Apethorpe Estates, and the three cornered piece, known as Howe Wood, where the bluebells were, was privately owned, but he didn't think that anyone would object to us having a closer look.

THE ARM OF COINCIDENCE

On Sunday I took Brynda and Jamie to the forest, taking the red dress in the rucksack with my camera gear. I carried my tripod to make sure I got some steady photos. Brynda got changed in the wood and I took a whole film of twenty-four exposures, some with Jamie in, but mostly with Brynda on her own. Jamie rode back on my shoulders with his bottom on top of the rucksack. Brynda carried the tripod. We got back in time for lunch, which Brynda had mostly prepared before we went. Our new Aunt had been cooking in our absence. Afterwards, I hadn't a clue what we'd eaten, I was too engrossed in watching Brynda. I hadn't heard anything from Terry by evening, so I didn't sleep in the pub bed that night!

Monday morning I went off to Oundle and got the wedding organised for Friday afternoon. Tony and Caroline agreed to be witnesses and Roger invited us to the farm for the weekend. He said he might have a surprise for us. Jamie was to go with us and Aunt Mavis reckoned she could cope with any self-catering that needed doing over the weekend. Her hand was improving with the treatment and we knew that she was quite capable of looking after herself.

I worked Tuesday, Wednesday and Thursday for Terry. Then came the most important day of my life! Brynda opted to wear the red dress to get married in. She wanted to re-use her wedding ring. She also wanted me to have a ring so that any potential rivals knew I was spoken for. We popped into Dorothy Gilks in Oundle and found one that was acceptable to her ladyship. The big surprise for me at the Registry Office was that Jamie gave his mother away! Apart from Caroline and Tony, the only other people there were Bunion and Aunt Mavis (I have to keep saying it to get used to not thinking of her as Mrs S!). We couldn't miss Bunion out. I'd got quite fond of the old boy. We went straight to Hertfordshire after the brief ceremony, arriving in time for tea. It didn't take Jamie long to captivate David, Bryn and Nesta, and it was most gratifying that Brynda and Sue hit it off, too.

'So, what's the big surprise in store then?' I asked Roger. He handed me an envelope with two tickets for the Saturday performance of Andrew Lloyd Webber's new show, 'Cats'. I was amazed. 'How did you manage that at such short notice?'

'I didn't,' he grinned, 'We booked them ages ago and we couldn't think of anything better to give you. I've booked again for ourselves in September.' I took the tickets and showed Brynda, and she was suitably impressed.

THE ARM OF COINCIDENCE

It was a bit more difficult than usual getting Jamie to bed, even with an hour's extension. He was most reluctant to part from his new friends. I was surprised that with the massive age gap they didn't seem at all anxious to get rid of him.

After lunch on Saturday, we drove down to Cockfosters and took the tube into town. When we had found the theatre, we went window shopping, content with each other's company and no wish to buy anything. We got to the theatre with time to spare and found our seats. We loved the show and Brynda reckoned we could fit 'Memory' into our programme.

Roger and Sue were still up when we got back, and we spent an enjoyable half hour chatting before retiring.

We were wakened by Jamie bouncing up and down on the bed. Just as well we'd been fast asleep when he crept in! We had a relaxing morning hardly seeing anything of the children. Jamie was most reluctant to leave after lunch, and we had to promise that he could come again before he could be persuaded into the car. We got home at tea time and I set to, moving my stuff over from The Walnut Tree. Rose and Jeff, whilst being sorry to see me go, were pleased that I wasn't going far. It's amazing how quickly you can become firm friends with some people, whereas others leave you cold.

There was a message from Terry – surprise, surprise – but he didn't actually need me till Tuesday for Melton Market. I rang him when I got home. 'Still in one piece, then?' he joked. He explained the job and I said I'd see him at the usual time.

On Monday morning I decided to go and see Robert and Jill as I hadn't seen them lately. Robert was strangely withdrawn and in the end I asked him if he'd got a problem. 'I'm in deep trouble, mate! Don't know what to do.'

'Well, if you'd care to share the burden, I might be able to help.' He shook his head. 'I doubt it, Jill will kill me if she finds out!'

'So?'

'Oh, I'll tell you. I might feel marginally better.' He paused and sighed. 'I took four calves over to Keith Morris last week, and when I got there he wasn't about, just Gloria. The wash line was full of panties, some quite saucy, and I made a stupid remark about the washline looking like the Capital of Cyprus – 'knickers here'. Anyway, she laughed and said, 'Well, I'd come to the end of the road, none to wear. That's why I'm wearing a skirt. Jeans chafe you without something between!' Her skirt was pretty

THE ARM OF COINCIDENCE

short and when she bent over to pop a calf in the pen, I could see she was telling the truth. Anyway, to cut the story short, I finished up giving her a good shagging across some bales. Turned out that Keith had been there all the time with a camera, I'd been set up! They're not going to pay me. Threatened to send the photos to Jill,' he finished despondently. 'Blackmail is a very serious offence, you know,' I told him. 'I think I can soon make them back-track on that.'

'How?'

'Can't tell you mate, you'll have to wait and see.' He went off marginally more cheerful, and I went to find Jill. I knew something that Robert didn't know! Now was the time to put it to the test. I explained the situation to her and suggested that she should come with me over to Morris's and play them at their own game. 'I'll get Caroline to pick you up, as if you're going somewhere with her. Come to think of it, she could take us to Morris's, there's bound to be one of them there.' I phoned Caroline and she said she'd be over as soon as she could get Fiona ready. I went off to find Robert and told him that Caroline was collecting Jill for a quick shopping trip to Corby. He nodded absent-mindedly. I guess he was still chewing over his stupidity.

Caroline arrived with Fiona about 20 minutes later and we set off. She grinned at Jill, 'See what comes of not being totally honest with each other?'

Jill grimaced, 'That's all going to change when we get the money and the photos.'

We found both Keith and Gloria in the calf shed. Were they surprised to see us! 'Jill here is not too chuffed with your blackmail attempt,' I went off without preamble. 'They treat blackmail as a very serious offence, you know.' They had both gone very pale.

'Now, I suggest that you get the cash a bit smartish AND the photos, and maybe we won't go to the police!'

They were a bit pathetic in their haste to comply. 'I suppose you thought that you'd get free calves for evermore, didn't you?'

Keith shrugged. 'We hadn't thought that far, I must admit. It never entered our heads that Robert would tell Jill.' He was about to add something else when Gloria came back with a packet. I looked in, then counted the cash. Not only the prints, but the negatives as well. I nodded and passed the envelope over to Jill, who popped it into her handbag.

I turned to the pair of them, 'I think this episode is best forgotten, don't you? Business as usual from now on?' I've never seen people so relieved!

We turned away, climbed into Caroline's Fiesta, and went off. 'We'd better call into Corby for half an hour and buy something,' I said.

'No need,' replied Jill. 'I'm going to put this little lot on the bedside table just before we go to bed; after I've had a jolly good look, of course. I don't think it's going to break us up.'

We dropped Jill off at the top of the farm drive. Caroline drove on, chuckling. 'Boy, is Robert in for a surprise.' I got out at the corner by Bunion's house. He was busy in his garden and we waved to each other.

I went off to find Brynda and tell her the story. She laughed until she could hardly stand up. Then she got serious. 'We aren't going to have secrets, are we?'

'Definitely not,' I answered, 'We shall adopt Caroline and Malcolm's philosophy'.

'What's that?'

'Never do anything we can't tell each other about.'

I dragged her to me for a cuddle. It wouldn't have taken long for things to progress, but this wasn't the time or the place! Anyway, we'd have all night.

After lunch, Aunt Mavis reminded us that it was Bank Holiday Monday, and said could we take her to Southwick Hall, as she hadn't been for a long time. We all packed into the car and set off. I parked on the grass where other cars were and we went in. We didn't need to pay for Jamie as he was under school age.

Aunt Mavis gave us a 'misguided' tour of the house. She seemed to know most of the people who were guiding in various rooms. Jamie liked the spiral stone stairs the best, because they went up a real tower and you could go out on top. Brynda liked the Parlour and I liked the Great Hall with its huge fireplace. It also housed a Bechstein grand piano, which I was allowed to play. I played the Rustle of Spring from memory and found I had an audience when I'd finished. When we'd been all round the house we had a cuppa and a piece of cake. Jamie had orange squash, then we went round the outside. I took some photographs of each side. Each aspect was so different that it hardly seemed like the same house.

It had a stable yard and an inner courtyard. I had to put a wide-angle lens on my camera to get a shot of the oldest part of the house: a circular tower dating from 1300. On top of a gable end hung with tiles

THE ARM OF COINCIDENCE

was a bell dating from the eighteenth century. We were told that it was rung when it was time to start work. I hoped it was rung again when it was time to stop!

We went all round the grounds and it was my turn to point out the various trees, until Jamie found an 'elephant tree', a huge silver birch with a low branch like an elephant's trunk with an 'eye' on either side. To me it looked like one of those trees you sometimes see in cartoons, with someone inside, edging down the street, hoping not to be seen! There was an enormous sycamore with an elder bush growing out of a fork, two Atlas blue cedars, and a Deodar cedar. There were some trees I couldn't identify without my books.

On the terrace I saw a coast redwood, which someone told me had grown from the stump of a previous tree, blown down in 1947. When we went round the back of the stables we found a Persian Ironwood, similar to the one at Halston. Jamie wanted to climb it, but I didn't think it appropriate for visitors to go climbing trees. There was a terrace running the whole length of the stable block, which Aunt Mavis said wasn't there last time she came. In a niche in the wall on one side of the steps sat a most peculiar piece of stone. It looked almost like a primitive Buddha, with arms, legs tucked under, and a quiff of hair! Jamie saw a mouth and a tummy button!

A chap came out of the back door and I was surprised to recognise Henry's mate from the market. He told us that it was made by years of water rushing round it. It had come from an old ironstone quarry at Nassington and was anything up to 150 million years old. He said that there was a bridleway going from New Sulehay to Old Sulehay right through the quarry where you could still see all the different layers of strata.

Looking at the picture on the front of the booklet, there should have been some tall trees to the east of the stable block. I asked him what had happened to them. 'They got Dutch elm disease and had to be felled. Beautiful Jersey Elms, straight up, a bit like Lombardy poplars. They were the first to get the disease, some of them were 120 feet high. It was a real shame.'

He went back in and we decided that we'd about seen everything and went home.

We had a call from Terry in the evening to say that his man would be back in the morning and he'd call in sometime during the week with a bonus for me!

CHAPTER VIII

Tuesday morning we had a phone call from Jill. It would seem they were both down off their pedestals! And no secrets from now on! They hadn't got much sleep that night, and she could hardly walk!

I got to Peterborough at 9 o'clock to pick up the posters and admittance tickets then I went to the Peterborough evening paper to place an advert for our gig. That done, I put posters up at strategic places on the way home. After lunch I went round all the local villages and Oundle, putting up posters.

I made a note of where each one was so I could remember to take them down again afterwards. Nothing worse than posters being left up until they get tatty and blow away.

When Brynda and I arrived at the pub in the evening, Caroline had our uniforms all ready with 'Halston Swingers' in stitchwork on the breast pocket. 'You've lost that job, Brynda,' I said.

'Good! It's better than I'd have done it anyway!'.

Rose said we could use my old room to get changed in if we wanted to give them a trial run. The girls went first, then Tony and I. I was chuffed with the result, the legs had slight flares so as not to look like overalls, and the cuffs sported a bit of red braid to match the belts. Nice touch that. We went down together and caused quite a stir when we went into the lounge.

One thing that emerged during practice was that it was virtually impossible to learn everything off by heart in the time, so we decided to have music stands so that we could have the words in front of us. That was a load off our minds, and gave us quite a boost in confidence. Caroline said she knew someone who would copy our sheets for us. Very useful girl that, there wasn't much she couldn't get fixed.

I also thought we should have a second guitar so that when Tony and I were singing together, Caroline could take over the keyboard. Brynda asked if she could have a tambourine for some of the numbers, 'I don't want to be the only one not playing anything.'

'OK. I'll pop into the Stamford music shop tomorrow and see if they've got a decent guitar and a tambourine to hire.' I promised.

THE ARM OF COINCIDENCE

'Maybe they'll put a poster up for us?' from Caroline. I nodded.

'When do you think we can start a bit more intensive practice at your place, Caroline?' I asked.

'As soon as I get some extra music sheets photocopied. I'll probably get them done tomorrow, so unless you hear different, why don't you come round at eight-ish tomorrow night and we'll have a go. Malcolm is still away working, so we won't aggravate him.'

Having agreed on that, we stowed our stuff away and I arranged with Rose to pick it up next day and take it to Caroline's. It was getting late and I was looking forward to getting snuggled up with my wife.

In the morning my ever-practical lady suggested that a trip to the doctor's was due, to make certain that she was in fact pregnant, and that I should get myself on the surgery books, just in case. She phoned through as soon as the surgery opened and got us booked in for 10 o'clock. More than enough time to take Jamie to playgroup, then on to Kingscliffe to the surgery.

I looked out my papers to get the address of my doctor in Hertfordshire, so that they could send for my medical history. Looking at me now, no one would have any idea of the amount of time and effort it had taken to get me back together again!

Brynda got her sample in a clean sterilised bottle and off we went to Tansor with Jamie. Needless to say, we got to Kingscliffe early, so we had a walk round to kill time. The old part of the village was almost all stone and Collyweston roofing. The council houses were brick.

We went in to see the doctor together and were delighted to have the pregnancy confirmed. I got signed in at reception and we went home to pass on the news to Mavis. She seemed as pleased as us.

I went off to Barclays in Oundle to get my account transferred from the Hitchin branch. Brynda and I had decided to keep our own accounts for the moment, and the bank manager told me to remind her she needed to get her name changed on her account. When I reminded her, Brynda wrinkled her nose playfully. 'Loring's a much posher sounding name than Evans! I don't know whether I'll bother.'

Aunt Mavis snorted, 'I'll have you know that my mother's maiden name was Evans, and, as young Wellington says in the cartoon, I won't have you casting Nasturtiums.'

'Was it really? That's another coincidence to chalk up.' I remarked.

Brynda made us a coffee and, as there was another hour before lunch, I went off to find Tony to see what could be done to get ready for our gig. No use leaving everything to the last. I followed my ears and found him using a huge industrial vacuum cleaner in the grain store. 'You can take over from me, if you like, and I'll go and knock up some steps to get onto our stage trailer.'

I took the pipe from him and carried on. It was easy enough to see where he'd been. After about 15 minutes it didn't seem to be going so well, so I guessed it needed emptying. I guessed wrong; the filter was blocked solid with fine dust. I had to take it outside and stand upwind while I knocked the dust out. The transformation was unbelievable, but in less than 20 minutes it needed doing again. Still over three quarters of the shed was done by lunch time and I had had to empty it once. Tony had nearly finished the steps. He'd cut up a couple of scaffold planks for the job. 'Plenty more where they came from,' he grinned. 'Doubt if the old man knows how many there are!'

We finished the job after lunch and put a four wheel trailer in place at the end of the shed, facing the doors. We had to have a shunt by hand to get it as tight to the wall as possible. We put the handbrake on and removed the drawbar. It was only on with a long bar and pin. That went under the trailer, out of the way. The steps would need to be fixed to the trailer half way along the side. I left him to it and nipped off to Peterborough on another Donna mission. This time I headed for Westwood, but once more drew a blank. I went back the way I'd come: A47 to Wansford. When I got to Yarwell I decided to have a look at the Quarry where the 'Buddha' had come from. I went up a narrow road towards Old Sulehay and parked on the corner where the bridleway went off to New Sulehay. I found the quarry easily enough, but quickly realised that I'd need to get permission from whoever owned the area before going into the quarry itself.

There was a strong smell of garlic in the air from large patches of Ransoms (wild garlic). When I got home, Brynda had already started to prepare the evening meal and I was set on to peel the spuds.

Mavis had bought a new colour television and Jamie was watching a children's programme, so engrossed he didn't even notice me go into the room.

We still hadn't heard anything from Caroline by the time we'd got Jamie to bed. I'd completely forgotten about going to Stamford. I'd have to go tomorrow. I wasn't too popular when we got to Caroline's. 'Well, neither of you reminded me,' I pointed out to Brynda and Tony.

THE ARM OF COINCIDENCE

Nevertheless, we had a good session until Fiona woke up demanding attention and we called it a night.

When we got home it was to find that Terry had called and left me £50, which was a nice bonus. Mavis was curled up comfortably in front of her new toy, watching something vicious, so Brynda and I slipped off to the comfort of bed.

As soon as we'd had breakfast the next morning, I shot off to Stamford. I managed to park in a side road leading down to the Cattle Market. Someone directed me to the music shop and I thought my luck was in. They'd got a very good hand-built guitar, but wanted £200 deposit before they'd let me take it away. Can't say I blamed them. I had to go round to the bank and withdraw £150 to go with the £50 Terry had given me. I found a really nice tambourine for Brynda. They agreed to exhibit one of our posters and suggested that I took one to the Information Centre and one to the Museum. They also wanted a reference, so I suggested they ring the Walnut Tree. As luck would have it, they had been several times for meals and knew Jeff and Rose, so they didn't bother. I came away with my finds and headed for home.

The evening practice took on a whole different aspect. We started to get really with it and were well pleased with our efforts by the time it was bedtime, Fiona once again bringing us back to reality.

When we got home, Mavis said there was a message. Could I ring a Tony Bowley at Barrowden, no matter how late we were. She had written the number down. I looked at my watch: 9.45. I dialled the number. He answered straight away. Apparently one of his men had phoned in sick and could I do a load into Kettering Market in the morning? If I could be at his yard at six o'clock, he'd give me all the details. 'How did you know about me?' I asked him. 'Oh, I rang Terry to see if he could do the run for me, but he was already booked. He told me.'

'OK, fair enough, give me directions of where you are and I'll be there.' Once I had written down his directions I followed Brynda to bed.

I found myself with a six wheeler in the morning, double drive, with differential lock on both axles. When I got to the farm, the animals were still in the field and the farmer had only just got up. Good thing I'd only got his to take in, otherwise the next client wouldn't have been amused. It took us half an hour to get loaded. In the Market I found myself alongside Henry again, and after we'd washed out we went for a cuppa together. I finished up with a load for West Ham. This lorry had a sheep deck on the roof. You only noticed it when the sides were up. They sloped inwards so that the animals couldn't jump over. So I had sheep on the roof and cattle inside. As luck would have it, Tony's firm, which was called Garretts, had another lorry going to the same place. The driver promised not to lose me! I phoned Brynda to say I'd be late back so wouldn't be able to practise. Couldn't have the lady of my life wondering where I was.

'We'll have to turn up the Harborough Road then cut back to Northampton Road down Gypsy Lane,' I was told, 'otherwise there'll be a heap of sheep in the road by the railway bridge!'

We went through Northampton to the M1, checked the animals before we went onto the motorway, then away. It was quite a trip and getting on for ten o'clock by the time I got home.

My car was due for a service so I rang Oundle Motors and got it booked in for Monday morning. Brynda would pick me up after taking Jamie to playschool. Apart from the essential jobs like watering, we didn't do anything in the nursery over the weekend. Fortunately Mavis had only ever supplied the wholesale market so we didn't get inundated with the general public. We all went to Stamford shopping on Saturday and Bunion went with Brynda, Jamie and myself to Barnack Hills and Holes on Sunday afternoon with a picnic. The Hills and Holes were also a designated SSSI and Bunion told us how much it had improved since they'd started sheep grazing after all the flowers were over in the autumn. Jamie was in seventh heaven, tearing up and down the tracks. Bunion and I were more interested in the wild flowers, which included Pasque flowers, Man orchids and Bee orchids. Brynda was kept busy with Jamie. We found a nice spot for our picnic where we wouldn't be flattening any rare plants. I had to take a few photos and thought I might have a good shot of Bunion with his favourite appendage well alight! The stone that had been quarried here was known as Barnack Rag and the magnificent Peterborough Cathedral was built with it. The site had never been levelled and reclaimed. Bunion told us that the Soke of Peterborough, in which Barnack was a village, had been for years considered as part of Northamptonshire and the Northants Trust had taken over the site at some stage before the Soke had been moved to Huntingdonshire. It was obviously a favourite place for dog walking and Jamie fell in love with a friendly mongrel collie and decided that he would like a dog. We said we'd think about it! Keeping a dog was a big undertaking. It would need feeding, bathing, and lots of exercise.

We didn't go home until about 6 o'clock, by which time Jamie had run himself into the ground.

I took my car in for its service at nine o'clock next morning and Brynda picked me up in the 'Yellow Peril'. I had to be careful not to call it that when she might hear. I expect it was as safe as any other car, just a bit unconventional.

We spent the morning preparing plants for sale, then Brynda took me to pick my car up, then onto Tansor for Jamie. After lunch I had a couple of hours making signs to indicate where our car parking, etc, would be for Saturday. Then I took myself off to Peterborough, heading for Bretton this time. I struck gold, I saw Donna's mum collect two boys who would have been strawberry blondes if they had been girls. I left my car and trailed along behind. They didn't have far to go, and I kept my eye on the house they'd gone into until I could read the number. I went on past then came back down the other side. I took a note of the street and went back to my car. Pretty obviously Donna had got a job. I suppose she would have needed to. It wouldn't be any use going to the house until evening. I wanted to make sure that Donna would be home. I went home and told Brynda. 'Great, do you think it would be a good idea if I came with you? At least she knows me.' I thought for a moment. 'Yes, perhaps between us we can persuade her that Tony did try to find her, if she wants to know, that is.'

We went off as soon as we'd got Jamie settled, having decided not to tell anyone else in case we were on a wild goose chase. When we knocked on the door, it was Donna who answered. Her eyes popped when she saw Brynda. 'Surprise, surprise. We've found you. Can we come in? By the way, this is Jim, my brand spanking new husband.

I held out my hand. 'Pleased to meet you at last, I've been looking for you for some time.'

She held the door open. 'Has something happened to Tony?' she asked anxiously. 'No, no, nothing like that, except he's missing you and didn't know where you'd moved to.' We went into the sitting room where her mum sat knitting.

'Well he only had to ask the people who moved into our old house,' her mum said tartly.

'Oh, he did and they claimed they didn't have a forwarding address, all they knew was that you were still in Peterborough on a new estate.'

'You left the address, didn't you, Donna?'

'I thought you had,' Donna exclaimed. They looked at each other. 'Oh, dear, Brynda, looks as though we each thought the other had left the address.'

'Poor Tony, he's been going spare, hoping you'd come back, and Jim here has been waiting outside school after school, looking out for you.'

'The thing is, Donna,' I said, 'Tony would have liked to have had the time to search, but didn't dare leave the job for any length of time. He went to the council offices and they either couldn't or wouldn't tell him anything, so I offered to try. I figured that if you were still in Peterborough the children would be at one of the new schools and one of you would meet them out of school'

Donna nodded, 'Yes, I've got a job at Freeman's packing orders so Mum does the school. I'm so sorry, pride got in the way. I thought he didn't care. I'd only intended to shock him into demanding more money off his Dad. He's a miserable old skinflint. He pays Steve better than Tony!'

I looked at her thoughtfully, 'Look, I can't promise results, but Brynda, Mavis and I can go to work on the man when he gets back from Canada. I daresay that Caroline will join in, too. I'm afraid the money situation will remain the same until then, though.'

'Yes, I can see that, does Tony know you've found me?'

'No, I haven't said anything. I'd hate to have raised his hopes, only to find out that it was all over.'

'Well, it's not all over! But I expect I'll be expected to work out some notice or lose money.'

I grinned at her, 'I've got an idea. I don't expect you've heard that there's going to be a gig in the grain store at Halston on Saturday night?' She shook her head. 'Well, Tony, Caroline, Brynda and myself have been practising mostly 60s songs and we're trying to raise money to rebuild the millwheel. You could come to the dance and make quite an entrance!'

She shook her head. 'I haven't got the right sort of dress, and how would I get there? There's only one bus a day past the Halston turn.'

'No problem. Brynda and I will find you a dress and I'll get a taxi for you. It won't cost you a penny.'

'Would you really do that for me? What would you get out of it?'

Brynda smiled at her. 'We'd get the pleasure of seeing you and Tony together again, where you belong. When you get to know this wonderful man of mine, you'll find he just can't stop helping people!'

I knew my ears had gone pink. 'I only help people who are in need through no real fault of their own,' I laughed. Brynda gave me a hug. She smiled at Donna, 'He tells fibs as well when he needs to.'

'I didn't even know you were courting again. Where did you meet?'

'It's a long story, but he and my husband, Pete, were best mates. Jim only just survived the explosion that killed Pete and he was told he'd be a cripple for life. You've only got to look at him to see he had other ideas.'

'So, Donna,' I cut in, 'are you game? Size 14, green or blue velvet if we can find something?'

Donna giggled, 'You'll have to watch him, Brynda, looks like he's got an eye for figures! Yes, size 14. I could do with losing a bit, perhaps I shall when I have to start cooking myself again.'

I turned to Donna's mum. 'How's it going to affect you?'

'Oh, I'm not going to be devastated if that's what you mean. I've got a fella lined up to move in with me.'

'Mum! You never said a word! I didn't realise we were messing up your love life'.

'Get along with you. If you can't take in your own daughter, it's a poor tale.'

We exchanged telephone numbers and Brynda and I departed. 'Well, that was a good day's work,' remarked Brynda.

'Yes, well I was beginning to think I wouldn't find them. What a hoot, each thinking the other had left the address.' We were soon on the Soke Parkway and twenty minutes later we were home.

In the morning I suddenly remembered that I hadn't done anything about tables and chairs. I phoned around, but the sort of numbers we would want were all booked out. I went to find Tony.

'Well, there's only one thing for it,' he said. 'We shall have to put bales of straw all round the sides and put a complete ban on smoking. Anyone who wants to smoke will have to go outside.'

'What about tables?' I asked.

'Four bales, two and two, with scaffold planks on them. That should do, just to put their drinks on.'

'I suppose a few won't like the no smoking bit, and we shall have to have some fire extinguishers on hand in case someone gets stupid.'

'I think we've got four water extinguishers and one powder one. That should do. Anything else, boss?'

I grinned at him. 'No, I think you've got it covered. If there's a trailer handy, I could start sorting bales. I expect there'll be a few broken ones.'

'The old 135 and two wheeler are in the shed. Just chuck any broken ones out of the way. We can use them in the stockyard when the animals come in again for the winter.'

I set to work. I only took 40 at a time, no point in reaching up too high when it was only a couple of hundred yards from the Dutch barn to the grain store. I put them end to end from one end of our stage to the sliding doors, and then round the other side the same. Tony came to show me where the scaffold planks were kept. I had a rough count, at least 40. 'What on earth does your dad want all that lot for?'

He laughed. 'Got them cheap in a sale, can't resist a bargain. He said they'd come in one day. That day has come!'

I loaded them onto the trailer and drove into the shed. I started laying them out on the bales. The planks were all twelve feet long and five planks side by side covered the straw. Tony came in with some laths, saw, hammer and nails. 'I've been to Coles in Oundle. Reckon we need to make sure they can't separate, so I'll tack a piece along each end.'

By the time we'd finished the job looked half tidy. If we got the numbers we were hoping for, people would have to take turns for a sit. Always supposing they wanted to.

After lunch I popped into Oundle to the Oxfam shop, but they hadn't got anything suitable. Brynda had a lorry coming about four, so I went home and helped her load the trolleys up ready. We'd only just taken the last trolley round when the lorry arrived. Surprising how long it takes to transfer all the trays onto the lorry. By the time Brynda had got her receipt from the driver, it was nearly tea-time. Jamie had gone for a little walk with his gran. She could go quite a distance now as had been proved in Stamford the other day. Brynda started to prepare the evening meal. I got set on peeling spuds and cutting them into chips; reminded me of early army days with the chaps who got put on jankers. They were always looking for people to put on spud bashing as it was called.

After Jamie was settled down, off we went to Caroline's again. At the end of the session we had recorded eight numbers and played them

THE ARM OF COINCIDENCE

back. Considering the tape deck wasn't of a professional standard, we were well pleased with the result. We decided that we'd have a final rehearsal on Friday evening in the grain store when we'd have everything, hopefully, set up.

When we were walking back, Tony said, 'I don't suppose you've got any nearer to finding Donna and the kids, have you?'

'Not yet,' I lied 'but there are still several schools to try. I'll have another look tomorrow.' We parted from him at his cottage and went home.

Next morning I set off to Peterborough, after taking Jamie to playschool. At least it was market day and if it came to it I might find something there. I went straight to the Oxfam shop, but unfortunately they hadn't got anything I thought suitable. However, they did tell me that there was a Salvation Army shop in Broadway. All I had to do was to keep going straight on, past Cathedral Square, past the Library, and keep going till I found it. Only just into Broadway on the right. I couldn't believe my luck! Blue velvet, size 14, pointed gathered waist with a big bow on the back. It was so cheap I had to scrutinise it very carefully to convince myself that there was no damage on it. I paid for it, well pleased.

I noticed taxis coming and going near the market and asked one of the drivers if he could be booked for a trip out into the sticks on Saturday night. It was a bit expensive, but I couldn't be bothered to shop around. I gave him the address in Bretton and told him to be there at eight o'clock, and drew him a map of how to find Halston. When I'd done that, he grinned at me, 'I might manage half a pint in the Walnut Tree.' Some people are rotten! Anyway, I paid him up front and got a receipt off him.

I went back to the car and took the dress up to Bretton and handed it over to Donna's mum. She had a sniff and wrinkled her nose. 'I'll see if I can get it smelling a bit sweeter before she gets home. Amazing how nearly all Charity Shop clothes have the same smell.'

'Do you think she'll like it, and will it fit?' I asked.

'Oh, looking at it, I should think yes on both counts. I bet it cost someone a lot of money not so long ago.'

I'd done all I could. Now it was up to Donna. I headed out of the north end of Bretton, past the crematorium to Marholm, turned left and headed for Castor. This lane took me past Milton Park to the A47 at the bottom of Castor Hill. I was following a lorry out of Ailsworth, approaching a fairly sharp right hand bend when a small lorry coming the other way went out of control on the bend. His back end came round, forcing the other lorry off the road. He went into the field on his own side down a bank and the lorry toppled over onto the driver's side. I stopped and got out. I was about to go into the field when the driver climbed out of the passenger door unhurt. He exchanged particulars with the other driver, who had some damage from the hedge, and gave my name and address as a witness. The crashed lorry driver didn't even seem to know what had gone wrong. Someone coming the other way in another lorry said he'd give him a lift into Ailsworth to the phone box. I was quite pleased that I hadn't been on the bend when he came round.

Looking at the map, the short piece of road between this bend and a left-hander was part of Ermine Street, the old Roman road from London to Lincoln. Perhaps he was trying to avoid a platoon of Roman soldiers! When I got to Nassington, damned if there wasn't a lorry load of last year's straw jammed under the railway bridge! The driver reckoned he'd have to let his tyres down to get out. I wished him good luck and left him to it. Highest load of straw I'd ever seen! Quite an eventful morning one way and another.

Bunion was busy in his garden as I drove past. Brynda had a saucepan of home-made soup on the Aga hob when I went in. I looked round the kitchen, suddenly struck by the thought that if we had to move on at some time, Brynda would no doubt want something like this. Aunt Mavis came in from the sitting room with an old shoebox full of photographs, which she said she was sorting. She was going to throw out the ones of people she couldn't put a name to. Some of the photos were really old, and I persuaded her not to throw any away. Most of them were in good condition and were a record of the way people dressed years ago. Some of them I reckoned dated back into the nineteenth century. There were even some of the old Hall in its heyday, and some with the Poles, who had been billeted there. Most of the photographs had been in the house when her husband and Dan had bought the village and land, just after the war. There was a photo of Mrs Ainsley-Barden, the last member of the aristocratic family who had been here for three hundred years. Both of her sons had been killed in the war, and her husband had been thrown off his horse and killed in 1938. She had moved over to the farmhouse when the Hall had been requisitioned for the Poles. The farm manager hadn't been very efficient and, at the end of the war, the old lady, instead of doing nicely, was practically bankrupt. Maybe he had been efficient on his own behalf! Bunion had worked on the estate, but wasn't in a position to do anything other than what he was told! The whole shebang had been put up for auction and perhaps the state of the Hall had put buyers off, coupled with the fact that now the war was over most people thought that farming would be allowed to slide in the same way it had after the First World War. There had been a big depression and lots of farmers had gone bankrupt. The net result was that Jack Spenser and Dan Woodward had got the whole lot for £16 per acre with nothing extra to pay for the village.

Mavis hadn't a clue where they'd got their money from, according to my calculations about ten thousand, four hundred pounds. Farm wages then would have been about five pounds a week, 2080 weeks wages, multiply that by 80, which are farm wages now, that's one hundred and sixty-five thousand four hundred. Land is currently worth about £3,000 per acre, 650 acres would therefore be worth one million, nine hundred and fifty thousand pounds, some profit!

It had been cheap, even then.

Mavis knew that Jack and Dan had met whilst they were POWs in Germany. They had escaped a few months before the end of the war and managed to get some booty back to England after the war. She had never known what it was.

Mavis and her sister Anne were both in the Land Army, based at Southwick, and had been working some of the time at Halston, which is how they had met Jack and Dan. Apparently, Mrs Ainsley-Barden had died intestate soon after the sale, all her assets claimed by the Crown, as there were no traceable relatives. Amazing how a family could actually dwindle to nothing. After all, in theory at least, 500 years ago, we all had a million ancestors! Work it out. About four generations per century, five hundred years, twenty generations, 2 parents, 4 grandparents, 8 great-grandparents, 16 great-great-grandparents. 20 generations on the binary system is over a million!

Enough of this nonsense, all that remained of the Ainsley-Bardens were a few tombs in the church and churchyard, and their coats of arms in the stone gateposts.

After we'd had our soup, Brynda said that she had a few jobs to attend to where I would only distract her, can't think why! So I took myself off to find Bunion. He'd got a metal detector, looking for a

THE ARM OF COINCIDENCE

lost penknife. He found it amongst the potato leaves. He said it only detected coins down to an inch or so, but larger pieces six inches or more. He was going to have a scan over the sugar beet field where he'd found a few Roman bits and pieces in the past. 'You can sweep over about 6 rows at a time without losing your mark.' He grinned, 'and if it bleeps between the rows, I'm allowed to have a scratch. When I get fed up I put a stone on top of another so I know where I've got to. Tell you what, I'll get me trowel and we can go and have a go, if you like?'

'Why not, I've never been metal detecting for fun before, and who knows, I might bring you luck. My nickname wasn't Lucky for nothing.'

'If we find anything valuable, really valuable that is, and it's declared Treasure Trove, I have to share it with Dan. We've got a written agreement. Who knows, a guy found what's known as the Water Newton Silver over on the Roman township of Durobrivae. Mind, he reckoned at the time that he'd found it without a detector. Still, there's plenty of broken pottery of the type they distributed from there and tons of slag from the smelting, all in small fragments.'

It didn't take us long to get to the beet field and it took us all afternoon to find 20 cartridge cases; two old Victorian pennies; and a round disc about ¼" thick with two spikes and what appeared to have been sprung leaves on them. Would have pushed into something and stayed there. We had no idea what it was, but I said I'd take it to an archaeologist to see if I could find out. Bunion said that there was an archaeologist at Prince William School. I put it in my pocket and we went home.

CHAPTER IX

I had a phone call from Brian over at Kettering, asking if I could fetch the amplifier gear today rather than tomorrow as previously arranged. It suited us better as well, gave us more time to get ourselves sorted properly. I found Tony after breakfast and swapped vehicles with him. He wasn't expecting to need it, but I gave him the keys just in case. It took about three-quarters of an hour to get to Pytchley Road. Brian explained how it all linked up. Fortunately, all the connections were numbered and there was no danger of making wrong connections. There were two big speakers. He sent six vocal microphones in case any went wrong; microphone stands; microphones for the guitars; and, most importantly, the mixer/amplifier. When I got back to Halston I took the gear straight into the grain store and started setting it up. We had a multi-socket extension cable to power the gear, my keyboard, and any extra lighting we would need. We wouldn't know exactly how it would sound on the night, because there's a considerable difference between an empty building and one heaving with bodies!

I spent the rest of the morning getting it all set up and making sure everything worked. I fetched my keyboard from Caroline's. She reminded me to take the music stands: be a bit tricky playing a guitar and holding the music. We needed the sheets to give us confidence with the words. Some songs were more difficult to remember than others, and we had been trying to learn so many in a short space of time.

Lighting for the building itself was very good. There were six tube lights in the roof and a floodlight above the doors on the outside.

After lunch I worked out a parking strategy for the paddock opposite and put up a notice indicating that motorcycles could be parked on the concrete apron in front of the shed. The rest of the directional signs could wait until Saturday morning in case some joker removed them.

In the evening we met up and had a long session, going through all our numbers. We decided that we would leave it at that and not have a practice on Friday night, otherwise we'd be heartily sick of the whole thing by Saturday night. If we made mistakes, we'd have to cover them as best we could.

Friday we had a busy day in the nursery, the last of the bedding plants were going, and a large consignment of perennials for the Saturday markets. I went round to the pub in the evening to check that people who had promised to help were still available. Jeff and Rose said the bar would be all under control. Robert asked whether we had taken into consideration the possibility of a power cut. Of course we hadn't.

'You've always got to remember Murphy's Law,' said Robert. 'If anything can go wrong, it will. I'll bring my generator up when I've finished milking. Essential equipment when you've got milkers or automatic feeders.'

I nodded, 'Thanks very much, it's amazing how many things there are to think about when you're entertaining Joe Public.'

Saturday morning the toilets arrived and we build a 'Gents' out of bales and an eight-inch piece of gutter. It wouldn't get dark outside until late and we reckoned there would be enough light from the floodlight when it did get dark. The ladies loos all had individual lights to connect to the mains. I went and put all the directional signs out, then we were as ready as we were ever going to be.

The cadets arrived at half past seven and had only just got themselves organised when the first cars started to arrive. Malcolm was kept busy on the door. The admission tickets were on a roll so that he could easily keep tabs on the number. If we got up to four hundred, which we knew we could hold, then he'd have to play it, not by ear, but by sight as to whether it was crowded or not. We had a really big notice at the entrance: 'Strictly No Smoking in the building'. I put an instrumental tape in the machine to keep people happy until we started at eight o'clock.

Just before we were due to start, Malcolm had already admitted over 350, and Jeff's friends were doing brisk business with the bar. They had a barrel of Adnams set up as well as crates and crates of bottles.

I had been elected, i.e. press-ganged, into being compère for the evening, and at eight o'clock I switched off the tape and we all took our places. I switched on the mike and introduced the girls, Tony and myself.

'I hope you like our style of playing and singing. We make no apology for not sounding the same as the original artists. We'll start with Abba's

THE ARM OF COINCIDENCE

Money, Money, Money and you're welcome to dance or sit as you wish.'

I played the intro and off we went. After the first number we got a good reception, which gave us extra confidence. The building was really filling up now and Donna made her entrance at about half past eight when the girls were giving their version of Memory from the new show 'Cats', which Brynda and I had been to see. She was halfway to the stage before Tony saw her, then he put down his guitar and leapt off the stage to meet her. He swung her round and round, crying and laughing at the same time. People who knew them and the situation started to cheer and pretty quickly others joined in, even if they were complete strangers.

As the girls came to the end of their almost drowned out song, Tony seated Donna on the edge of the stage. She looked absolutely smashing and I asked the audience for a show of hands as to whether they'd like an uninterrupted repeat of 'Memory'. Almost a unanimous 'yes' vote, so they did it again.

Only about 15 minutes later a group of motorcyclists pushed Malcolm to one side and trooped in. I counted a dozen and jumped down from the stage and met the leader in the middle of the floor. He stopped and removed his helmet. He was a big man. I looked him straight in the eye. 'You can do one of two things,' I said quietly, 'you can either pay, stay and behave yourselves; or go quietly now.' He gave a great guffaw and turned to his mates grinning. 'Did you hear that?' Then he spun round and took a swing at me, the oldest trick in the book. Before he knew it, he was on his back on the floor and I had my foot on his throat. I felt a slight movement and increased pressure.

'Don't even think about it!' I warned him, 'or you'll be very seriously hurt or even dead'. He lay still and I eased off the pressure slightly. I looked at the others, 'Don't think about a rescue unless you want him hurt! Now, I repeat, you pay, stay and behave; or you leave quietly in one piece; or we put you out. Now what's it to be?'

The next in line slowly removed the helmet to reveal a girl. She turned to the others. 'I vote for the first option'. Helmets were removed to reveal five more chaps and five more girls. They agreed, so I removed my foot and allowed the big fellow to scramble to his feet. He rubbed his neck ruefully. 'How the hell did you do that?'

'Now, you don't really expect me to tell you that, do you?' I grinned at him. I turned to the others. 'Right, I want all your helmets under the stage, then you can go and pay.' They trooped up and did as I'd asked. I got back onto the stage. We restarted the number and carried on as if nothing had happened.

When we got to the interval, I was about to put our tape on when Tony indicated that he wanted to say something. 'Ladies and gentlemen, there's a bit of entertainment that the rest of the gang here know nothing about! Before we put our tape on and take our break, I'd like a very warm welcome to our own resident Country Yokel, Cyril Williams, better known as Bunion!' People started to clap as Bunion stepped into the store and made his way to the stage. He had on an old pair of boots, coarse material trousers tied below the knee with genuine old binder twine, a collarless striped shirt with bandanna tied at the neck, and an old trilby hat with the crown knocked out, 'Diddyman' style, the inevitable pipe between his teeth. He climbed up the steps and took the mike from Tony, making a great performance of putting his pipe into his shirt top pocket.

'If I catches fire, perhaps someone will put me out! Now I'm going to do a few little ditties I got from an old domino partner who unfortunately died last year. I'll try to do him justice. The first one goes something like this.' He started to sing: 'Mary Ann is after me, full of love she seems to be. My mother says if that be so, she wants you for her young man. But Father says be thankful do, there's one bigger fool in the world than you, and that's Mary Ann.' The way he performed it had everyone in stitches. When it had quietened down he started again. 'Mary Ellen at the church turned up, her ma turned up, and her pa turned up, her rich uncle Bert and her fat sister Gert, and the Parson with his long white shirt turned up. But no Bridegroom with a ring turned up, but a telegram boy with his nose turned up, with a telegram that read, that he didn't want to wed, and they'd find him in the river with his toes turned up.' When it quietened again, 'Now ladies, gentlemen and others, the next, and you'll be pleased to know the last, is a bit tricky and I may not have the wind for it, but here goes.'

I can't write it down properly and I most certainly can't perform it myself, I'll just try and give the gist of how it went. There was an old man and he had an old sow (followed by a couple of raspberry type sounds) idel-de-dow, Suzannah's a funniful man. Sing lastical rings to relie. Suzannah's a funniful man (more raspberries, whistles and snorts) idel-de-die. Suzannah's a funniful man.

THE ARM OF COINCIDENCE

'Now this old sow she had little pigs, igs, digs, idel-de-digs (and so on through all the Suzanna's and raspberries, etc).

'Now these little pigs, they had curly tails, ails, tails, idel-de-ails. Suzannah, etc.'

He managed six verses before he ran out of puff. I think it was the most difficult thing to perform I'd ever heard and he deservedly got a standing ovation as he stepped down from the stage. I put the tape on and we all went for a drink.

The big motorbike chap came up, 'Don't suppose you do Rock Around the Clock, do you?' I shook my head, but Caroline thought we had a copy in the file, which Tony and I could share.

'But we haven't even tried it,' I protested.

The biker grinned. 'We don't mind a few mistakes, we can improvise, you know.'

When the tape ran out, we got back on stage and I announced that by special request we were going to try Rock Around the Clock. The twelve bikers took to the floor in their pairs and stood expectantly waiting. It was like going back to the late fifties, they were really with it, swinging their partners between their legs up and over, you name it, they did it! They, too, got a big ovation from the rest of the crowd. We then carried on with our prepared programme.

Steve came over to see if Donna wanted to dance and she looked at Tony for guidance. He nodded, I was pleased to see, not dog in the manger. After that, she had several partners and Tony even got to dance with her himself while the girls were performing Dolly Parton's 'Jolene'.

The evening went better than expected and we had to do some repeats as people showed no signs of wanting to go home. We played Auld Lang Syne at 5 to midnight and slid open the big doors. I didn't see anyone obviously the worse for drink and, apart from that little hiccup with the bikers, we'd had a marvellous evening. Malcolm had sold four hundred and forty-six tickets, which was only just short of nine hundred quid.

The big biker came over and shook hands, apologising for the way they had come intending to make a nuisance of themselves. Everyone left with the minimum of fuss and it was all quiet by half twelve. We locked everything in the big shed for the night, but Robert took his generator home 'Justin Case'. (He was the bloke who wrote the book 'Why men have tits'!).

Donna was staying the rest of the weekend till Sunday night, what a surprise! Malcolm and Caroline took Fiona home from Aunt Mavis's care. Apparently she was now well used to the bottle and Caroline was gradually weaning her and gradually not making so much milk herself.

Sunday morning I took all the Kettering stuff back and recovered my extra security deposit as nothing was damaged or missing. Then I went round and took down all the signs and posters. The afternoon I spent in lazy contentment with Brynda, amusing our son.

Tony came round just after tea with Donna and their two boys. She had been allowed to finish work at the end of the week without loss of earnings. She wanted to know if I wanted the dress back! No way!

On Monday I dismantled the tables and put the scaffold planks back where they'd come from, reloaded the straw and restacked it in the Dutch barn. It's amazing how it always seems to take longer to put things back where they came from! I popped over to Stamford with the guitar and tambourine and got most of my £200 back.

After lunch I swept up all the loose straw and put it in the cattle yard. They came and collected the portable toilets and I dismantled the gents. The four wheel trailer could stay until it was needed for hay bales, but all the grain tunnels and partitions had to be put back into the store. Steve and Tony helped with this. When harvesting started they would be put into position to separate the different commodities and so that air could be blown through to stop the grain from going mouldy or heating. The drier the grain was harvested, the easier it would be to keep it in good condition.

The only thing to show for our gig now were the car tyre marks in the paddock and it wouldn't be long before they grew out.

So far, Brynda had had an ideal pregnancy, no morning sickness. She didn't have any with Jamie either, a fact that Caroline and Jill were quite envious of! Robert was going in shortly for a vasectomy as they had decided that the two boys were enough and Jill had been on the pill long enough. Caroline, on the other hand, was hoping to get pregnant again ASAP so that she and Malcolm wouldn't be too old and there would not be too big an age gap between children.

Towards the end of the week, both Tony and Robert started silage making. Tony, of course, had Steve, so I gave Jill a break from trailer duty whenever Brynda wanted me out of the way. Trouble being that we still couldn't keep our hands off each other! The different ways we found of making love were nobody's business. When the first grass was

THE ARM OF COINCIDENCE

cut for hay it rained. 'Seed time and harvest never fail,' intoned Bunion, 'but hay time you'd better look out!'

Saturday 13th June was a fine day, so we decided to go to the medieval fair at Ashton. We managed to squeeze Donna and the boys in with Mavis and Jamie. Just as well we weren't noticed by those people the Irish call the 'Polis'. Donna had the blue dress on and Brynda wore the red, not exactly authentic, but they looked more the part than the rest of us.

It was surprising how many people were dressed quite authentically. We got there at half past eleven, in time for the opening parade and ceremony. There were loads of stalls with people dressed up, selling their craftwares. There were entertainments taking place throughout the day at six different venues.

In the big field was a marquee, a green, a square and a stage. Some events were being staged in the village chapel and some on the village green in front of the Chequered Skipper, the village pub, named after a rare butterfly.

Spoilt for choice! At various locations we managed to watch the Northampton Morris Men, the Southwick Handbell Ringers, they had two bells in each hand – no mean feat. We saw the Stamford Puppets, a Punch and Judy show; the Capriole Mediaeval Dance Theatre; Glapthorne Dancing School, and the Kings Cliffe Dancers. You'd have needed to go both days to see and hear everything on offer. So far as I was concerned, the icing on the cake was a nuthatch's nest in the hole of a tree, right in the middle of all the activity. Aunt Mavis enjoyed herself, meeting old friends she had not seen since her stroke. It was good to see that she was still improving. The children enjoyed themselves with Jamie trying to keep pace with Donna's two. From eight until midnight was to be a dance led by the Eleanor's Cross Country Dance Group. Mavis offered to sit if Brynda and I wanted to go back for it, but we didn't take her up, we were nearly as tired as the children!

Both farms operated what was called the 'flat eight system' for collecting hay or straw bales. A cleverly designed 'sledge' with two wheels was towed behind the baler which filled up four compartments of two bales in balanced order so that the last bale of eight operated a trip and all eight bales were released at once. When they were carted off, Tony used the Sanderson and Robert the old Super Major, both fitted with a custom built grab. You swept the bales sideways and forwards to compact them and curved tines were thrust into each bale hydraulically. You could then lift them up and deposit them onto trailers. The big four wheel trailers could hold about 200 bales between the raves.

Robert made more silage than hay and Tony made the same about of each. Because Robert concentrated on dairy, he didn't have any arable except for a few mangolds and some sweetcorn for extra silage.

Robert had an uncomfortable few days after his operation, walking about as if he'd had an accident in his trousers, but he didn't take any time off, except for the actual day, when I stepped into the breach once more.

Jill said she wouldn't mind a good seeing to before she came off the pill! I laughed, 'You'll have to get permission off Brynda first.'

'Well I might just ask her,' Jill threw back as she took another trailer-load of bales back to the farm. That night Brynda and I were cuddled up in bed when she murmured, 'I had an unusual request from Jill just after tea.'

'What!' I sat up and switched on the bedside lamp. She had a smug expression on her face, 'I was wondering how much I should charge for letting you out to stud!'

'You're joking, aren't you?' I asked uncertainly.

'Not entirely. I must be odd, because it really turns me on, thinking about you giving her a really good shafting. There's only one condition. If you want to take her up, I get to watch without her knowing.'

'What on earth have you told her?' I demanded.

'Oh, only that it's up to you. I won't be throwing a tantrum.'

'So long as you can have a go with Robert while you're safe, eh?'

'Not at all. I don't fancy him. I wouldn't say no to Tony, though, but I doubt if Donna would rate me making a pass at him.'

'I think you're right, didn't she look great at the dance, though, with her shoulder-length red hair and the blue velvet dress. I half expected Tony to sing 'Blue Velvet'.'

'So, you wouldn't turn her down, then?'

She snuggled up a bit closer and reached for JT again. 'It's nice to think naughty, isn't it?' she whispered.

'Umm, but I'm not sure that the reality would be a good idea. Hey, be careful what you're doing with that or you'll make a mess!' She pulled back the bedclothes and straddled my legs. 'That's just what I'm aiming to do.' I let her get on with it and when it finally let rip it

THE ARM OF COINCIDENCE

went everywhere, right up onto the pillow. She quickly straddled my face and I gave her the satisfaction she sought.

We slept late in the morning, to be woken by an impatient Jamie who'd dressed himself ready for playgroup.

Brynda needed a hand for an hour or so after I'd taken Jamie to Tansor, she returned to last night's discussion. 'Down on the married quarters it all happened. Some marriages broke up, and some got better.' There was a serious glint in her eye when she said, 'If we keep our feet on the ground and don't mess up anyone else's life, I think it would work for us!' I churned it over for a few minutes.

'How about you and Pete?' I wanted to know.

'Well, you know Pete was a good-looking guy, it was inevitable that he'd get it thrown at him in the pubs from time to time. I don't think he ever took anyone up, but I wouldn't have minded.'

'You are one incredibly sexy unusual female, Brynda Evans! I can tell you that both of us had offers, but we didn't for the simple reason that we may have got more than we bargained for! We had no wish to catch anything nasty or have to defend ourselves against other irate males. Look what happened when that lad reckoned I was making eyes at his girl!'

June was passing at a rate of knots and I hadn't given another thought to our sexy conversation. On Monday 22nd, which was a lovely day, I'd been turning hay for Robert to bale. He'd had just about finished the field when Jill came down with the two four wheel trailers behind the old Ford. How she'd hooked it all up herself, goodness knows. She released the trailers some distance apart then started loading bales with the loader. As I had finished rowing up for Robert, I got onto the trailer to arrange the bales so that we could get the maximum on. When Robert had finished baling for the day, we had loaded one trailer, so Robert took the baler back to the farm and brought the Land Rover down and the trailer back. He said he would start milking when he got back. I looked at my watch, almost half past three.

When we had finished the load, Jill rested the contraption on top of the load and I climbed on, expecting to be lifted down. Instead, she pulled the engine stop, turned off the key and climbed up the loader arm! Well, I suppose I knew what was coming before she'd even pulled the shirt over her head. She stripped right off and threw her clothes to form a 'bed', then she reached for the buckle of my belt. JT was fully to attention. Brynda wouldn't get to watch, that's for sure. She pulled me down onto the bed of clothes with her, lay on her back and invited me in. How could I resist? Afterwards I couldn't help but wonder how Robert would react. She pulled a piece of paper from her jeans pocket and handed it over. Written permission from Robert, so he had known what the minx had in mind. 'My turn to ride,' she murmured, and getting astride proceeded to do just that.

'What do you think was going through my mind?' she asked playfully.

'No idea,' I laughed.

'I was pretending that you were putting me up the stick!' That sobered me up a bit quick!

'It had better have been only pretending, otherwise we're in big trouble.'

She promised that it was so. 'I wouldn't do that to Robert after he's just had the op to avoid that very thing! Now I'm coming off the pill I shall have to behave myself anyway.'

We got dressed and got down, hitched the tractor back onto the trailer and went back to the farm. The first trailer was alongside the elevator, ready for unloading. Jill went and fetched some gloves and I started the Briggs and Stratton on the elevator. She soon climbed up the rave (harvest ladder) at the front of the trailer and started to unload. It was hard work for me on the stack because I had to carry every bale quite a distance before putting it in place. It was a bit like bricklaying! It had to be done so that it wouldn't fall down by crossing the bales across the joints. Jill had to fetch the boys from Woodnewton. They had an arrangement that if Jill wasn't at the school when they came out, they would go with friends and play with them until someone picked them up.

When they got back, Jill left them watching a video while we unloaded the other trailer. When Robert had finished milking, we took the trailers back to the field and loaded them again before we called it a day. There were only a couple more loads left in the field to be collected.

We were about to part company when Robert grinned and made an unmistakable gesture of putting his elbow in his groin and raising a clenched fist. When I got home I thought I'd better tell the boss straight away. She wanted to know every detail and had to have a demonstration in the Dutch barn on Tony's hay bales!

On Tuesday morning I popped down to Glebe Farm after breakfast and gave Robert a hand with the last bales from that field. No mention was made of the episode with Jill and I didn't see anything of her.

THE ARM OF COINCIDENCE

Robert was going to start mowing another ten acre field after lunch and I said I'd take over from him just before half-three. He was still using an old fashioned 'finger' mower on the 135. The blades needed sharpening quite regularly and if you hit a stone you'd have to rivet a new blade onto the knife. Robert had four knives so although I might have to change a knife I wouldn't need to do running repairs unless all four got damaged.

When I got home it was to find out that a huge Horse Chestnut tree had fallen down in the paddock where we'd parked the cars for the gig! Tony said it was the second time he'd known one to fall down for no apparent reason, on a perfectly still day; something to do with the sap rising and the tree not being able to cope with the weight of the foliage. Bunion and Steve could have the firewood but it would have to wait until there was time to cut it up. The main trunk depended upon whether any timber merchant wanted it.

I volunteered to cut it up if Brynda, myself and Mavis could have a share for the living room fire. Tony was a bit dubious about letting me use the chainsaw, said he'd feel responsible if I had an accident. I told him that I'd been trained in the army. The chainsaw was a Stihl, one of the best, and they had all of the safety gear. I agreed to use the trousers, but didn't want the helmet or earmuffs. I preferred to be aware of what was happening around me. I remember my Uncle saying he'd hurt himself more on the so-called 'safety frames' they insisted tractors had to have than he'd ever hurt himself before without them!

On Wednesday Bunion and I took the 135 and tipping trailer round to the field. I'd already sharpened the chain with the special file and guide provided and filled up with two-stroke petrol and chain oil. This oil was especially sticky so that it didn't fly off the chain straight away. I started by cutting off the boughs, which Bunion stacked for burning, then sawed off logs starting with the thin end of a branch, working my way back to the trunk. We had a log splitter to reduce the size of the big pieces before they were thrown into the trailer. We had a really big load by lunchtime which we took round to Steve's house.

It took us two days altogether to saw up all the branches and burn up the rubbish. We each had a big load of logs. Spencers of Brigstock said they would buy the trunk if we could deliver it. It wasn't worth them coming out for one tree. We took the back rave off one of the four wheel trailers and loaded it up with the Sanderson. I took it to Brigstock with the Ferguson 590 on Friday morning.

THE ARM OF COINCIDENCE

When I got back, Brynda told me that Caroline and Malcolm had a static caravan at Hunstanton and had had a cancellation for next week, could we go? Mavis could take care of the nursery as no big orders were in line.

So the following morning found us on the way to 'Sunny Hunny' soon after breakfast, an early breakfast at that. Jamie was very excited, he'd never been to the seaside before. Two hours later we had found the caravan; it was bigger than I'd expected and was connected to mains electricity, although the maximum you could use at a time was 15 amps, otherwise it knocked the trip out.

Jamie couldn't wait to get onto the sand, so we bought the mandatory bucket and spade, took a couple of deckchairs and got onto the beach. Someone was operating ex-wartime amphibious landing craft for sea trips. I reckoned on a trip on one of them before we went home.

Brynda and I were both strong swimmers, so it wasn't long before we had Jamie in the water giving him his first lessons. He was an amazingly quick learner and had grasped the rudiments before the day was out. He wasn't the slightest bit nervous. I suppose this was partly due to the fact that we were both very confident in the water.

In the morning we discovered that the couple in the next van were from near Oundle. They were younger than us, but their little boy was about the same age as Jamie. They played together on the beach, competing to see who could make the best sand castle, which meant that we didn't have to assist.

In the afternoon we all went out to sea on a 'Duck' (properly a DUKW, ex-wartime handling craft). Both boys thought it great fun. It wasn't until the next morning that I realised that I'd forgotten my camera. I couldn't believe it! I took a snap of Brynda and Jamie sitting on a rock with our new friends' Polaroid camera. It was a bit fuzzy. I didn't really understand what the attraction of the things were until our new friends pointed out that you didn't have to send your pictures away to be developed. As I developed and printed my own, that aspect hadn't occurred to me.

When the girls had taken the children to get ice cream he showed me some snaps of his wife with her friend, both of them proudly showing off their assets. He quickly put them back in his wallet as they came back carrying ices for us as well.

In the middle of the week our friends suggested a trip to the next village, Holme Next the Sea, because it had sand dunes and was more

THE ARM OF COINCIDENCE

private. Not so many people. It transpired that the girls wanted to do a bit of nude sunbathing and we chaps were expected to watch out for anyone coming near. Ralph winked at me and asked if I minded him using his Polaroid?

'I think you should ask Brynda rather than me. I wouldn't put money either way.' Seeing that both girls were completely naked and not fazed by both of us seeing them, it was no big surprise when Brynda agreed.

The week passed quickly and soon it was Friday, our last night. Brynda asked Ralph, Janice and Ricky in for a meal. Both boys were tired by seven o'clock so Brynda suggested putting them both to bed in our caravan. Brynda found a scrabble board in a cupboard full of games and jigsaws. We hadn't been playing many minutes when Janice suggested that we double up points for 'rude' words. I couldn't object without appearing a spoilsport.

As the evening wore on I began to suspect that the two women had something up their sleeves. When we packed up about 10 o'clock, Brynda asked if I'd mind if she went to the other van with Ralph and Janice stayed with me. And there was I thinking that it was mostly men who instigated these sort of goings on. In view of the episode with Jill, what could I do but agree? After all, Janice was easy on the eye, with or without clothes.

'What if the boys wake up and come out of their room?' I wanted to know.

'I doubt if they're old enough to take much notice,' Janice reasoned.

'Anyway,' added Brynda, 'They're both sound sleepers.'

Ralph just stood there grinning as Brynda took him by the arm and led him off. Janice made her way ahead of me to the bedroom and started to undress: first her tee-shirt, then her bra. That was when I first realised that her tits were larger in proportion to the rest of her. 'Come on, then,' she grinned, 'or do you need me to undress you?' I quickly slipped my things off and joined her on the bed. She proved to be a real sexual athlete. Fortunately she was on the pill and Brynda was safely pregnant. She and Brynda must have had everything worked out between them because when I awoke at about half-five next morning it was to find my wife with me and not Janice!

'You're a pair of minxes, very naughty girls,' I told her.

'I know, but it's nice to be naughty. Someone once said that stolen fruit tastes the best. This isn't better, it's just exciting. I was imagining you giving Janice the full treatment when I was doing it with Ralph.

Good job he didn't know. I think I could just manage a good shafting before the children wake up.'

Afterwards I did some serious thinking.

'Bryn, darling. I'm not so sure that this swapping is such a good idea.'

'Perhaps not,' she said thoughtfully, 'Do you realise there were two firsts in your sentence! First time you've shortened my name and first 'darling' I've had from you? Anyway, why isn't it such a good idea?'

'Well, for a start we've only just met Ralph and Janice. You've only got Janice's word that they aren't all that promiscuous. We could easily get more than we bargained for. That was the one thing they dined into you in the army. Another thing, sex, or as I prefer it, making love is something that needs a lot of understanding of your partner. I doubt whether many people can be instantly compatible with everyone they meet.'

'I guess not. Anyway Ralph didn't come up to your standard. He didn't bother to find out what I wanted. I suppose he assumed that as I had agreed to Janice's suggestion I must fancy him like mad. All right, I agree, been there, seen it, done it, and if you call me darling more often I'll put up with being called Bryn.'

The boys were stirring so it must be time to get up. Only half past six. Still, they hadn't stirred all night, which was a blessing. Another three and a half hours and we would have to be out. Still we could stay on the beach till late afternoon.

CHAPTER X

We had a big surprise at half past nine when Caroline and Malcolm arrived with Fiona. We had assumed that another 'letting' family would be coming. We no longer needed to rush and spent all day on the beach with them. Jamie was engrossed with Fiona, making her giggle and generally keeping her amused in a very gentle way. Ralph and Janice had left about 10 o'clock as they wanted to stop off in Kings Lynn on the way home. I was glad that they hadn't made any reference to last night's activities before they left.

I paid a visit to the Joke Shop and bought a couple of wigs, a red one and black one. I figured that if Brynda wanted to act a different personality, changing hair would be a good start.

We got home to Halston about teatime. Jamie had bought a tin of shortbread for his gran, and she made a great fuss of him. We had enjoyed the seaside, but it was good to be back. We had a walk round the village after tea so that, hopefully, Jamie would sleep when he got to bed. We met Bunion walking the old Rectory dog, which reminded him that he would like a dog.

After we'd got him reluctantly to bed, I broached the subject with Aunt Mavis. To my surprise she seemed almost as keen on the idea as Jamie, and suggested that we all went to Wood Green Animal Shelter near Royston in the morning.

We told Jamie after breakfast and there was no peace until we were on our way. We went to Kate's Cabin to get onto the A1, then A14 through Huntingdon from the top of Alconbury Hill to Heydon where the shelter was based, being about 5 or 6 miles east of Royston. We all fell in love with the same dog, a Border Collie cross who was so pleased to see us that we couldn't resist him. Only just a year old, the people who had him as a pup hadn't expected him to grow! We bought a large dog basket and supply of dog food, which I stowed in the boot. Our new friend, who answered to Sam, sat proudly on the back seat between Jamie and his gran.

I never knew a dog so anxious to please as Sam. He seemed to know what was required of him without fuss. It was obvious that boy and dog were going to be firm friends from day one. When it came time for Jamie to go to bed, boy and dog refused to be separated, so we had to put the basket, most reluctantly, into Jamie's bedroom. When we got up in the morning Jamie's room was empty. The basket had been lugged downstairs into the kitchen. Jamie sat at the kitchen table with his pad and crayons. Sam sat beside him watching proceedings.

'Sam was a very good boy,' Jamie announced. 'He woke me up and told me he needed to go outside.'

'How did he tell you?' Brynda asked.

'Oh, after he'd woken me up, he just went to the door and looked backwards and forwards from me to the door and put his paw on the door handle and opened the door. I let him out the back door and left it open a crack. When he came back in he shut the door. I had fetched his basket down but he wanted to watch what I was doing so I got him a chair.'

'How long ago was that?' I asked.

'Oh, well, not long. I've only done one drawing.'

Brynda looked at me and raised here eyebrows. 'Looks as though we've got ourselves the sharpest dog in the country. If he carries on like this, he'll soon be doing the cooking.'

'No he won't, dogs can't switch the cooker on,' said Jamie with the natural logic of small boys.

We were wondering what would happen when Jamie went to play-group. Sam solved that one by following me out of the house to the car, calmly getting in when I opened the door. I went down to Glebe Farm to see if they needed help. Their guard dog was in the yard. Sam got out with me and they stood eyeing each other up, then both tails wagged in unison and they had a good sniff round each other. When Jill came out with the boys, both dogs leapt into the back of the Land Rover as she drove off. Ten minutes later she was back with both dogs in the front with a seat belt round them. Robert said their dog went to take the boys to school every day.

As soon as Robert had had his breakfast he got the forage harvester out and I took the 135 and tipping trailer. Dogs in the trailer of course! As soon as we got started, the dogs began to look for rabbits in the grass. They chased several but didn't catch any. Rabbits are actually faster than hares over a short distance and, living underground, can usually reach safety very quickly. Hares can outrun most dogs except greyhounds and lurchers.

By the time my trailer with its extra high mesh sides was loaded, Jill was down with another one. She preferred to catch the chopped grass than to empty. I had to drive up one end of the clamp, spread the load as I tipped, and back down the other end. On the occasions when too much came out in one place, I had to level it with the old Super major and muck loader. By lunchtime we had done enough for the day and the clamp had to be compacted and allowed to heat up. Robert had a temperature gauge, which he inserted into the clamp to make sure it didn't overheat. Once it reached the required temperature more would be added until the clamp was complete, when it would be covered with black polythene and weighted down with old tyres from the tyre centre. Here endeth the first lesson on silage making!

Sam was back in the car, having appeared from nowhere as soon as I opened the door. He leapt across onto the passenger seat and pulled the seat belt clamp round in his mouth for me to fasten for him!

The pattern was set. Sam came with me whatever I was doing in the morning and stayed with Jamie the rest of the time.

After lunch, Jamie carried his football over to the paddock and he and Sam chased the ball round. Sam dribbled the ball with his nose. I daresay he could have hogged it all the time, but he let Jamie have a kick now and then. What a dog!

On Sunday we all went to Wicksteed Park and no one seemed surprised to see Sam scamper up the slide steps and slide down with Jamie. When the boy went on the swings the dog lay down, crossed his front legs, rested his jaw on his paws and watched. We bought a frisbee and Sam soon became very adept at catching it in the air and returning it to be thrown again. We'd taken a folding chair for Mavis and a picnic rug for ourselves. We spent the whole day in the free area. Not once did Jamie mention the train, perhaps he thought Sam wouldn't be allowed on.

Brynda was blooming, although obviously it would be some time before her pregnancy would show.

On Monday morning I went into Owen & Hartleys in Oundle and looked at what was available in video cameras and recorders. JVC had an outfit which had three components: a camera, a recorder and a tuner. The tuner stayed with the television and when the recorder was attached to it you could either record programmes off the television or play back other videotapes and anything you had filmed. You had to carry the recorder from your shoulder by a strap and the camera had a cable to connect with. Although quite heavy to carry, it wasn't as heavy as the previously available recorders, which you couldn't record off the television with either. It cost well over a thousand pounds, but I thought it would be worth it to have moving pictures of my new family as well as still photographs. Mr Hartley thought he could get one by the end of the week and would ring and ask me to call in for it. He had instructions not to tell anyone what I had to collect, should Brynda or Mavis answer the phone, as I wanted it to be a surprise.

When I got home, I went up to my dark room, a small box room with only a small window, which I'd blacked out. I got some super pictures of Jamie and Sam on the slides. We'd already got so that we couldn't imagine being without that dog. Good thing that with a bit of luck Jamie would be grown up before anything happened to him.

I spent most of the week learning in the nursery. Someone would have to take over when Brynda got advanced with her pregnancy and her tummy got in the way, to say nothing of the time after the baby was born. I decided that I would attend the antenatal clinics with her so that I knew what was happening. I bought a book on childbirth, JUST-IN-CASE! I needed to cover as many eventualities as possible, because I always felt that Murphy was never far away: Murphy's Law being roughly that if anything could possibly go wrong, it would.

I got my outfit on Friday, quite professional looking. I forced myself to read all the instructions before trying it out. There's another saying which goes: 'When all else fails, read the instructions'. I managed to film Brynda at work and Jamie and Sam playing football without them noticing.

I got the tuner connected to the TV and tuned a channel on the TV to the video channel. The aerial now went through the tuner before connecting with the TV. After our evening meal I got everyone seated in front of the TV and got everything switched on. It was worth the money just to see their faces when first Brynda, then Jamie and Sam, appeared on the screen. I reckon Sam recognised himself, as he took up his favourite position of jaw resting on crossed paws. Anyway, his tail thumped the carpet every time his nose got onto the ball. One thing that became obvious was that when panning round one needed to move slowly. Once or twice the subject whizzed across the screen at a rate of knots! One other thing that was surprising was the amount of birdsong recorded. Walking around you hardly notice it until some-

THE ARM OF COINCIDENCE

thing very loud or unusual chimes in. Sitting in front of the television, you're immediately aware of it.

Next morning, Saturday, Bunion came round to see if I could give him a hand to take the sheets off the steam ploughing engines. The boilers were to have their annual test at the end of the week and he wanted to check them over beforehand. Some care was needed to get the sheets off so that nothing got damaged. Apart from some dust they looked fine to my unpractised eyes. I gave him a hand to remove the ends of the boilers to reveal the tubes. 'Every time we put them away I treat them with Ensis fluid, gets between any water and the metal and stops them going rusty,' Bunion explained.

'What on earth is Ensis fluid? I've never heard of it.'

'Dunno, mate. Don't know how to spell it either! Dan bought about 20 gallons years ago to stop plough mouldboards from rusting. Anything else that needed protection come to that.' He winked at me. 'Any road, I nicked a can and hid it away for the engines. The rest has been used up years ago.' So far as I could see it had done a good job. 'They had their ten year pressure test last year, so I reckon they'll see me out. So long as I don't let the rust set in, that is.'

'So what's going to happen on the day, Bunion? Will people come just to see two steamers ploughing?'

'Maybe not many,' he said thoughtfully. 'But I reckon I know someone who'd bring his Shire horses and plough, and we could get the Allis out with a trailing plough, and the 1952 Fordson could have a hydraulic lift plough. Then people could see the way ploughing has developed over the years.' He grinned suddenly. 'And if Steve had the Cat with his six furrow reversible, we'd have the field ploughed completely in an afternoon!'

'You know, Bunion, that might just draw a decent crowd. Capture the curiosity of people and you're in business. When did you think of having it, was it the week before Peterborough Expo?'

'Yep, we aren't going this year, can't see the point if there's nowt for the engines to do.'

We spread the sheets back over the engines but didn't tie them down. Bunion showed me the plough, the mouldboards had been treated with his special fluid and no rust showed on them, even though it was outside, sheeted over of course. It was twice as long as modern reversible ploughs because instead of each set of furrows being on top of each other and revolving, this had two sets of six furrows facing each other.

THE ARM OF COINCIDENCE

It pivoted on a heavy duty axle in the middle and when one set of six was in the ground the other was up in the air. There were two seats and a steering wheel on each side so that the plough could be kept in the correct position as the cables towed it from one side of the field to the other. The distance between the engines was governed by either the width of the field or the length of the cable, whichever was the shortest.

The stuff that was actually packed into the vintage shed was something else. Apparently there was some method in all this vintage madness. An old trailing Claas combine which was power-driven from the tractor towing it could be used for harvesting thatching straw. It didn't break up the straw like modern machines, in fact the straw came out the back all the same way round. Dan's old Claas had a 'trusser' on the back, which tied the straw into bundles. Some threshing drums were used with a similar device when thatching straw was needed. The man feeding the drum had to put every sheaf into the beaters the same way round.

According to Bunion, Dan had been growing about 10 acres of longstraw wheat for several years. He didn't grow any more because there was always a danger it would go flat in rough weather and be spoilt.

When these combines first came out, someone had to ride on them, bagging up the corn. It was a dusty job, as bad as threshing, which was always a filthy job! Fortunately this one was a later model and had a tank like modern combines so the corn could be emptied straight into a trailer. The straw would be stacked in a bay in the Dutch barn and Thatcher John Underwood from Cotterstock fetched it as required. I was looking forward to seeing it in action.

When I got home Brynda asked if we could go to Wicksteed Park again in the morning and Mavis said that perhaps if she didn't go we could see if Donna and the boys would like to go with us. I went round to the cottage and Donna opened the door before I had a chance to knock. 'Tony's in the shed round the back,' she informed me before I had a chance to say anything. 'Tell him his lunch is ready, please.' So I went round to the shed to find him working on one of the boys' bicycles.

'Donna's given me destructions to tell you that lunch is ready.'

He grinned, 'Sure it's not constructions? I'd better come then.'

'You got a motorbike under that sheet, mate?' I asked him.

THE ARM OF COINCIDENCE

He grinned. '1955 Triumph Speed Twin, not allowed to ride it now. Petticoat government. I thought I'd told you I'd got a bike.'

'Don't remember. If you did I must have been thinking about something else.' I went into the cottage and issued the invitation.

'We haven't got anything spoiling,' said Tony slowly. 'If we take the Land Rover as well, Auntie can come too, anyway, and there'll be plenty of room for the woofing machine.' So that was quickly settled; we would leave about ten when we'd done the necessary jobs and Tony had checked round his cattle. 'Come round after lunch and have a look at the bike if you like,' Tony offered.

'Oh, thanks, I'd like to have a decko.'

I told Brynda that Tony had a Speed Twin in his shed and I was going to have a look after lunch. 'Will you buy it off him if he wants to sell?' she asked.

'Depends how much money needs to be spent on it and whether you'd mind me having a bike.'

'No, I don't mind. According to Pete you used to do stunts, but didn't take chances.'

'That's right, in the Signals White Helmets it's all about teamwork. Everyone's safety depends on everyone else getting the timing exactly right. The stunts aren't as dangerous as they look.'

Jamie wanted to have a look at the motorbike too, so we went round to Tony's and guess who came too? Sam, of course. When we pulled the sheets off I was surprised at how clean the bike was. It would most likely need new tyres, but then again maybe not. Tony had kept them pumped up and covered up, so the light hadn't perished them.

'It hasn't been started for about five years,' Tony told me. 'So I expect the petrol is well and truly stale. That's if it's got any left in it. Probably evaporated.'

I took the bull by the horns. I couldn't resist it. 'How much do you want for it, boyo?' I asked.

'Well, it was going OK when I put it away, so to you mate, seeing how well we get on and everything, how about a tenner?'

'Aw, come on. I know it's worth quite a bit. I'd feel guilty if that's all I gave you.'

'No need for that, I'll be chuffed to bits if it stays in Halston and I can see it being ridden. You have asked Brynda, haven't you?' This last somewhat anxiously. I could see that he really wanted me to have it,

THE ARM OF COINCIDENCE

so I assured him that it was OK with the boss, and gave him the ten quid there and then.

'Why don't we push it round to the workshop. You can check it all over in there. In fact, do what you like.'

I nodded. 'Actually it may sound a bit daft, but I'll take it all to pieces and check everything before I even try to start it.' We got it out of the shed and down the path to the road, sat Jamie in the saddle and pushed it round to the workshop. There were a couple of carpenter's stools in there, a bit like trestles, only not so high. We put an old door on top, then lifted the bike onto it. Quite heavy, it took all we'd got to get it up there, but it would be easier to work on.

'You may as well come back for the sheet to keep it covered. I shall have some extra space to move around in the shed, now'.

On Sunday morning we whipped round the jobs and set off with both vehicles about ten o'clock. We had Tony's youngest, Ben, with us. Sam was relegated to the back of the Land Rover with a mesh across the back to make sure he didn't fall out. He didn't seem to mind, particularly as he could see us following behind. It was a really nice day and the children had a marvellous time. The water chute was a favourite, and I got some good footage of the three boys and two mums getting somewhat damp! I think Sam thought we were all a bit crazy as he adopted his favourite pose.

When it came to train ride time, Sam took my seat and I took a video of them going round. Amazing how clear they were through the viewfinder, even on full telephoto, although it was a bit of a strain holding the camera steady. The only disadvantage I found was that with a black and white picture in the viewfinder it proved very hard to pick up things like butterflies, they seemed to merge with the surroundings.

We went back to the motors for lunch and spread blankets on the ground under the trees. While we were eating, a couple came on an old Matchless G9 500 twin, so I wandered over to have a look. It was immaculate and I asked the chap how he went on for spares. 'No problem mate, I get everything I need from Ernie Merryweather at Northants Classic Bikes in Irthlingborough. It's in Victoria Road, which runs more or less parallel to the High Street.' I thanked him for the info and congratulated him on the condition of his machine, then rejoined the family.

THE ARM OF COINCIDENCE

Tony grinned at me, 'Reckon you can get the old Speed Twin looking like that?'

'I don't know, but I'll have a damned good try. I'll give Northants Classic Bikes a ring in the morning to see if there's a workshop manual available.'

After lunch, Mavis opted to stay in the shade with a book and we decided to walk all the way round the lake. There was a boating lake where children could go in pedalos and, as we stood watching, debating whether Tony and Donna's boys were big enough to have a go, two boys started fighting in their boat. One boy fell out, hitting his head on the side of the boat as he went. Sam was in the water like a flash. The parents came running and couldn't believe their eyes as Sam got the boy by the collar and towed him to the bank. I dragged him out of the water and started pumping water out of his lungs. He came to, coughing and spluttering and within about fifteen minutes appeared not much the worse for his misadventure. The other boy had, in the meantime, taken the boat back and came running round. The parents were both in shock and I advised them all to go to the first aid centre and get the boy checked over. Our boys were making a great fuss of Sam, they were sure he was the cleverest dog ever. They also decided that they didn't want to go in the boat because, as yet, they couldn't swim properly.

'I can swim,' said Jamie proudly. 'I learnt at the seaside, but I can't swim as well as Sam.' It was further round the lake than one was aware of riding on the train, and I gave Jamie a shoulder ride for part of the way. Tony took over the camera and recorder and I showed him how to operate it, warning him not to pan round too fast.

When we got back to the main buildings, everyone, including Sam, had an ice cream. Sam had his in a saucer. The intrepid four then set off for the swings and slides with mums in pursuit. Tony and I went back to the cars to see if Mavis was OK. Fast asleep in the chair, so we went back to the others. I saw the chap whose boy Sam had pulled out of the lake hurrying towards us.

'I'm glad I've found you! We never thanked you for saving our Brian. We were just so shocked at the time.'

'Think nothing of it, mate. You've got our dog to thank really. While we stood gawping, he did the business, in the water like greased lightning! He was either well trained by his original owners or he has fantastic instinct.'

'Oh, we thought you'd trained him.'

'No, we've only had him five minutes as the saying goes. We found him at Wood Green Animal Shelter down near Royston. Reckon he's training us! If you fetch your boys over they'll find our lot on the swings and slides and they can thank him themselves. We're pretty sure he understands every word.'

He went off and it wasn't long before Jamie had got five mates to play with.

We decided to have tea at home and see what video we'd got, so we said our goodbyes, woke Mavis, got loaded up and went home. We all went to the farmhouse where Brynda and Donna made a pile of sandwiches and a large pot of tea. The video was mostly the antics of Sam and the children. Unfortunately I hadn't thought to use the camera when Sam went to the rescue. Too concerned about the boy's safety, I expect.

When Donna and Tony had managed to prise their two away from Sam and Jamie, it was Jamie's bedtime. Both he and Sam had a bath, the latter being a bit niffy from the lake water. Once they were both settled down, we rejoined Mavis in the front room and had a game of scrabble.

On Monday morning I took all the boys, well three and a dog, over to Irthlingborough. I'd decided not to bother to ring. I found it easily enough and was very impressed with the range of bikes for sale. Ernie was very helpful and found me a workshop manual for the Speed Twin. I also bought a new battery, set of points, and a gasket set.

When we got back, Jamie collected his football and all four of them went off to the paddock. Jamie might have been the youngest and smallest, but he could hold his own.

I went to the workshop and set to work on the bike. First I drained down the oil from engine and gearbox, then started to dismantle, being careful to put all the parts in order as I took them off! By lunchtime I was ready to take the engine out and by evening I had it stripped out. It still had original pistons, but looked as though it would benefit from new piston rings. I took the pistons and brake shoes over to Irthlingborough and bought new rings and replacement brake shoes on Tuesday morning.

By the end of the week I was ready to strike the bike up. Decarbonised, valves ground in, all new gaskets and new oil in the engine and gearbox.

THE ARM OF COINCIDENCE

The wheels were trued up by adjusting the spokes and the tyres had been checked for any signs of perishing.

I put some new petrol in the tank and she started like a dream. A little bit of fine tuning and we were ready for MOT on Saturday morning. Mr Bould at the Kingscliffe garage performed the MOT, which she passed with flying colours. All ready to get it insured and taxed from the 1st of August.

When I got back from Kingscliffe, Tony and Steve had got the big Claas combine out, ready to harvest the winter barley in the field nearest to the farm where it was proposed to do the ploughing demonstration. They were duly impressed with the way the bike was running and I was impressed with the sheer size of the combine and the air conditioned cab.

As soon as it was deemed dry enough they got started. I fetched Jamie to watch. The big machine fairly ate into the field. Steve operated it and Tony had the 590 and an eight-ton trailer for Steve to empty his tank into. A flashing orange light on top of the combine indicated to Tony when the combine was getting full. It was a twenty or so acre field, but at the rate they were going I guessed they'd have it finished by the end of the day.

On Sunday they were off to the next field. I did a bit of video for posterity, then Brynda, Jamie, Sam and I went for a walk into the forest. I managed to get some relatively close pictures of a herd of fallow deer until they got wind of us and took to their heels. There must have been about twenty of them crashing through the undergrowth.

On Monday morning Tony asked if I would care to do some baling so that he and Steve could carry on combining the winter barley. How could I refuse when he had just virtually given me the bike? After breakfast I got the 595 attached to the baler and got started with the flat eight sledge on behind. After a couple of rounds I thought to check the twine box. In the knickers of time! It was on the last rolls. I filled up the box, carefully joining the rolls together so that it would carry on tying up the bales straight from one roll to the next. It was quite satisfying work, seeing each of eight bales leaving the sledge and hearing the gate clunk to at the back for the next set.

Wednesday was Royal Wedding day. Mavis watched the whole thing and I recorded it on the video to watch on a wet day!

By Thursday, all the winter barley had been safely harvested into the grain store and Tony and Steve got busy with the bales. They had carted some off every morning while they waited for the dew to dry off. My motorbike insurance came through from Ernie Merryweather's recommended broker, so on Friday morning I nipped off to Peterborough to get the bike taxed and re-registered in my name. That done, I went to give a hand with the bales. Tony had taken on a teenage lad from the council houses and he was unloading bales onto the elevator while Tony and Steve stacked them in the Dutch barn next to the hay bales. The horse barn could wait for some wheat straw. Tony said they could manage but why didn't I go and give Robert and Jill a hand? They baled up other people's unwanted barley straw and carted it in because they hadn't got enough acreage to grow cereals themselves. I took myself off to Glebe Farm where I found Jill unloading and Robert struggling on his own on the stack. Were they pleased to see me! 'A little help is worth a great deal of pity any day,' was Robert's greeting.

Their boys had gone to grandparents for a few days so that they could get on without having to worry about them. I spent the rest of the day and all day Saturday helping them, by which time they had a fair stock in. They got the straw quite cheaply because it saved their neighbour the hassle of burning unwanted straw, the only advantage of burning straw being that it killed a lot of weed seeds and left a nice clean field for ploughing. The general public got fed up with it. The ash tended to blow away and settle on people's washing and paintwork. Very aggravating for someone having their house painted! There were also some irresponsible farmers who didn't take adequate safeguards and some quite serious fires resulted. Whole hedgerows were destroyed and sometimes the wind changed and blew smoke across roads making driving difficult. Tony said that on one occasion a whirlwind had taken up burning straw and set fire to a field of standing corn in an adjacent field. Another time a whirlwind had cleared an acre of straw and littered it all the way to Oundle and beyond. He had no doubt that eventually public outrage would get it banned.

Sunday was a very hot day. Robert's boys were home from their grandparents and Brian, Ben, Jamie and, of course, Sam, were invited to Glebe Farm to help Bill and John build a den in a spinney near the farm. Bill apparently was to be senior NCO, at eight trusted with a bow saw to cut some pieces for the frame. According to the blueprint it was to be covered first with hazels then with bracken. Robert assured us that a discreet eye would be kept on proceedings. Brynda and Donna agreed that they could go, Brynda telling Jamie that he and Sam had got to be good boys, only to be told by an indignant Jamie, 'Sam and me are always good boys, aren't we Sam?' Needless to say, Sam thumped his tail in agreement. All of which left Brynda and I free to go for a spin on the Speed Twin. First time on a bike for Brynda so I told her to simply go with me and not try to sit upright round the bends! She took to it like a duck to water and when we got back I had to let her have a go at the controls up the Chase past Caroline's.

CHAPTER XI

On Monday morning Bunion came round with a suggestion. 'Reckon we should pop over to Barrowden and see Bill Story, ask him if he'd bring his traction engine and threshing tackle to our ploughing day. If he agrees, I know where I can borrow an International power driven binder. We could cut about 4 acres of the thatching wheat with it and get the sheaves loaded up on trailers ready for threshing.'

'Only problem I see with the idea, Bunion, is what if the trailers are needed for bale carting?' Tony put in.

Bunion winked at me, 'Reckon I can borrow a couple of trailers. I know where there's a couple haven't been used lately, so long as the tyres are OK.'

'Well, you better check on the trailers first, Bunion,' said Tony. 'No good asking Bill Story or borrowing the binder if we've got nothing to load the sheaves on.'

After breakfast Bunion directed me to the farmer who had the trailers. He had three, the tyres were OK because they'd been covered with old bags to keep the light off, but the floors were very dodgy. 'No problem,' declared Bunion, 'There's some sheets of plywood in one of the sheds at Home Farm we can lay on temporarily.' His friend agreed that we could borrow them but we had to give him a disclaimer in writing not to claim if we fell through the floor.

Next he took me to the farm where the binder was. They were going to use it themselves later on in the day, but we could use it when they'd finished their small field. I gave him our phone number and he agreed to give us a ring as soon as it was available.

Next we went to Barrowden where we found Bill Story senior. It didn't take long for Bunion to talk him into coming over to Halston. They'd leave the tackle till the following Friday then take it to Expo at the Showground. Bunion was quite chuffed with his morning's work. He reckoned that the extra attraction would bring in a few more punters. Bunion explained to me that we would use the binder as soon as it was available because it was best for the corn not to be as ripe as for the combine. If it was completely ripe, the grain would fall out before it got into the threshing drum.

We were able to fetch the binder at lunchtime the following day and it was agreed that we could use their Super Major as they, the tractor and binder, were a matching pair.

I drove the tractor and Bunion operated the binder. It went like a dream, didn't miss a single sheaf, and we were finished by six o'clock. We packed the machine up, putting the transport wheels back on, and took it straight back to its owner. I managed to get him to accept £10 to cover the cost of fuel and string. He wouldn't take any more. Bunion promised me a stooking lesson in the morning. He grinned at me, 'Be thankful it's not barley. If you get barley awns round your nuts you get a fair old rash! I got one in me tummy button once, had a hell of a job to get it out.'

Tony and Steve came with us in the morning. They fell about laughing at my first efforts at stooking. The idea was to lean the sheaves together like a tent, four rows of sheaves into one row of stooks. Brynda brought Jamie and Sam to have a look. He wanted to crawl through a stook and, of course, the inevitable happened. He got scratched knees from the stubble and it collapsed on top of him halfway through. Brynda's efforts at rebuilding it were worse than mine.

We had a few days grace before the combine needed to start on the wheat so Tony suggested that we try to get the water wheel out of the mill. I was dispatched to Sacrewell to get some advice. Their wheel was similar to Malcolm's in some respects but it was inside the mill rather than on the end. David Powell, the manager, thought I'd best go and see Maxey mill, owned and run by Donald Stable. I was in luck. I was introduced to Fred Bird from Glinton, who agreed to come over next day and take a look. Mr Stable assured me that what Fred didn't know about mills wasn't worth knowing.

When I got home, I rang Caroline and told her what arrangements I'd made. 'I shall be out,' she informed me, 'but I'll leave the key under a stone near the main door.'

There were no signs of Mavis, Brynda, Jamie or Sam. I went round to the garage to find that the 'Yellow Peril' was out. I didn't remember them saying anything about going out. I hoped that nothing was wrong, then I heard the car coming back. Brynda headed towards the garage, but stopped for everyone to get out before putting the car away.

'I'd forgotten I had an appointment at the clinic. Fortunately Mavis reminded me in time so that I wasn't late. They all came for the ride and guess what, there's a strong possibility that we're going to have twins!'

To say that I was dumbfounded would be the understatement of the year. 'I'll find out for sure next visit,' said Brynda happily. 'Then we shall have to sell the business.' Seeing my look of puzzlement she added, 'No more children, three's enough for anyone, or at least it should be.'

Tony and I met Fred Bird at nine o'clock at the mill as arranged. Caroline had remembered to leave the key. After a thorough inspection, Fred asked whether we had considered rebuilding the wheel ourselves. 'Most farmers I know are a pretty versatile lot,' he said. 'The cast sections of the wheel look alright, it's just the buckets that have rusted away. If you buy sheets of 3mm or 1/8' thick steel you could cut them up with a disc cutter, weld ends in, drill holes, and bolt them on. Two or three coats of red oxide paint, and you're in business. That's if either of you can weld?'

'I can weld,' said Tony. 'Learnt at Agricultural College, very useful on the farm. Looks to me as though the wheel is four foot wide, which is what the sheets come in, I believe.'

Fred nodded, 'Yeah, eight by four usually. If you cut the heads off the bolts and get one of the few buckets off which haven't rotted too badly, you should be able to make a template to bend the new metal to the right shape.'

'It looks pretty heavy to me,' I remarked. 'Any suggestions how we get it out?'

'You'd either need a crane or one of those big diggers on tracks. Once you've taken the tops off the axle bearings, it will need to be moved upwards and sideways more or less at the same time. It'll be heavier when it goes back in, getting on for a ton at any rate.'

We took him to have a look at the rest of the machinery. After a thorough look round, he announced 'Some of the wooden teeth in the cogs need to be replaced, fortunately not in the big wheels. I'll put you in touch with a specialist firm in Lincolnshire. They are made either of apple or hornbeam, depending upon what is available. Both pairs of stones will want redressing. I can teach you how to do that. You'll need a wooden template to work to because these stones have been worn down too far to judge the grooves accurately.'

He reckoned they were Derbyshire millstone grit, possibly off Froggat Edge. I remembered going there once and seeing an unfinished, or

THE ARM OF COINCIDENCE

failed stone lying at the bottom of the cliff. He explained what we'd have to do to get the stones into a position where they could be dressed. I took him back to the farmhouse for a coffee and to square up with him for his time and expertise. In the meantime, Tony collected a formidable array of huge wrenches and a blow lamp in case any of the nuts were reluctant to undo. In the event, the outdoor ones all had to be heated before they would come undone. It was a great relief that none of them sheared off. The bearings inside the mill came loose without trouble.

Tony phoned Bradshaws of Stibbington to see how much it would cost to get one of their big diggers to lift it out. We couldn't believe our luck. They were fetching one home tomorrow from a job and would be coming past Halston turn and we'd only have to pay the hire for the time it took from the end of the road to when it got back on course. There wouldn't be much room to spare getting over the bridge as the tracks of the machine overhung the sides of the transporter on both sides. The best bet was to cross the first bridge and go down on the same side as the pub.

Once the wheel was lifted out of the millrace it could be put down anywhere and Tony could move it with the Sanderson forklift. Unfortunately Tony's machine couldn't reach far enough to lift the wheel from its position and, even if it could, it wouldn't be able to move far enough sideways to get the axle out of the side of the mill.

When Malcolm arrived home on Friday night, he was amazed to find that the wheel was now in the workshop and some of the minor gear wheels had disappeared into the depths of Lincolnshire. Tony playfully spoke for both of us, 'You and your crackpot ideas of getting this mill going again, our wives will expect free flour for life when we get it going.'

On Monday morning combining got underway on the winter wheat. Bunion and I fetched the four wheel trailers from his friend with the Land Rover, not quite legal, we had all three, one behind the other. Two empty trailers were legal, but not three. Inevitably we met a police car, but it was going so fast that it either didn't register or they were on some emergency. We pulled up outside the workshop and, using the compressor, got all the tyres up to fifty pounds per square inch. Bunion figured that we'd have a fair bit of weight on by the time we'd loaded it all. Brynda came with Jamie and Sam to drive the Land Rover, with one trailer at a time, from stook to stook.

THE ARM OF COINCIDENCE

Bunion loaded while I pitched the sheaves to him. Good job Bunion had warned me to wear gloves otherwise I'd have had blisters; my hands weren't used to this sort of work. He certainly knew how to load and it was a good job we'd remembered to put the – not plywood as Bunion had thought – but thick hardboard out of old grain silos onto the trailers. When he'd finished a load, no ears of corn showed on the outside, and he'd carefully counted the stooks to make sure we'd hold it all on the three trailers. I was quite glad there were only four acres.

When we'd finished the first load we had to take it back to the farm so that Bunion could get down by a ladder. The loads were quite high and I got the job of carrying sheets up the ladder onto each trailer so that they could be made safe against the weather. We wouldn't be able to get them all in the barn and, anyway, the space would soon be occupied by bales of wheat straw for bedding the cattle in winter.

Next day Tony asked if I would go grain carting while he got the old trailing Claas out and combined the other six acres of thatching wheat. He didn't want Bunion to do it because it would be too dusty. He took one grain trailer and parked it in the field ready, saying that he would empty it himself when he'd got it full. He reckoned that Steve wouldn't have to wait many minutes for me to get back from emptying my trailer. The new combine had a big tank and I hadn't got too far to travel back to the grain store.

Wednesday saw a break in the combining. The next field wasn't deemed to be quite ready. Steve got busy with the baler. Tony, Bunion and I carted up the trussed thatching straw. This time Tony loaded while Bunion drove the tractor. Each time we got to a truss I lobbed it up onto the trailer. As soon as we'd got a load we went and unloaded it. We used the same elevator as for the bales. Bunion unloaded onto the elevator. I took them off and Tony stacked. We only used about a third of a bay in the Dutch barn, so we quickly gained height. Although there were only six acres, it took quite a time to clear because of the number of times each truss was handled. Tony reckoned there would be enough height left to add the trusses we'd get from the threshing machine. Tony decided that we may as well fetch a load of bales and make a start with filling the rest of the pole barn with wheat straw for Dan's hunters to lie on. They were cleared out every day so they got through quite a lot of straw in the winter months. Bunion didn't come with us for this job because the bales were too heavy for him now. We didn't want to kill the old boy off. Tony operated the

THE ARM OF COINCIDENCE

Sanderson with the flat eight loader whilst I made the load safe for travelling.

Thursday I was let off, Tony got the lad from the council houses again to help. The lad was a good worker and was keen to earn a few bob. Tony was allowed to employ him as his dad had used him the previous year. It left me free to have a play with the water wheel. I had a good look round to see if there was anything likely to catch fire if I used the disc cutter. A lot of people were under the misconception that you couldn't start a fire with a disc cutter. People had often used them near hay and straw stacks and caused serious fires. I managed to turn the wheel until I found a bucket that was more or less intact. It would be a waste of time to try to undo the bolts, so I used the nine-inch cutter to cut the nuts off. I had to be careful not to break the cast spokes when knocking the bolts out. I gave each a good soaking in easing oil, some had to be heated with the blowlamp before they would move. It was going to take quite a while to get all the bolts out. I wore goggles whilst using the disc cutter, but didn't expect to get a piece of metal in my eye when I was knocking a bolt out. I went round to the house and Brynda rang the surgery. We were advised to go straight to the hospital. They said that they'd ring the hospital to expect us.

Finding a parking place was quite difficult, and in the finish Brynda parked her car on a piece of grass. Once in the hospital we were directed to the eye clinic. On the way down Brynda spotted Ralph and Janice waiting at Clinic 5. She waved to them and was somewhat miffed when they ignored her and turned their backs. While we were waiting in the clinic, Brynda asked one of the nurses what happened at Clinic 5 as there was no other notice. She grinned, 'It's the clinic where no one wishes to be seen; the VD clinic!'

I looked at Brynda, 'Looks like we had a narrow escape,' I whispered. 'It underlines the risks taken with promiscuous people you hardly know.' Brynda nodded. She'd gone a bit pale.

'I guess you're right. How long does it take to show itself?' she asked anxiously.

'Reckon we'd have known by now,' I replied. 'Anyway I vote we don't take any more chances.'

She shuddered, 'No, we won't. I must admit I hadn't given it much thought. It was something that only happened to other people.'

My name was called and I went in. They managed to remove the

THE ARM OF COINCIDENCE

piece of metal without any further damage, but warned me that I'd been lucky. 'You'll have a sore eye for a few days,' the doctor said. 'Let it be a lesson to you always wear goggles if there's the slightest risk of getting something in your eye.'

One way and another it was a somewhat chastened couple who returned to Halston. I didn't sleep too well that night; it was difficult to stop myself from rubbing my eye. I stayed indoors out of the sun for most of the day. I learnt quite a bit about building with Lego, Jamie was a very inventive exponent! In the evening we had a visit from Terry Grant. His wife had been whizzed into hospital and was undergoing major surgery. They had booked a holiday in Robin Hood's Bay months previously and now couldn't go. They had paid a fairly hefty deposit, which they would lose anyway. If we were free to go, all we need do would be to pay the balance. Mavis said straight away that we should go because there was nothing that she couldn't take care of in the offing. I asked Terry if we'd be able to take the dog? He pulled all the information about the cottage out of his inside pocket and we read it through. It didn't say 'Dogs welcome'. On the other hand, it didn't say 'Sorry no pets'. We decided to risk it, after all, I doubt if anyone had a better behaved or sharper dog than Sam.

I offered to refund him the deposit money but he wouldn't hear of it. 'The reason you've got the offer is because you've always come when I've asked for help. I'm glad the cottage isn't going begging.' He left us all the details, where to find the key, etc. Someone would come to collect the balance on Saturday evening.

Brynda immediately started packing. 'I want to get as much ready as possible so we can make an early start. You get the video and your camera ready and anything else you want to take.' She gave a sudden grin. 'You may have to put up with me driving your car if your eye isn't better in the morning.'

In the event it was much better and I thought I'd be OK so long as I wore dark glasses. The sun would be behind us most of the time anyway. We got away about 8 o'clock and took the A1 north. Traffic wasn't too bad and it only took a little over two hours to get to the A64 turn off to York. We stopped off in York for an hour and a half to have a look in the museum and drink our coffee near the river with Clifford's Tower behind us. From York we headed to Scarborough and then took the coast road towards Whitby entering Robin Hood's Bay via Fylingthorpe. We found the terraced cottage easily enough but had

THE ARM OF COINCIDENCE

to carry our stuff from a car park, as there was no vehicular access to the cottage itself.

Once we'd unpacked we went to explore. It was easy to imagine it as a pirate stronghold in days gone by. We bought an ordnance survey map and had a look in the museum. When we went back to the cottage we met an old boy, who lived a few doors away, making a violin. He was a retired civil engineer who had been clerk of works over the building of Fylingdale's early warning 'Golf Balls'. Very interesting man.

On Sunday morning Brynda packed some lunch and we set off to walk to Boggle Hole just a bit further down the coast. Some of the walk was along a disused coastal railway line. We had to have Sam on a lead for some of the way because, although he was very obedient, there were notices reading that dogs must be on a lead. When we came back we clipped his lead back on, but on the way down the cliff walkway met a dog, not only not on a lead, but very ahead of his owners. It promptly went for poor Sam. I grabbed it on either side of the neck and hurled it off the walkway. The scree wasn't too steep and it reached the bottom without undue fuss. The owners came charging up with the man very aggressive. I pointed to one of the signs, and he started swearing about it being their land and he wasn't going to be told what to do by bloody grockles. I asked him, I thought mildly, would he like to join his dog? He took a swing at me and I belted him straight in the solar plexus. He went down like a pole-axed steer. I turned to his open-mouthed wife, 'When he gets his breath back, tell him he's lucky not to have gone the same way as the dog.' We continued on our way leaving her to assist him to his feet.

Monday we drove out to Grosmont and took a ride on the North Yorkshire Moors Railway; if not the longest preserved railway in the country, close to it. It chugged its way up to Goathland, a very steep climb for a steam engine. We stopped off at Goathland, it seemed a good point to video the train. When it moved off we were standing on the footbridge to get a good view. Some sparks from the engine set fire to grass on the trackside and someone had to run from the station with a beater to knock it out. Surprising how fast it was spreading, he only just got there in time to stop it getting out of hand. I captured it all on video.

We had a walk round while we were waiting for the next train to take us on to Pickering. I managed to get some video of the engine gasping its way up the hill, then one boy and his dog scrambling into the carriage. Brynda was more elegant, but then she had longer legs.

Jamie loved Pickering Castle, looking out through the slits in the wall, pretending that we were being besieged. We ate our picnic in the castle enclosure. We could hear the trains coming and going, but only had brief glimpses through the trees. Jamie vetoed a visit to the museum, he'd seen one already on this holiday. He was more interested in the train ride. I'm ashamed to admit that I couldn't identify any of the engines, one steam engine being pretty much the same as another to me, except for the shape, that is.

We decided to drop off at Goathland again and walk back to Grosmont. All downhill, part of it at least followed the original route of the railway. It was a lovely walk and I got some more video of my family. The cottage was equipped with everything we needed and was very comfortable. It even had television, so I was pleased I'd brought the complete video outfit so we could watch what I'd filmed.

On Tuesday I remembered that I hadn't ordered the portable loos for the weekend, so I rang Mavis to give Tony a message. She thought he'd already done it, but would check. Malcolm had bought a second hand caravan to do the teas from. Now that was a useful idea.

We decided to go into Whitby to see the harbour where Captain Cook sailed from to Australia. Jamie insisted upon climbing all the steps from the harbour to the ruins of Whitby Abbey. Sam went up at least twice to our once, I suppose he wondered why we were so slow. It wasn't a good idea for Brynda to rush too much.

We had our lunch on the beach and it wasn't too long before Jamie and Sam picked up with another little boy. Sam was very good at scratching out tunnels under the castles they built. The boy's parents told us they were staying in Whitby and had been to Middlesborough on the single track BR line. They said it was worth it just for the scenery. You got more panoramic views than on the preserved line and it took you past Ayton where Captain Cook was born.

We decided to try it on Wednesday. It really was a wonderful ride following the River Esk through Eskdale. In fact, if you wanted, you could link up with the preserved line at Grosmont by walking from one station to the other. Jamie had his nose glued to the window for most of the trip. At Middlesborough I have to admit we didn't leave the station, but caught the next train back. At one point on the journey, the driver had to leave his cab to alter some points. He forgot to remove

THE ARM OF COINCIDENCE

his keys and a sudden gust of wind closed his cabin door. He couldn't get back in. Apologising, red-faced, he explained that we would have to wait for someone to bring a key. His job prospects didn't look too good, his train could have been driven off by anyone who knew how. It turned out that a senior executive was travelling on the train and had a key. We were saved a long wait and the driver got away with a severe ticking off and a promise that this time, it would go no further.

On Thursday morning all Jamie wanted to do was to go back to Goathland and watch the trains. In the end we decided to drive out and park up at Goathland. There was a really nice walk along the original railway track from Goathland to Moorgates where it met with the line proper. Jamie wanted me to video every train in each direction as we walked. We returned to the station on the same track and ate our lunch on the platform. I think Jamie was secretly hoping for another fire.

After lunch I persuaded him that we should look for a Roman road I'd heard about to the west of the village. We drove part of the way as Jamie had done quite a lot of walking for short legs already. When we found the road, it was amazing how intact it was; only a short stretch across the moors, but most of the stones still in the same position as they were laid all those hundreds of years before. To a child, of course, one year seems to be a lifetime, so we knew that Jamie wouldn't be able to grasp that length of time. When we got back to Robin Hood's Bay we went to a green at the top of the village and sat watching the sea while boy and dog frolicked about on the grass.

In the morning we decided that we'd go home after tea so that we could help get ready for Sunday. Brynda suggested we spend the day in Scarborough. We packed up and stowed everything in the car, put the cottage to rights, leaving it as we found it, and returned the key to the caretaker.

Brynda remembered her Gran taking her to Scarborough as a child for a holiday once. I had never been before. I doubt whether I went further north than the farm in Hertfordshire until I joined the army. Scarborough has quite impressive cliffs and a sandy beach. Jamie as usual soon made friends with some other children to build sandcastles. I thought I recognised someone, I was sure I'd seen him in the pub at Halston. Every time I looked his way he was looking mine. Eventually he got up and came over.

'I'm trying to work out where I've seen you before, I'm sure I have,' he greeted me with.

'Halston pub?'

'Of course, you're the guy who was playing keyboard in there on Tuesday evenings earlier on this year. I'd have liked to have got to your gig, but I'm a long distance lorry driver and I got stranded in Scotland with a breakdown which couldn't be fixed till Monday.'

'Where do you come from?' I asked him.

He grinned, 'Woodnewton, next village to Halston. Small world isn't it?'

I agreed and watched as he rejoined his family. I didn't think his wife accompanied him to the pub. Perhaps couldn't get a sitter.

When Jamie got bored with building sandcastles, we climbed up to the castle ruins. He and Sam had a fine old time, playing catch me if you can round the ruins. We left as soon as we'd had tea, taking the A64 initially. We went down the B1249 to Driffield then down to Beverley. We stopped and I took some photographs of the newly opened Humber Bridge before we paid the toll and crossed it: a very impressive bridge, mind boggling in fact. We then followed the A15 through Lincoln, Sleaford and down to Market Deeping, the A16 as far as West Deeping and then down the old Roman road, King Street, which originally would have gone through where the village of Upton now stands, to the Roman answer to Stoke-on-Trent, Durobrivae. The Romans distributed the local pottery which archaeologists now call Nene Valley Ware all over the country from this township. Ermine Street passed through it. Bunion has some quite sizeable chunks of this pottery he has found around the iron workings in Halston parish. The rough pottery, which looks older, is in fact, according to our old friend, much younger. The secrets of how to make good pots disappeared with the Romans.

By the time we got back to Halston, both boy and dog were fast asleep. We managed to get Jamie to bed without properly waking him. Sam woke as soon as he heard the car door opening. He followed us upstairs as soon as he'd had a little walk, and waited for me to fetch his basket. Tucking his nose under his tail, he went back to doggy dreamland.

CHAPTER XII

Saturday wasn't a very good day, dull with some rain, nevertheless we got everything in place, ready for the Big Day. We borrowed Robert's four wheel trailers to load the bundles of straw as they came off the trusser on the back of the threshing drum. Bunion and Tony put the ploughing engines in place, one at each end of the field. They did one trial run, pulling the plough first one way then the other. The two Shire horses were housed in the stables, no need for them to have a trial run. We had to keep everything crossed for a good day tomorrow and that everyone who had promised to help turned up.

We needn't have worried! Sunday was a glorious day, everyone turned up at half past nine, quickly followed by the first spectators. The tannoy was in place and Tony had the mike on his engine on the far side of the field where, with a bit of luck, he would be able to see everything that was happening.

I put my leathers and helmet on and at two minutes to ten started the bike and took it to the centre of the field where we had a square temporarily roped off. I heard Tony announce that as a prelude to the real action, some nutcase had volunteered to start proceedings with a bit of stunt riding. That was my cue and I roared the bike straight into a wheelie across the square, down, turn round and wheelie to the other side. Next I set the throttle to a sedate pace, climbed onto the saddle and balanced the machine with my arms held out on either side. My final stunt was to ride round the perimeter of the square sitting on the handlebars backwards. I made my exit still sitting backwards, stopped at the edge of the field and, riding normally, took the bike through the barn and parked it by the house. I got rid of the leathers and helmet, quite chuffed that I'd managed to get the heavy old bike onto its back wheel and hadn't fallen off, then went back to the field.

By this time, everything was under way. The steamers were towing the six furrow plough backwards and forwards across the field with two of Bunion's mates operating the plough. Steve had the Caterpillar in the next field. Barry from the council houses on the Allis Chalmers; Robert on the Fordson Major in the centre of the field with the Shire horses furthest from the noise. Most of the spectators had cameras. The two Bill Storys, father and son from Barrowden, were busy with their helpers threshing wheat off the first trailer. I went to my allotted place, helping load the straw bundles onto Robert's trailer. As soon as one trailer was empty, another took its place. At least we didn't have anyone sacking the grain up, with no sacks available. We were cheating! The grain dropped into a tank and was augered into the grain trailer to go into the store with the rest of the wheat.

It was a job to estimate the number of spectators because people were moving around all the time and as some left others arrived.

Threshing was dusty and thirsty work and I for one was quite pleased when everything stopped for lunch. The horses got their nosebags on. The three tractors had to be stopped for safety reasons. Tony and Bunion had their tea and sandwiches by their engines to make sure no bright sparks decided to have a go!

Brynda, Donna and Caroline seemed to be doing brisk trade at the sandwich bar caravan. I wondered how Mavis was getting on with Jamie and Fiona, not to mention Sam, when I spotted them viewing from the edge of the field. Jill was with them, with her two boys and Tony's boys.

The smell of newly turned earth mingled with the unmistakable smells of burnt TVO, diesel, coal smoke and steam. The two Shire horses were great favourites with the children, very few of them minded the smell of sweaty horses!

I was amazed at how straight everyone's furrows were, but then this reddish brown earth was some of the easiest working in the area. Had we been on the higher ground where the boulder clay had been deposited by the retiring ice age, it would have been a different story. I remember Bunion telling me about a guy at Southwick trying to plough with two furrows behind a wartime Fordson. The plough was bouncing in and out of the ground like a yo-yo and the front wheels of the tractor were off the ground as much as on it. Steering a straight line was out of the question. When the little grey Ferguson tractors first came on the market, it was claimed that they could do anything that other tractors could do. They had a demonstration on a farm at Apethorpe, the plough was let down, the tractor went a couple of yards, the front wheels came up, and that was as far as it went! The demonstrator turned to the foreman and complained, 'You've taken me to the worst field on the farm!' to which the foreman replied: 'We can already plough the best. According to your advertising your tractor should be able to plough the worst.'

'If the Ferguson can't plough it, I don't call it land,' grumbled the salesman.

'Well, in that case we've got a lot of acres that aren't land,' replied the foreman.

Actually they were wonderful little machines, thousands of them were produced and sold. Like everything else, they had their limitations, but hundreds of them are still going strong today.

I was kept busy all afternoon, it was part of my duties to make sure that the grain trailer didn't overflow. I had to move it occasionally to get even loading. We had another trailer on standby. At £120 a ton we didn't want any spillage!

About twenty past three I noticed Robert leaving to milk his cows; our friend from Southwick had taken over from him on the Fordson. By four o'clock most of the field was ploughed. All the grain was threshed and people had started drifting away.

The Shire horses were housed in the stables for a well-earned feed and rest. The Allis and the Fordson Major were driven into the shed. The Caterpillar came trundling along. Steve's field was completely finished, including the headland. He would put our field to rights in the morning, finishing off the oddments and the headlands. The steam plough was disconnected at Bunion's end and Tony's cable rewound onto his drum, being cleaned and greased as it went. He trundled the engine over to stand it near Bunion's. They would let the fires die down until there was just enough steam left to put them away.

The girls had shut up the caravan and departed to collect their offspring.

I heard a yell from the farmyard and looked round in time to see two teenagers picking themselves up off the ground near the pole barn. They ran off and Tony and I simultaneously saw smoke coming from under the roof. The fire spread so fast that we knew it would be hopeless to try to save it. Our top priority was to save the nearby buildings. I had an idea and shouted to Tony 'You and Steve drag Bunion's cable round the barn. I'll get the chainsaw and cut off the poles.' He understood immediately what I intended should be attempted.

'Barry, you help Steve with the cable,' he yelled and together we belted to the machinery shed. I grabbed a handful of six–inch nails, a hammer and the chainsaw. I knew it had fuel in it because I was the

THE ARM OF COINCIDENCE

last to use it. Tony dragged a huge pulley wheel and shackle from under the bench, reached for a coil of straining wire and we dashed back to the barn. It was well alight. I passed the hammer and nails to Steve, yelling, 'One in each post about two foot up.'

I started the chainsaw and started cutting through the poles. Thank God I'd sharpened it before putting it away.

Tony pulled the pin out of the pulley, put the cable into the wheel, replaced the pin and connected it with the shackle to the end of the cable. The shackle pin he threaded the straining wire through. As I cut through the last pole, Steve and Barry rested the cable on the nails to keep it up. I heard Tony yell, 'Take the strain, Bunion,' the cable tightened round the poles, the whole lot of hay and straw was well alight.

'Give it some wellie, Bunion,' from Barry.

'Uppen it out!' from Steve.

'GIVE IT THE ONION, BUNION!' Damn near deafened me from Tony!

Slowly but surely the whole mass started to move. The mighty engine was belching steam and black smoke. As the blazing mass moved further from the other buildings into a safe area, we all gave a great cheer. At least the rest of the farm was safe.

When the fire started to get too close to the engine for comfort, Bunion slackened the cable and Tony pulled out the shackle pin with his length of straining cable. We had to knock bits of burning hay off the cable as it came free. The shackle stopped the cable from pulling through the pulley wheel and so far as we could see the precious cable wasn't damaged. The threshing tackle was fortunately sheeted down behind the grain store, far enough away as to be in no danger.

The fire brigade arrived and Tony had some difficulty in getting them to leave the fire to burn out! He reasoned that there would be less to clear up and, even if they succeeded in putting it out, nothing would be salvaged. Tony told them that we would make sure that there was no danger, even if we had to stay up all night.

Whilst we had been dealing with the fire service, Bunion had driven his engine out into the open field and Steve and Barry had pulled the cable out again to check, clean and grease it. The pulley, shackle, hammer and chainsaw were returned to the workshop. I took my shirt off and examined it ruefully, ruined! It had loads of small holes in it where sparks had fallen whilst I was sawing the poles off.

THE ARM OF COINCIDENCE

I was just checking the area where the barn had been, it hadn't cleared all the hay and straw away and I didn't want to risk it igniting, when a green Jaguar drove into the yard. The driver got out and strode towards me. 'What the bloody hell's been going on here!' he snarled. Well, I don't like being snarled at. So I turned my back on him and started to walk away.

'You! I might have known it would be you!' I turned round, but he was running back to his car. He went to the passenger side and reached inside. When he turned around, he was holding a gun! I went into automatic self-preservation, dived towards the open barn door, went into a roll and came up running. I heard a bullet whining off the barn wall as I shot out of the opposite door. I slammed the heavy oak door and threw the bolt, just as another bullet thudded into the door. I tore to my bike, thank God for the time spent fine-tuning it. She started first kick and I was away.

I turned out of the drive and wound up the revs. As I was going over the bridge I glanced in my mirror in time to see the Jag pull out of the yard in pursuit. With scant regard for safety to other road users I roared up through the gears only to realise as I approached the chicane that he was gaining on me! Of course this was no ordinary car and my bike would only do about 90 mph flat out. I felt a thud as I screamed the bike down through the gears and through the double bend, catching both footrests in the process. Then I heard the screaming combination of brakes and tyres, then crashing through bushes and I knew that he'd crashed. My brain had gone into overdrive as I wheeled the bike round and went back. The Jag was nose first down the brook bank, almost vertical, with the bonnet jammed under a huge ash tree root, which had become exposed with constant erosion of the bank over the years.

I could see the driver slumped over the wheel with his head touching the windscreen. I yanked the bike onto its stand and ran back over the bridge. The first thing I saw was the gun, a German Luger with home-made silencer. I kicked it down a rabbit hole under the tree stump, which had brought the young motorcyclist to grief a few weeks back. I was about to start down the bank to try and get him out – I wanted some answers – when the car, which incredibly was still running, gave another lurch. There was a strong smell of leaking petrol. The engine stopped as the battery shorted out as the bonnet crushed down. I only just got back to safety when the whole issue ignited!

I tore back over the bridge and yanked the locked gate off its hinges and opened it enough to get the bike through. Once through I put it back on its hinges and set off down the track on a low rev towards the hall grounds. I heard the Land Rover roaring along the road, but knew no one could see me because of the hedge. I managed to get back to the farm without seeing anyone and hoped that I hadn't been seen. Sweat was pouring off me, running into my eyes, making them sting.

I pulled the bike onto its stand where I'd left it before. I was shaking from head to toe. I wiped the sweat out of my eyebrows, then I saw the bullet hole in the back of the seat! That's what I'd felt, a really close call. Fortunately for me he'd been so engrossed with trying to shoot me that he'd forgotten his speed. With only one hand on the wheel he hadn't stood a chance.

My brain was in a mess, the gun I realised I'd seen before somewhere, that homemade silencer had put the fear of God into me! He had obviously either recognised me, or thought he had. In view of my certainty of the gun, it must have been the former. I retrieved my shirt and dried myself off with it as my heart returned slowly to normal speed. I put the bike away. I wasn't ready for questions yet, so I didn't want anyone to see the seat.

I heard the fire engine with its siren going, another fruitless journey; nothing could have saved the driver of that car, who I assumed was Dan Woodward.

Shortly afterward I heard the Land Rover returning. Tony and Steve got out.

'Where have you been?' I asked.

'Didn't you see all the smoke down at the skew bridge?' Tony replied. 'We went down to see what had happened and found the old man's car going up in smoke. He must be here somewhere, someone must have pinched it as soon as he got here! There were huge skid marks on the road, whoever was in there must have been going like the clappers, expecting to be chased, I expect. I wonder why he's come back early, we better see if we can find him.'

'How 'd you know it's his car?' I asked.

He held up the front number plate in reply. 'We found this lodged under some brushwood. We better find Bunion and help put the engines away. Perhaps the old man is with him. He'll be as mad as hell about the pole barn and his hay. Don't suppose you recognised those two who ran away?'

THE ARM OF COINCIDENCE

I shook my head. I had a suspicion that one of them was a girl from the council houses, but nothing definite. 'I think there was one of each sex. No doubt they went up there for a bit of nookie, then decided to have a fag! I doubt if it was deliberate arson, otherwise they'd have set fire to the bottom of the barn instead of the top!' I replied. By this time we'd got to the vintage shed where both engines were being attended to by Bunion.

'Seen anything of the old man, Bunion?' enquired Tony.

'No, why, is he here? Thought he wasn't coming back till October.'

'So did I, but his car's definitely here. It's burnt out down on the skew bridge. Whoever was driving was going much too fast and didn't make it. He's going to be bloody furious when he finds out!'

I stayed with Bunion as Tony and Steve moved off, presumably to look for Dan.

'Bunion, do I remind you at all of anyone who's been here in the past?' I asked him. He knocked his pipe out on his heel.

'Not that I can think of,' he said thoughtfully. 'But that little lad of Brynda's is a lot like Jamie who was taken off by his father and aunt.'

We hadn't told anyone that Jamie was mine, so Bunion would assume that he belonged to Brynda's first husband.

'Do you remember if that Jamie had any distinguishing marks or anything?' I asked.

Bunion leaned against the wheel of his engine and carefully stoked his pipe. 'If I remember right,' he said slowly, 'he had a strawberry birthmark about half-inch across on his left, no his right, shoulder. Why did you want to know?'

I closed my eyes. I had a birthmark on my right shoulder! It occurred to me that Mavis had never seen me without a shirt and neither, for that matter, had Bunion. Either I was Jamie Spenser, or was it just chance? No, it had to be. I had seen that gun before! I put my hand on Bunion's shoulder. 'Just something that happened made me curious that's all. I'll give you a hand to sheet over in the morning when they've cooled down properly.'

'There's a bit more than sheeting to be done in the morning! They've got to be cleaned up and the boilers treated.'

'OK. Well, I'll still give you a hand. See you tomorrow.'

I went home, already half convinced that I was in fact Jamie Spenser, but I still couldn't remember anything before I was seven.

News travels fast! Mavis and Brynda already knew that some major

146

catastrophe had occurred. Jill had been on the phone to tell them there had been a crash and a fire on skew bridge. Funny how in my mind it had been chicane as on a racetrack, and locals referred to it as skew bridge. Apparently the police were still there and Tony and Steve had gone down with the Sanderson to get the remains of the car out.

I wanted to delve back into the past before my involvement was revealed. I wasn't looking forward to telling Tony and Caroline that their father had been trying to kill me, even if there wasn't much love lost between Tony and his dad. I still didn't understand why he had completely flipped his lid when he saw me, nor why he had returned unannounced so far ahead of schedule. At the moment only I was thinking that it was Dan Woodward in the car.

Tony came round to tell us that the remains of the car had been taken away for forensic and to get the remains out of the car for possible identification. I don't think that he was at present entertaining thoughts of it being Dan's remains in there.

I woke suddenly in the night, wet through with sweat. I must have screamed because Brynda switched on the light.

'Whatever's the matter?' she demanded. 'You look as though you've seen a ghost!'

'Perhaps I have,' I muttered. The image of two bodies; that gun! In a building that I now recognised as a dovecote, still in my mind. I got out of bed and went to the loo, dried myself off with a towel and went back to bed. Cuddling up with Brynda I determined to investigate the dovecote at the first opportunity!

In the morning I took Jamie and we went to the vintage shed where Bunion was already at work on his beloved engines. You wouldn't believe the state they could get into in one day's work! I bet they didn't get this amount of care when they were working throughout the ploughing and cultivating season. Bunion was very proud of them, being the third generation to operate them. His grandfather used to take them round to other farms once the estate land was ploughed up.

The engines were all cleaned and sheeted over by lunchtime.

'What are you doing after lunch, Bunion?' I asked.

'Not a lot, why?'

'I thought maybe we could do a bit of metal detecting?'

'Sure, got somewhere special in mind?'

I grinned at him. 'I'll tell you after lunch,' nodding towards Jamie.

'He and Sam are going over to Glebe Farm this afternoon with the rest of the gang.'

After lunch I took Jamie, Sam, Brian and Ben down to Jill's. They all took themselves off to the 'den'. I went back to Bunion's and he was surprised, to say the least, when I told him that our destination was to be the dovecote! We picked up a pretty loud signal near the centre of the floor and went over to the workshop to get spades and bars to lift the slab. It took quite a bit of prizing and easing, getting the slab up without breaking it.

'What are you expecting to find, boy?'

'I'm not sure.' I started to scrape away the soil where the signal was loudest, and revealed a large brass buckle in the shape of a snake.

'Well, I'll be damned,' exclaimed Bunion. 'Only buckle I ever saw like that was Jack Spenser's.' I took my shirt off and turned round so that he could see my back. 'Well damn my rags, you are Jamie Spenser, well you sure kept quiet about that.'

'No, Bunion, I didn't. I didn't know myself, didn't even suspect, till yesterday! Let's put the slab back for the moment. You may depend that Anne Woodward is under there, too. I need to call a family conference and I guess the police will have to be informed.'

Bunion nodded. 'We'll put the gear back and go round to my place first for a cup of coffee. I need one, even if you don't. All these years we've been thinking that Jack and Anne had gone off together and taken you with them. An' they hadn't gone anywhere.'

As we turned the corner to go into Bunion's, Tony drove up in the Land Rover. He stopped outside Bunion's and got out.

'I've just come from the police station. They've identified the body from dental records. It's the old man! I can't believe the old bugger's dead. Nor what the hell he was doing going in that direction at such a speed!'

'I think Bunion can run to three coffees. You'd better come in. I can now explain some of the mystery.' We went in and Bunion went to the kitchen to put the kettle on. 'Your dad came back yesterday and started shouting at me, something about what the hell was going on? I turned my back on him. I'd taken my shirt off and he appeared to recognise me! Anyway, when I turned round again he was running back to his car. He went to the passenger side and got a gun out and tried to shoot me. No doubt he would have succeeded if it hadn't been for army training. There's a flattened bullet somewhere in the barn, another in the barn door and another in the motorbike seat! He was chasing me when he crashed. I was going to try to get him out but the car went up in flames. His gun is down a rabbit hole, under that big tree stump.'

Tony sat dumbfounded. I continued.

'Between then, and what we've discovered today, I now know that I am in fact Jamie Spenser. My father and your mother, we think, are buried in the dovecote. Definitely my father. I had a nightmare last night, a blast from the past, brought on by the sight of that gun. I was dreaming about it and two bodies in a dovecote. Bunion and I have been to investigate.'

Bunion nodded. 'Definitely Jack Spenser's belt buckle is there, we didn't investigate any further. Jim reckons that it'll have to be official'.

Tony nodded. 'Aunt Mavis always thought it odd that they'd taken her Jamie and left Caroline and me behind. Now it seems they didn't go anywhere. But what happened to you?'

'I'd like to be able to remember that, too. At the moment I've no idea. The gun obviously struck a chord somewhere, otherwise I wouldn't have had the dream. We're going to have to talk to Caroline, and Mavis is in for a shock, seeing she must be my real mum! Amazing coincidence, Brynda coming here. I don't expect I ever would have otherwise.'

I turned to Bunion. 'What can you tell us? Anything we don't know?'

'Not a lot. I remember Jamie was coming up for his sixth birthday, big lad for his age. I was putting up sheep netting the day they disappeared. Reckon it was Dan put me on that job.'

'Could be I'm younger than I think then! They thought I was about seven when Marjorie Evans found me in her shed.'

Tony stroked his chin. 'I'd better go and see Caroline. You best go home and break it to Auntie that she's got a son again. We'll come round later when we've all had time to unscramble our brains!'

We thanked Bunion for the coffee and went in our separate directions. I decided to talk to Brynda first. I found her in one of the greenhouses. She looked at me. 'You OK? Still thinking about your bad dream?'

'Not exactly. That dream came from the past. I've found out exactly who I am! Remember when we got married, you had your birth certificate but I had my adoption certificate. Well, I think we may be able to find my birth certificate. I could even be a year younger than I thought!'

Brynda looked puzzled. 'How come?'

'Well, I think it's pretty definite that Mavis is my mother! That was Dan Woodward who got burnt in his car yesterday. Tony got confirmation today from the police. Dental records, they said. Anyway, he was trying to shoot me when he crashed, and Bunion went with me to the dovecote because I saw two bodies in a dovecote in my dream. Jack Spenser is definitely buried there, and most likely Anne Woodward. Shot with the same Luger pistol he was trying to kill me with.'

Brynda was staring at me round eyed. 'Then Mavis really is our Jamie's gran. What a mess! What are you going to do, now?'

'Well, first of all, we have to tell Mavis. Tony has gone to see Caroline. We are going to have a family conference tonight, but no doubt the police will have to be brought in.'

We went into the house together. Fortunately Jamie and Sam were still at Glebe Farm.

'Best put the kettle on, Bryn. Mavis is going to need a strong cup of tea.' I went through to the sitting room where Mavis was watching the telly.

'Anything special?' I asked her.

She shook her head, 'Just passing the time.' So I switched it off, knelt in front of her chair and took both her hands in mine.

'I've got good news and bad news,' I told her. 'Which shall I begin with, both are going to be a great shock.'

She straightened her shoulders, 'I'll have the bad news first!'

I didn't beat about the bush. 'Your husband and sister are both buried in the dovecote. They never went anywhere.'

She went very still, her eyes on mine. 'And the good news?'

'I've just found out that I'm Jamie Spenser.' I pulled my hands free and took off my shirt, turning so that she could see my back. When I turned round, tears of joy were streaming down her face. She cupped my face in her hands.

'I can hardly believe it! I never though I'd see you again! What happened to you?'

'I wish I knew. I must have seen Dan shoot Dad and Aunt Anne. I had a dream about that last night. Dan recognised me by the birthmark yesterday and tried to kill me with the same gun. He got pretty damn close!' I told her ruefully. 'There's a bullet in the motorbike seat.'

Brynda came in with the tea and we each had a cup.

'You know, I always thought that just too many things went wrong that day for it all to be coincidence,' Mavis mused. 'I had a really funny turn in the bank, thought I was dying. They took me into the manager's office and made me a cup of tea. That must have been when Anne was shot. Being identical twins, I don't think it's unusual for one to feel something if the other one dies. I ran out of petrol just out of Oundle on the way home and I had to walk to Oundle Motors to get a can of petrol. I remember wondering how it had come to be so low when I'd filled it up the week before. Then, when I got home, I found the note.'

'Have you still got it?' I asked.

'I think so. Have a look in the bottom drawer, right hand side of the bureau.'

I found it at the bottom of the drawer and opened it out.

'We are sorry to do this to you, Mavis, but Anne and I are going to Australia to start a new life. We've taken a thousand pounds out of the account and we shall leave the Land Rover at Peterborough Station with the key under the seat. Hope you and Dan can get together.'

I turned to Mavis (mother – it's going to take some getting used to). 'I bet Dan wrote this. I'll get samples of both of their handwriting if you can find them and take it to a calligraphist for analysis.'

Mavis was still shocked, so we had another cup of tea. 'There's something else, good news, which we can tell you,' said Brynda. 'Jamie really is your grandson! Pete and I tricked Jim because Pete was infertile. Jim didn't know till just before we were married!'

Mavis dabbed her eyes and turned to me. 'He's just like you were as a little boy. I think it's just wonderful.'

'There's just one thing,' I cautioned, 'we haven't told Jamie as yet that I'm his real Dad. We're going to wait until he's old enough to understand.'

'I don't mind, he calls me Gran, anyway.' I looked at my watch. 'I'd better go and collect the boys from Jill's, otherwise she'll think we've abandoned them on her.'

CHAPTER XIII

Jamie was safely in bed asleep with Sam in his basket before Tony and Caroline came round.

'I suppose we ought to ring the police now,' began Caroline. 'We wouldn't want you to get into trouble for withholding information, Jim.'

Everyone seemed in accord with that, so I rang direct to Corby and asked whether any of the police who had attended the accident at Halston yesterday were on duty. After a few moments, they came back to me to say they were out on patrol in the Oundle area.

'Could you contact them and ask them to come to Home Farm House, because there's a lot more information we need to give them.'

I gave them our phone number and replaced the receiver. Caroline came over to me and gave me a hug. 'Welcome back into the family, cousin! It looks as if Dad did some terrible things, but we shan't hold it against you.'

'And I've got my boy back,' smiled Mavis.

In less than five minutes we saw some headlights turn into the driveway and I opened the front door to admit the two policemen.

Tony shook hands with them. 'Bit of luck your being on duty so close.'

'Yes, sir. I suppose it is. Now, who's going to tell us what this is all about?'

'Me,' I said.

'And who are you? We didn't see you yesterday.'

'Well, between yesterday and today I've found out that my birth name is James Spenser, although I've been known by my adoptive name of James Evans for as long as I can remember.'

I regaled them with yesterday's events, not forgetting to tell them that the pistol would be down the rabbit hole. I told them of my dream and how Bunion and I had investigated the dovecote.

'Why didn't you come forward yesterday, sir?' one of them wanted to know.

'I suppose partly because it's a very hard thing to tell your friends that their father was trying to kill you, and partly to give myself thinking time. I had thought at first that it was a case of mistaken identity, but the gun must have triggered something off in my brain, hence the dream. It's a German wartime Luger, with what appears to be a homemade silencer. The silencer is very effective; it only makes a dull plop. The bullets make more noise when they strike.'

'Reckon we'd better call back to HQ,' one of the policemen said to the other.

'Why don't you wait till you get back?' interposed Caroline. 'The bodies have been there all these years, nothing is going to change overnight. I, for one, would rather this stayed as low profile as possible.'

'So would I,' said Mavis. 'I can make a full statement tomorrow on my memories of the day my husband and sister disappeared. It's been a day of shocks for me, and it's not every day that one finds they've been sharing house with their son unbeknown to either of them.'

The two coppers looked at each other. 'OK. I expect it will be in the hands of CID anyway, and as you say, nothing is going to change overnight.'

They took their leave and departed.

'I've been thinking about that dream I had last night. I couldn't have actually been in the dovecote otherwise I wouldn't be here now. I'd be under the floor with them. I'll have another look tomorrow before the police arrive. Pity I can't remember anything else. I've got no idea how I came to be in London, or how I got to be in Marjory Evans' shed.' I turned to Mavis; it was going to take some time to think of her as Mum. 'I expect you've still got my birth certificate, haven't you?'

'Of course, it's in the bureau with all my other bits of memorabilia of you. We'll get everything out tomorrow. It's been quite a day for me. I think I'll go to bed.'

After she had gone, Brynda said, 'Are we going to have to change everything to Spenser now, do you think?'

'I don't know. It would somehow seem disloyal to that wonderful lady who adopted me and brought me up as her own.'

'You can always get posh,' Caroline put in. 'Go double-barrelled, 'Spenser-Evan; would sound quite good.'

Tony grinned. 'I don't know. They'd be too posh to associate with us country yokels. You know, I haven't come to terms with the fact that I shan't be getting the old man finding fault with everything I do. He didn't get a chance to give me a bollocking about our ploughing

THE ARM OF COINCIDENCE

day and losing his horse fodder. Come to think of it, I don't expect we shall have the horses back anyway, unless you want them, Caroline?'

'No, definitely not. You know I never had ambitions to have a pony, never mind a horse. I think Dad only went hunting to be in with the Joneses if he spoke the truth. I must say, I never thought of him killing anyone, although I expect he killed a few Germans in the war.'

'Well, I doubt if killing my Dad and your Mother was spur of the moment. He must have put a lot of planning into it, and if it hadn't been for me I doubt if anyone would ever have found out. We'd better get to bed, I shouldn't be surprised to find the police on the doorstep bright and early.'

Caroline got up and gave Brynda and me a hug. 'Welcome to the family,' was her parting remark. We also got a hug from Tony. It's a wonderful feeling when you realise that your friends are also your relations. After all, as someone once said, 'You can choose your friends, but not your relations.'

It was a long time before we got to sleep, cuddled up together chewing things over. If I hadn't set the alarm clock, I'd have overslept. As it was, we got across to the dovecote before anyone else was stirring. I made for the corner far left of the doorway and almost immediately could feel a draught through a couple of holes. They had no 'bottom' to them like all the others, which were designed for the birds to lay their eggs in. It looked as if a section of masonry should open into the dovecote from the corner. It fitted so snugly that I only noticed it because I was looking for it.

It wouldn't budge, so we went back to the house. Brynda got a torch while I took the driving mirror off the Speed Twin complete with its arm. When we got back to the dovecote Brynda held the torch in the hole nearest the corner and I poked the mirror into the other hole. By angling it round I could see the steps going down into a passage. We swapped positions so that Brynda could see.

'Well, that explains how I saw the murders,' I said. 'I expect it led to the old hall and I must have escaped before Dan could get to me.'

We went home and found that Jamie was up and dressed and had opened a tin of dog food for Sam and got himself some cereals. Brynda made a pot of tea and took a cup up for Mavis, who was just thinking about getting up. We were just having our breakfast when half a dozen policemen arrived. They were all in plain clothes, so they must all have been CID. Brynda made them all tea whilst we finished our breakfast. I told them that we had found a secret passage over in the dovecote.

We all went over to the dovecote. It seemed pointless to exclude Jamie; after all he knew that something momentous was going on. We picked up some tools from the workshop: spades, crowbar and a couple of big screwdrivers. We had just lifted the first slab when Tony arrived. It was only a matter of seconds to reveal the belt buckle again, and we removed another four slabs, two each side of the buckle. One of the policemen took photographs as the work proceeded.

First Jack's skeleton was revealed and removed and then Anne's. There was a bullet hole in the back of Jack's skull and one in the front of Anne's, which was what I'd expected. The skeletons were carefully loaded into a police van together with fragments of clothing which had survived.

Mavis recognised enough of the material of Anne's clothing to realise that she had been wearing identical clothing to the dress she herself had worn to go to Oundle that day. You didn't have to be a genius to realise that anyone who had seen them that day wouldn't have known who was which. The police had recovered the pistol on the way out last night, we were told. Two of them stayed whilst the others departed with the bones.

I showed them the bullet hole in the oak barn door and we found the flattened-out bullet in the barn. We had to cut the motorbike saddle to recover the bullet. It wouldn't cost the world to buy a new saddle.

We all went into the house and Mavis told them everything she could remember about that fateful day back in 1954. No doubt it was Dan who had made sure the car would run out of petrol. I don't expect we shall ever know how he got the Land Rover to Peterborough and himself back without being seen. Most likely he left the village via the Old Hall drive. I had another thought. 'I bet it was Dan who sabotaged Robert's ladder. He was down at Glebe Farm when Robert was shovelling out the food bin.'

'What are you talking about, Jim? Nobody said the ladder had been sabotaged, we thought it was an accident.'

'No, well I realised somebody had deliberately weakened it soon after Robert was taken to hospital. The only person I told was Robert. That's why he bought the dog. We ruled out Dan because he was in Canada, but when you think about it, he would have known that Robert

THE ARM OF COINCIDENCE

wouldn't have been using the ladder again for another month when his stock ran low again. He'd made no secret of the fact that he wanted Glebe Farm. I daresay he'd have been back sooner if the accident had been fatal. Someone must have been keeping him informed with events, because when he came back he was definitely expecting to find someone other than family. He shouted something like 'You. I might have known it would be you.'

'Well, I certainly wasn't in touch with him,' declared Tony. 'And I'm pretty certain that Caroline had no more idea where he was than me. If she'd spoken to him, she'd have mentioned it.'

I agreed. 'The original killings were well thought out, and so was Robert's accident, but he obviously flipped completely when he saw me. If he'd succeeded in killing me, I doubt if he'd have got away with it.'

The police didn't think there would be any further investigating to do, but of course, none of the bodies would be released until after the inquest. We signed our statements and they went back to Corby.

'You know, Anne and I being identical twins turned into a tragedy,' mused Mavis. 'We both fell in love with the same man, but only one of us could marry him. We tossed a coin and I won. Anne married Dan, even though she didn't really fancy him. I daresay she always intended to go on seeing Jack, with or without his knowing which of us he was with. I think that both Jack and Dan eventually got so they could tell the difference, but very few other people could.'

Tony and I decided to get back to the dovecote, fill the hole in, and put the slabs back down. The police hadn't said anything about leaving it and there would be no need for further forensic on site. We took a wheelbarrow and collected molehills from the paddock to make up the soil deficit. It didn't take long. You could hardly tell where the grave had been.

'Got any ideas on how we could get that stone door opened?' I asked Tony. He crossed over to the corner to have a look.

'Might be easier to try and find the other end. It must go under the wall somehow round to where the house was. I suppose we could take a bit of wall down or dig a hole at the end of it.'

'Hand or machine job?' I wanted to know.

'Hand, I'm afraid. We got rid of our old JCB when we'd done all the ditches; it was about clapped out. We never bothered to get another. There didn't seem to be enough work to warrant it.'

There's no time like the present, so we took the barrow, spades and crowbar to the end of the wall where it would have joined onto the corner of the house. An hour's digging and we had uncovered and cleared a hefty slab. It took some prizing and heaving to get it up without breaking it. We had struck the jackpot. About six or seven foot down we could see steps up towards the wall, down to where the Hall had been.

We went over to the house for a drink and to fetch a short ladder and the torch. Brynda made a pot of tea and took a cup in to Mavis, who was looking for the birth certificate and any old photographs she could find.

'If we take some easing oil spray and a scissors-action car jack, we may be able to open the dovecote end,' I suggested.

We lowered the ladder through the opening. It was a tight squeeze to get down into the hole. I went first and Tony passed me the torch and tools. In the event, the torch wasn't necessary as light filtered through from cracks in the stonework just below the arched roof. We got to a right-angled bend where the wall turned back towards the dovecote. There was old mortar on the floor where a repair had been made to the wall. Where the steps went up to the dovecote it became very narrow and it was obvious that you wouldn't get right to the top without opening the door. There was just enough room for me to get my head up and peer through the nearest hole. I reached up and sprayed easing oil into the joints in the stone where I thought it should pivot. We sat on the bottom step to give it a chance to penetrate.

I positioned the jack between the two stone surfaces as near to the crack as possible and wound the handle to exert some pressure. It didn't move, even though I nearly bent the jack handle. We decided to go back and fetch the one from my car so that we could have one top and bottom.

I reached up but had to remove the jack before I could spray some more easing oil into the joints. We laughed at each other's filthy clothes when we got out. We had collected a few hundred cobwebs. Tony waited while I fetched my jack, then we set off along the tunnel once more. This time we were successful; the combination of more oil and two jacks enabled us to get it open far enough to be able to lever it from the other side.

We retraced our steps once more, taking our gear with us. When we'd lifted the ladder out we lowered the slab in place and shovelled

THE ARM OF COINCIDENCE

the soil back over it. At least curiosity had been satisfied. With the crowbar we managed to open the door completely and, after copious amounts of easing oil (we emptied the can), and much easing backwards and forwards, we were able to close it and open it at will by pulling on a hole. Perhaps the monks had used it all those years ago to collect the eggs when it was raining!

It was nearly lunchtime when we'd put our tools and the wheelbarrow away.

'I shall have to get on with some work this afternoon,' Tony announced.

'Anything you want a hand with?' I asked. He shook his head.

'No thanks, Steve's ploughing and I'm going discing. We're going to try some oilseed rape this year. The old man didn't like it, but he can't dictate now, can he?'

When I got in, Brynda and Mavis were looking through an old shoebox. The birth certificate took pride of place on the table.

'Wasn't in the bureau where I thought it was; found it on top of the wardrobe in my bedroom in this box of old photos.' I picked it up.

'Good Lord. It was my birthday on the day my mum found me in her shed! Sorry, Mavis.' I smiled at her. 'Marjorie Evans will always be remembered as my Mum.' I returned my attention to the certificate. 'And I'm a year younger than they thought. They fixed my birthday on the day I was found and put me down as seven. The only reason Marjorie was allowed to keep and finally adopt me was, so I've been told, that I screamed the place down every time the welfare people tried to take me away. Anyway it was quite convenient with her being a schoolteacher. She'd have been married, but she lost her man in the war and never found anyone else who matched up. We loved each other and her brother and his son treated me as if I were real family, so I never thought any different. When Mum died, no one complained about her leaving everything to me.'

After lunch I pottered around in the nursery for a while with Brynda, then we collected Jamie and Sam and went for a walk.

'I don't think we're going to be able to avoid the media you know,' I told Brynda. 'There'll have to be an inquest and no doubt someone will pick it up from there. Tony's got to get in touch with his father's solicitor so we may as well get him to sort what name we're going to have now we know who I am.'

THE ARM OF COINCIDENCE

'Did it ever bother you? Not knowing where you'd originated from?'

'Not really, no one could have had a better mum than me. She encouraged me in whatever I wanted to do; she paid for music lessons for me; but, above all, she taught me to respect myself and help others less fortunate than myself whenever possible. I joined the army, not because I wanted to kill people, more to keep the peace from a position of strength. Having said that, you can only hope that one's government doesn't abuse that strength and go to war when they shouldn't.'

Jamie wanted a shoulder ride, so I hoisted him up. 'I shan't be able to do this for much longer,' I told him. 'You're growing fast, you'll soon be too heavy to carry far.'

'Do you think it was fate that brought us here, or is it just an amazing coincidence?' Brynda wanted to know. I grinned at her.

'Now, how would I know the answer to that, any more than you?'

'Well, what with you being found nearly dead on your birthday, it has to mean something, doesn't it?'

I shrugged, 'Certainly lucky for me, that's how I came to be called 'Lucky Jim' and then for most of my life, just 'Lucky'.'

We went through the forest and back round by the road. Jamie walked about half the distance, which was very good for a child of his age. I had to carry him for the last mile, but it was no hardship.

'I wish I could remember how I got to London, but I doubt if I ever shall. I don't expect it's important really. I just don't like not knowing.'

'Changing the subject slightly, do you want to know whether I'm carrying boys or girls?'

'I'm not bothered too much either way, all I care about is that you all come out of it all right. I'll leave it up to you as to whether we know or not.'

When we got back, Mavis said she'd heard from the police to say that the remains could be released any time, so we could arrange funerals. 'I had a word with Caroline and if you're in agreement, she'll make arrangements with Derek Gunn at Crowsons for cremation of all the remains. She wants the ashes scattered round the dovecote.'

I said that it was OK with me and had she asked Tony?

'Caroline's already done that, and he's in agreement, so I'll tell her to go ahead tomorrow.'

'I expect there'll have to be an inquest,' I remarked.

'Yes, the police said that the Coroner's Office had been informed in

THE ARM OF COINCIDENCE

Kettering, but the inquest wouldn't be much before Christmas. I hadn't realised it took so long. Anyway, it doesn't matter, because we know exactly how everyone died, and when, and positive identification has taken place. I must say that I'm quite relieved to know that Jack and Anne didn't really run away. I wonder what the old devil spent the thousand pounds on, and what he did with their clothes. Another question we shall never know the answer to.'

'The other thing we don't know,' I remarked, 'is what decided him to come back early. I've been giving it some thought, and I've a mind to pay a visit to the Morrises over at Kettering.'

The media hadn't got wind of anything as yet, and as the inquest wouldn't be for some time, it would be all over before they did. There had been a brief bit in the local paper about 'local farmer Dan Woodward dying in a car crash' but that was all.

The cremations were arranged for the Tuesday following Bank Holiday, with the customary efficiency of Derek Gunn. Seeing that no one was in mourning, we decided to go to Expo as planned at some time over the weekend.

Bill Story and son collected their traction engine and threshing tackle on Friday and Malcolm offered them a share of the takings from our weekend. Decent chaps, they would only take expenses. Bunion had entered the Allis Chalmer model 'U', so he trundled along behind them, taking his tent with him. The ever-amazing Bunion. I'd no idea he was into camping out. I suppose I should have realised, after all, they'd been taking the ploughing engines for years.

When Brynda, Mavis, Jamie, Sam and I arrived at Expo on Saturday, we got a big surprise: Caroline in WAAC uniform with her Jeep. She'd joined the 39/45 group. Malcolm had got Fiona on his back in a baby carrier. They had brought the second hand caravan, as they didn't fancy roughing it in a tent. Malcolm had towed it behind the Jeep, to which he'd clipped temporary wide mirrors.

We learned that most of the 39/45 vehicles had starred in several war films and the fees earned helped with the upkeep of the vehicles. Bunion said that if we came again tomorrow or Monday, Brynda could drive the Allis round the ring. Donna had had the offer previously, but didn't feel confident enough to take up the offer. Being a dynamic exponent of the Yellow Peril, I had no qualms about Brynda's ability to manage the Allis!

We took careful note of the route taken when the parade took place, but quickly realised that all Brynda would have to do was follow the tractor in front.

We decided that we would go on all three days as we wouldn't be able to see everything otherwise. Apart from exhibitions in the ring and in the air, there were Morris Dancers, and a steam fairground with steam organs and even a wall of death motorcycle exhibition, the power for the organs being provided by Showman's Traction Engines. Their music was reproduced from holes in pieces of special card. My newly discovered Mum decided that one day would be enough for her. She was pretty tired by the time we got home.

Brynda thoroughly enjoyed operating the old Allis on Sunday, then for her the icing on the cake was Caroline generously offering her uniform and a drive round with the Jeep. Jamie went passenger and Brynda had to put up with being announced as Caroline McCloud with her restored Jeep.

Tuesday, we all went off to Kettering Crematorium to pay whatever respects we could to the remains of Ann, Jack and Dan. There were no hymns; it didn't seem appropriate, somehow, just a few prayers by the regular priest. It crossed my mind that they would need all the help they could get, especially Dan, if they were to go to a better place.

It would be a few days before the ashes would be returned for scattering.

After lunch Tony came round to say the solicitor was coming over in the afternoon and would we all congregate in the Farm House as he was bringing Dan's will. Tony brought the solicitor round at half past two, and Caroline arrived a few minutes later.

The solicitor was clearly ill at ease. He took a single sheet of paper from his briefcase. 'I'm afraid it's very brief.' He went through the preliminaries, last Will and Testament, etc, then announced that Dan had left everything to Caroline! Tony went as white as a sheet and made to get up. Caroline jumped up and rushed over to him, crying, 'I don't want it! It's yours Tony. I don't want any part of it. What a dirty trick!' She looked at the solicitor. 'I don't think I have to accept anything if I don't want to, do I? Tony's worked like a slave all these years and Dad's taking it out on him because he thought Tony wasn't his.'

Before the solicitor had time to say anything, Mavis cut in, 'I think I can more or less prove that neither of you belonged to him. I think

THE ARM OF COINCIDENCE

Jack fathered you both.' She went to the shoebox and brought out a couple of photographs.

'This one is of myself and Ann when we were in the Land Army. As you can see, Caroline is quite a lot like us. This one is of Jack's grandmother when she was young.' She laid the photo on the table for us to have a look. Caroline was a dead ringer for her!

'Dan never met Jack's grandmother; neither did I come to that, she was killed in a bombing raid on Coventry during the war. I've only found this photograph since I've known that they're all dead.'

We were all stunned.

'Well thank God for small mercies,' said Caroline. 'I'd rather have a murder victim for a Dad than the murderer, especially a cold-blooded murderer. He didn't have to kill them, did he?'

'I think his idea was that if I married him he would get the whole farm. Thank God I didn't! In spite of all his pestering, he only owned half the farm,' declared Mavis.

The solicitor left the copy of the will on the table. 'I'll make arrangements to get a valuation done in compliance with your wishes,' he said. Turning to Caroline, 'Are you sure about this, hadn't you better consult your husband before you put it in writing? I understand that he's a barrister!'

'Well, obviously I'll tell him, but I know he'll agree one hundred per cent with my decision. He won't want any part of it. Tony's earned it.'

Caroline and Tony saw him to his car, then came back in.

'Thanks, sis, you're one in a million,' he said gratefully. 'And, just think, we and Jim are even more closely related than we thought, he's our half-brother. In fact, seeing our mothers were identical twins, he's as near as dammit our brother.'

I must admit I was very touched. They always say that blood is thicker than water, which no doubt accounts for why we got on so well together. Then thinking about it, not all brothers and sisters do get on together!

'Have you got any pictures of our Dad in there, Mum?' (I remembered) 'I've got no idea as to what he looked like.'

'We were only children when he and mum disappeared, so I for one can't remember either,' said Caroline. 'How about you, Tony?' He shook his head.

Mum had a rummage and came up with a photo of their wedding

day. 'I haven't had these out since they disappeared. I couldn't bear to look.'

'Reckon if Brynda had an identical twin I'd want them both, same as he did.' I remarked. Brynda suddenly fell about laughing, 'Boy, are you in for a surprise.'

'You haven't, have you?' I gasped.

'No, of course not, but wait here.'

She shot off upstairs and came back wearing the ginger wig I'd bought in Hunstanton and forgotten. Tony and I were both dumbfounded. She looked remarkably like Donna.

She grinned, 'You ain't seen nothing yet.' She went out and came in wearing the black wig. This time Caroline was as dumbfounded as we were, as she came face to face with her double.

As someone who thinks of himself as a photographer, I was amazed that I hadn't noticed the resemblance. Still, neither had Tony or Caroline. A change of hair and your whole appearance is changed; no wonder actors and actresses could portray so many different characters.

I went to put the wedding photo back in the box and could hardly believe my eyes, the top photo was one that I was very familiar with! 'Who are these people, mum?' I passed her the photo.

'The eldest one at the back was my mother, and the other two were her much younger sister and brother. My mother left home when she was sixteen. She'd been seduced by a married man and got pregnant. She couldn't face her parents so she went off and got a job as a maid. She did write to them and explain, but she didn't put her address because she knew there would be recriminations. In the event she had a miscarriage and eventually married one of the sons of the people she worked for.'

'Well, have I got news for you! Your mother's younger sister was my other Mum. She had a copy of this photograph. In fact, I've still got it at the farm. How the hell did I come to get in your aunt's garden shed? That has to be the coincidence to beat all coincidences!'

EPILOGUE

It's August 1991, ten years on. We've expanded the nursery into the field and now grow trees and shrubs as well. We have a keen young man working for us full time, and open to the general public on Sunday afternoons when the Mill is open.

Our twin girls: Megan and Rhonda, were nine in January. One thing we've never done is dress them alike. We've tried to get them to develop their own personalities. We wouldn't like history to be repeated. We've also discovered that if you never threaten children with something you don't intend carrying out, they'll know exactly where they stand. We try to be reasonable, but once either of us has said 'no', that's it, and they know we won't change our minds.

Fortunately Tony and Donna, and Caroline and Malcolm think along the same lines as us. Just as well, Donna had twin girls a month after ours; something to do with the night of the big dance! Caroline had twin boys in April! Donna's girls are called Olivia and Lucy; Caroline's boys are Andrew and Ian. Our two have Welsh names in accordance with their ancestry, whilst Caroline's are Scottish in deference to their father's Scottish blood.

It still seems incredible that we've all got twins. Must be something in the genes! I went for the 'chop' when the girls were a year old, as we definitely didn't want an increase in family.

Tony and Donna moved into Dan's half of the farmhouse as soon as everything was sorted. Tony had a hefty sum to pay in taxes because, apart from the value of his share of the farm, Dan had a considerable sum invested. He could have bought Robert out without a mortgage if Robert had wished to sell.

We found the reason why Dan was so keen to get his hands on it: gravel. There is now a twenty-five acre gravel pit at the river end of the farm, which has given Robert and family security for life. When the gravel runs out, it will become a leisure amenity.

We also discovered that Dan had been keeping in touch with Keith Morris, which was how he discovered that I had been inadvertently spiking his guns. He had also planted the blackmail idea in their heads.

Tony decided that, as he had no Woodward blood in his veins, he didn't wish to carry the name. They changed the whole family to Spenser on the grounds that he preferred to be associated with a victim rather than a killer. We became Spenser-Evans. It took months to get everything sorted out. After the inquest had been reported in the press, there was a surge of ghoulish interest in the dovecote. People seemed quite happy to pay to explore and we raised money for Oxfam through it.

It took over a year to get the Mill back into full working order. Malcolm had a double garage built on the end of the house, with extra bedrooms on top. Now that it's mellowed, it looks as if it's always been there. Fred Bird showed us how to dress the millstones and supervised the first millings. Malcolm, Tony and I are now fully conversant with all the workings. The Mill is open every Sunday afternoon in the summer, with one of us operating it. Caroline does teas from her kitchen and, if it's too cold to sit outside, they have kitted out the garage. She does quite a brisk trade in flour. People like the idea of knowing that the wheat has been grown on the farm, and that no 'nasties' are added.

Bunion is in his eighties, but doesn't seem any different, apart from wearing out his pipes. He's taught me all about his beloved Fowler ploughing engines so that when he's 'gorn' they will be properly maintained. Since Expo ceased, our ploughing day has become an annual event and Tony gets quite a bit of land ploughed on the day. Last year, by popular demand, we had a display of vintage lorries. Bailey's haulage and storage brought an old Dodge, still with its original Perkins engine, all painted up and looking like new. A big wooden box on the side of the chassis struck a chord with me, and when Bunion informed me that it was the very lorry which old man Bailey had operated from the Mill, carting potatoes on the fateful day from the farm, the jigsaw was complete. I knew how I'd got to London all those years ago.

Tony and Donna's two boys are great strapping lads. Brian is coming up for 17 and Ben is 15. They help around the farm, but don't have noticeable ambitions to follow in their father's footsteps. They are more into electronics; they reckon that's where the money will be.

Our Jamie got into motor-cross motorbikes at an early age and we've carted his various bikes to events over a wide area. He's won quite a few cups for the various age groups he's competed in over the years.

THE ARM OF COINCIDENCE

We usually carry his birth certificate with us because we often have to prove how young he is! This year is the first he's been legally allowed on a tractor. Now that he's a teenager he's proving to be more help on the farm than Tony's own boys.

Mavis has never looked back after recovering from her stroke. She turned her share of the property over to me in 1982 to avoid duties. We all still live together in our half of the house. It would have taken a very large family to fill it when it was all one house.

I lost my darkroom. Jamie claimed it for his bedroom, even though it's the smallest in the house. The girls share his old room.

The stables are full of ponies; all the girls ride. Not the grown ups, thank the Lord. It's expensive enough keeping ponies!

Tony had kept on George, the keeper, allowing him to run the syndicate of shooters. It brought in good money. I can't believe the amount of money some people will pay to shoot at a few pheasants. George also volunteered to look after the ponies, which let the rest of us off the hook!

We've also made the Old Hall grounds into an amenity. It seemed a shame that only a few people could enjoy the magnificent trees. We planted some extra trees which are now quite well established; we put in a footbridge by the skew bridge and another nearer the village back into the grounds, so that people could have a round walk. There's an 'honesty' box for people to put money in to help with maintenance. We don't get much, but it helps.

I've still got the Speed Twin, but it doesn't get used for stunt riding now. In fact, I leave all that to Jamie. He has a bigger repertoire of tricks than I ever had.

There's a famous proverb that says 'It's an ill wind that blows nobody good'. People who live in this village on the whole have a quiet life. The Yobbo brigade leave us alone. There's no quick getaway from here. Everyone looks out for their neighbour.

The nickname 'Lucky' given to me by Marjorie Evans proved itself time and time again; no longer in use, but not forgotten by Brynda and me. We still can't keep our hands off each other when the slightest opportunity arises, which is as it should be, considering the amazing string of coincidences which have brought us to where we are today.